THE NO-KIDS CLUB

Talli Roland

LAKE UNION
PUBLISHING

This is a work of fiction. Names, characters, organizations, places, events, and incidents are either products of the author's imagination or are used fictitiously.

Text copyright © 2014 Talli Roland
All rights reserved.

No part of this book may be reproduced, or stored in a retrieval system, or transmitted in any form or by any means, electronic, mechanical, photocopying, recording, or otherwise, without express written permission of the publisher.

Published by Lake Union Publishing

www.apub.com

Amazon, the Amazon logo, and Lake Union Publishing are trademarks of Amazon.com, Inc., or its affiliates.

ISBN-13: 9781477822920
ISBN-10: 1477822925

Cover design by Mecob

Library of Congress Control Number: 2013922869

Printed in the United States of America

To S, for making the past year wonderfully challenging and full of joy.

CHAPTER ONE

'I bet you were a really cute kid.'

Clare Donoghue met her boyfriend's warm brown eyes, her features contorting into a grimace as she rolled into the crook of his arm. 'Yeah, right. You should have seen me: a skinny little thing with bones jutting out everywhere! Mum used to say I'd scare a skeleton.'

Edward raised an eyebrow. 'Well, you've certainly filled out in all the right places.' He ran a hand down her body, and even though they'd made love not even a minute ago, Clare felt desire rising. She was about to reel him in for another kiss when his next words stopped her cold.

'You know, I wouldn't mind a miniature skeleton of my own someday.' He brushed back her hair with a cheeky grin. 'Reckon a bony baby's better than a blobby one.'

His tone was joking, but Clare's heart dropped. In the few months they'd been together, the subject of children had never come up. She'd figured her Perfect Match profile made it obvious kids weren't part of her life plan, but evidently not. Perhaps she should have clarified the topic sooner, but it was hard enough to find a decent single man in London after age thirty, let alone one who wasn't seeking the perfect wife plus 2.5 kids.

Clare bit her lip, a heaviness filtering in. She'd love to smile and say she couldn't wait to be a mum, like millions of other women.

Truthfully, though, the very thought of tending to a child 24/7 filled her with horror. Life was perfect now, and the sheer weight of responsibility as a mother didn't appeal. In fact, it *repelled*.

But how would Edward react when she said being a parent wasn't on her agenda? It didn't matter, she told herself. Whatever his response, having children was non-negotiable. And maybe, just maybe, he loved her enough to reconsider the baby skeleton?

She took a deep breath. 'Um, actually, I don't want kids.'

'Don't want kids?' Edward's mouth dropped open. 'Ever?'

Oh, God. 'No. Never.' No point pussy-footing around the issue. If she didn't feel the urge at thirty-nine, it was doubtful she ever would. And the longer she waited, the harder it would be to relinquish the freedom to do what she wanted, when she wanted. Her heart beat fast awaiting Edward's response, and Clare pulled the duvet over her bare arms, as if it could protect her from a coming blow.

'Wow.' Edward looked at her like she'd just proclaimed an urge to streak naked across Trafalgar Square. 'You know, if I'd met you ten years ago, you'd have been everything I wanted. Clever, confident, and no ticking biological clock. But now . . . ' He shook his head. 'I'm looking for a woman who wants the same things I do. And that means children.'

Clare held his gaze, shifting away from the warmth of his body as a chasm opened between them. She forced herself to nod, eyes filling with tears as she realised there was nowhere to go from this conversation except their separate ways. 'So . . . ' She let her voice trail off, unwilling to put her thought into words.

'So.' Edward smiled sadly as he raised himself up on one elbow, reaching out to push a lock of hair behind her ear. 'I guess this is it, then.'

'I guess so.' Clare's voice was flat as she struggled to take in what was happening. Just five minutes earlier, they'd been making love.

A tear streaked down her cheek as he drew close for a final kiss, and Clare wished with every fibre of her being that she *could* be one of those women who'd always longed to be a mother, that wanting to have children felt as natural as rolling out of bed in the morning. But she wasn't, and it didn't, and as much as she wanted a future with Edward, that would never happen.

He pulled on a fitted T-shirt and jeans, and she tore her eyes away from his trim physique, tracing the stitching on the duvet cover and trying to block out the hurt streaming through her.

Edward paused, glancing down. 'I hate to go.'

Silence filled the flat as they both struggled for something to say, anything that would bring them together again. But what words could bridge the gap between wanting a child and wanting to remain child-free?

Finally, Edward sighed. 'Well, let me know if anything changes, okay?'

Clare nodded, even though her stance on motherhood was about as likely to change as Rod Stewart's hairstyle. 'Okay.'

She watched as Edward slid a watch on his wrist, gathered up his wallet and coat, then left the bedroom. A few seconds later, the flat door clicked closed. Lowering her head onto the pillow, she breathed in his citrusy scent that still lingered as her heart throbbed painfully.

Better to find out now they wanted different things, Clare told herself, gulping in air to cleanse her heart of the past few minutes. Somehow, she'd find someone on the same wavelength—a wavelength that didn't include dirty nappies or screaming children.

She just needed to accept it wouldn't be Edward.

CHAPTER TWO

'You can't fault the man for wanting children, Clare. It's a biological urge.'

Clare smiled at her best friend and stifled a sigh. Of course she hadn't expected Ellie—now seven-and-a-half months pregnant—to understand the reason behind last night's break-up with Edward, but she *had* hoped for sympathy.

'I don't fault him for wanting kids,' Clare said, shredding her croissant into flaky bits. 'I just thought we were on the same page when it came to the future. Guess I was wrong.' She shook her head, still trying to come to terms with their break-up. Women were meant to be broody, not men!

Ellie shifted her belly on the banquette, and Clare felt a pang of guilt for dragging her heavily pregnant friend down to Carluccio's café to share her woes.

'Another one bites the dust. He lasted longer than anyone in recent history, anyway.' Ellie shovelled a huge bite of carrot cake into her mouth, then licked a dollop of cream-cheese frosting from her fingers. 'God, I can't get enough of this.'

'If you can't indulge when you're pregnant, when can you?' Clare had always thought the best thing about pregnancy would be satisfying each and every craving guilt-free. That didn't come close to balancing out what happened *after* pregnancy, though: a lifetime commitment. Even the notion made her shudder.

'I'm going to miss Edward.' The words left her mouth before Clare could stop them, and she tried to block out his sorrowful expression as he'd stood at the bedroom door, staring down at her. She wouldn't have thought it so difficult to meet someone with a similar mindset, but in the past year, all she'd managed to unearth were blokes who wanted a quick shag, men lumbered with step-kids, or just plain losers. Where were the normal guys who, like her, didn't want children? How ironic that Edward was the one man she'd considered a future with, and their idea of what the future held was worlds apart.

'Well, you still have me!' Ellie took a sip of her decaffeinated coffee and made a face. 'Ugh. Can't wait until I'm back on the real thing.'

Clare nodded, hoping her expression didn't convey the thought that since her friend had fallen pregnant, she'd seen her less than ever. The daily grind of Ellie's busy job at a high-end estate agency combined with doctor's appointments, antenatal classes, and 'getting ready for Baby' (the amount of preparation Ellie was putting in, you'd think it was a mission to Mars) meant Clare was lucky if she saw her every few weeks. And when Ellie had the baby, she'd probably disappear into the same black hole that had swallowed up all Clare's other acquaintances once they became parents. Clare would be alone then: the one childless woman in a sea of reproductively busy females.

As if on cue, Ellie glanced at her watch. 'Yikes, is that the time? I'd better get going. I've a "Mum to Bee" sewing class over in Sloane Square.'

'*Sewing* class?' Clare lifted an eyebrow incredulously. Last she'd known, her friend could barely stitch on a button.

'I know, I know, but they teach you to design these dear little teddy bears . . . At least I haven't joined the Bumptastic Gymnastics club! You wouldn't believe what they make you do on a trapeze. I swear, once you get knocked up, there's a club for everything.'

'Wish there was a club for people without kids,' Clare grumbled, thinking she'd enrol in a heartbeat. 'Not that there's anything wrong with having children,' she added. She knew Ellie didn't judge her life choices, but you didn't want to rile up a pregnant woman.

Ellie rolled her eyes. 'You don't need to throw in that statement for me, my friend. I'm very familiar with your stance on the subject.' Ellie was the one person who hadn't tried to change Clare's mind with accusations of being selfish or, as one woman had so kindly put it, 'a waste of reproductive space'.

'Maybe there *is* a club for people like you,' she continued. 'There certainly seems to be one for everything else out there. I was reading in *Metro* the other day about a newly formed organisation for people with a clown fetish. They dress up each month and meet in a pub.' She grunted as she struggled to her feet. 'If there's a club for that, there must be one for those who don't want children.'

'Bet there's not,' Clare said, sipping her espresso. 'From what I've seen, people who don't want kids aren't usually loud and proud about it. Dealing with others' reactions is more trouble than it's worth.' She sighed, remembering the psychologist keen to analyse her, sure there must be something wrong if she didn't feel the urge to procreate.

'Start one, then. Aren't you always saying you hate when people complain about something but never do anything about it?' Ellie gazed down at her, and Clare nodded. She *was* always saying that. Damn. Sometimes, having a best mate who knew you inside out wasn't an advantage. After more than twenty years of friendship— from when they'd first bonded over soggy chips in the secondary school cafeteria to their busy professional lives now—they'd become like sisters.

'I'll have a look and see what I can find,' Clare responded, thinking it wasn't such a bad idea. With Edward gone, a lack of energy to hit the dating scene again, and her friend about to give birth, she could do with meeting some new people. Some *like-minded* people, whose conversations weren't constantly derailed by baby talk.

'Good.' Ellie leaned down as far as her tummy allowed and kissed Clare on the cheek. 'See you later.'

'Bye.' Clare watched her friend join the crowds on Fulham Road, then gulped her espresso and darted across the street to the hospital where she worked as a doctor in the Accident & Emergency department. Joining a club might be just what she needed, she mused . . . if such a thing really existed. She'd check it out when she got home. First, though, she had an overnight shift to contend with.

⁊

Twelve hours later, Clare heaved a sigh as she unlocked the front door of her flat. Every muscle ached and her head throbbed with fatigue. More than a decade in A&E and she had yet to get used to working through the night. Still, she wouldn't trade her job for the world. She loved the adrenaline rush when the cases appeared in front of her, and the sense of pride and accomplishment when she caught something others had missed. Patients moved past her like a conveyor belt—they were in, they were out, and there wasn't time for messy attachments or clinging relatives, a definite advantage.

Even though she was dead tired, her brain buzzed. She peeled off her work clothes and tugged on her comfiest moth-eaten pair of jogging bottoms, along with an old T-shirt that had belonged to her father. Pulling it over her head, she could almost smell the soothing scent of home: cinnamon from her stepmum's cooking mixed with the spicy cologne her father slathered on each morning.

A smile tugged at the corner of her mouth as she pictured the two of them, perusing the Saturday morning papers as Tikki the cat tried to curl up on them—usually the Sports section, for some reason—while light streamed into the conservatory and birds chirped in the back garden. The cosy home in leafy Berkhamsted outside London had given her an idyllic childhood. Well, apart from Mum leaving.

No point dwelling on that, Clare told herself for the millionth time. If her mum had wanted to disappear, then she was better off going. Clare had a wonderful mother in her stepmum Tam, who'd stepped in to fill the gap and more.

Flopping on the queen-sized bed, Clare drew the laptop towards her and booted it up. Nothing like a little mindless Facebook surfing to dull the senses. As she scanned baby photo after baby photo, Ellie's words about joining a club for people who didn't want children filtered into her mind. Imagine, a place where she wouldn't be forced to lay eyes on yet another picture of so-and-so's little darling, where the talk wouldn't revolve around baby-led weaning (whatever that was) or cracked nipples from breastfeeding (*way* too much information!). Ellie had been definitely on to something.

Clare opened up a new tab and entered "no kids club" into the search box, her heart sinking when the very opposite of what she wanted—listing after listing of kids' clubs—filled the screen. All right, how about "club for people without children"? Search results uncovered a plethora of articles on couples without kids and whether their lives were happier because of it (an obvious answer, Clare thought), but nothing even the slightest to do with social organisations for those lacking offspring. Exactly what she'd predicted.

Start one, then. Ellie's voice drifted into her mind as Clare climbed under the duvet and sank into the downy pillows. Well, perhaps she would. If people could band together to indulge a clown fetish, surely she could find others who wanted to socialise past 8:00 p.m. Righteous indignation coursed through her. Quite frankly, there *should* be a group for people without children!

Was she the right person to spearhead it, though? Her personality was about as far from rah-rah as you could get. And with her busy schedule, some weeks she was lucky if she made it to the off-license for bread and milk. But now that Edward was gone . . .

Maybe she'd consider starting the club when she had a spare moment, Clare thought as her eyes closed. Right now, all she wanted to do was sleep, sleep, sleep—and thank her lucky stars she wouldn't be awakened by baby *or* man.

CHAPTER THREE

'Oh, God,' Clare groaned as she crawled from under the duvet late Monday morning. Her head throbbed with lack of sleep, and her stomach shifted uncomfortably. Normally after a night shift, she'd doze until well after lunch, but today was different. Clare groaned even louder at the thought of what was ahead: Ellie's baby shower, organised by one of her American colleagues who refused to let the occasion pass without celebrating the US custom. Ellie hadn't objected—who could turn down free gifts, she'd joked—but she'd begged Clare to come along, too. Never one to desert a friend in need, Clare had agreed.

But now she was dreading it. The only thing worse than facing a dozen women braying about children was facing a dozen braying women with four hours' sleep! She lurched to the loo and downed two Nurofen, then went back to the bedroom and crawled onto the bed. Across the room on the bureau, Ellie's carefully chosen present met her eyes: a gorgeous Jo Malone candle along with moisturiser, perfume, and bubble bath. She'd already given Ellie a set of sleepsuits and a fluffy lamb doubling as a white noise machine, and Clare wanted to treat her friend to something nice, too. God knows Ellie deserved it after hauling that baby around inside her for nine months.

At five to one, Clare hurried up King's Road towards Ellie's office, clad in her best jeans and sky-blue cashmere jumper. The invitation—slathered with storks, baby socks, and rattles—had said to wear clothing the colour you thought the baby's sex was, since Ellie didn't yet know. Clare could never understand people who wanted to wait. The technology existed, and it wasn't like you weren't going to discover the gender at some point.

'Hello,' Clare said to the polished receptionist at Langley Estates. 'I'm here for Ellie's baby shower.'

'Oh yes, just let me ring Amanda. She's organising the whole thing. Take a seat.'

Clare sank onto the plush leather sofa, eying the swank confines. She hadn't been by in ages, and despite the downturn in the property market, it seemed things were on the up when it came to high-end properties. Bottled water and an assortment of posh-looking drinks chilled in a clear-fronted fridge, an espresso machine gleamed in the corner, and a glass-fronted bar with elegant bottles lined one end of the room. The place looked more like a lounge than an estate agency, but given the kind of properties Ellie was selling, Clare guessed clients would expect nothing less.

'Hey there! You must be Clare. Thanks for coming!' An enthusiastic American voice cut through the soft background music, and Clare glanced up at a tall blonde woman. Her teeth were polished and white the way only American teeth could be and her blue eyes sparkled; Clare could almost imagine her baling hay in a checked shirt and pigtails, straight from *Oklahoma!*

'My pleasure,' Clare said, trying to sound sincere. She was all for gift giving, but someone should have told this person baby showers weren't the done thing here. And that was how it should stay.

'Just hang on a sec, I'll grab Ellie and the gang, and then we can head to the restaurant. I've got everything set up there. Too bad we only have an hour.' Amanda's face dropped, and Clare breathed a sigh of relief this wouldn't last all afternoon. She was about to help herself to an espresso when a chorus of voices heralded Ellie's arrival.

'Clare!' Ellie pushed through the surrounding women and gave Clare a hug. Clare squeezed back as tightly as the bump allowed, noticing that despite Ellie's flushed cheeks, dark circles ringed her eyes. 'Everyone, this is my best friend, Clare. Clare, this is . . . ' She rattled off the names so quickly Clare hadn't a hope in hell of remembering them.

'Right, let's hit Bonnington's!' Amanda linked arms with Ellie, and Ellie's mouth dropped open.

'Bonnington's? You booked Bonnington's? That's my favourite.'

'I know,' Amanda responded. 'I remember you telling me. Just wait until we get there and you see what's in store. You're going to love it.'

The women crossed King's Road and walked the short distance to the iconic restaurant. Frequented by the Duchess of Cambridge and other A-listers, it was one of London's top spots. Inside, dove-grey walls and cream mouldings made it seem a world away from the busy street outside. A crystal chandelier sparkled from the centre of the room, glinting off the shiny cutlery.

'Come this way, ladies.' The maître d' escorted the group to a private room, and the women breathed a collective 'ooooooh' of approval as they entered. Far from the garish balloons and banners Clare had expected, the large linen-covered table was decorated with tiny blue and pink baby shoes, miniature glass bottles, and the smallest rattles Clare had ever seen. Off to one side, a cake—featuring a stork with a precious bundle winging its way across a blue sky—perched on an ornate table.

'Put your gifts over there, everyone, and have a seat.' Amanda's cheeks were flushed with pleasure.

'Thank you so much, Amanda.' Ellie threw her arms around her co-worker. 'This is perfect. No, more than perfect.'

'It's nothing.' Amanda waved a hand. 'I'm happy to do it, you know that.'

As the group settled into their chairs, a tiny pang of jealously hit Clare. *She* was Ellie's best friend, not this Amanda character. Perhaps she should have organised something similar? The thought had never even crossed her mind. Ellie wouldn't have expected it, she reassured herself, since showers weren't *de rigueur*. Still, as she took in her friend's shining face and the beautifully decorated room, Clare couldn't help feeling she'd let Ellie down.

Waiters set tiered silver trays with tiny cucumber sandwiches in front of them, and Clare eyed the food with disappointment. She needed something to calm her stomach, and these poncy things weren't going to cut it.

'So.' Amanda flashed her shiny teeth at Clare as she helped herself to a sandwich. 'Do you have children? Is Ellie's little one going to have a ready-made circle of friends to pal around with? I always think it's great when best friends have kids about the same age. It's such a life-changing event. When my twins were born ten years ago, I'd no idea how different things would be.'

Clare darted a glance at Amanda's midsection. *She'd* had twins? It was hard to imagine her stomach accommodating two babies. Right now, the woman had all the curves of a diving board.

'I know,' Amanda chuckled. 'You're probably thinking I'm not old enough to have a ten-year-old, but I'm actually thirty-eight. And I'm going to start trying for another soon, too—I want to do it before I'm forty and become one of those high-risk cases, you know?'

Ellie swung to face them. 'Oh, Clare doesn't need to worry. She's not going to have kids.'

'Not going to have children?' A sympathetic expression slid across Amanda's features. 'You poor thing. I'm so sorry—I can only imagine how hard that must be. There's always adoption, but I'm sure you know that.'

'No, no,' Clare interrupted, before Amanda reached out to stroke her arm or something. 'I don't *want* kids.'

Amanda's broad brow furrowed. 'Don't want kids?'

Clare sighed inwardly. This really wasn't the time or place to explain her motives. 'It's just not in my life plan.'

'But—'

'Why don't we get started on the gifts now, so we have plenty of time to open them while everyone eats and before we need to head back to work?' Ellie cut in, and Clare breathed a sigh of relief. Besides the fact that they were here to celebrate pregnancy, she was beyond tired of having to justify her decision.

'Oh, okay. Good idea.' Amanda put down a sandwich, rose to her feet, and clapped her hands. Silence fell as the women looked up at her. 'All right, ladies, it's gift time! Now, we're going to play a little game.'

Oh, God. Clare rolled her eyes in Ellie's direction, sure she'd see a similar expression on her friend's face, but Ellie was staring up at Amanda with a fixed smile.

'Ellie is going to open each gift before looking at the card, and then she'll guess who it's from. For every one she gets right, she'll add a ribbon or bow to this hat.' Amanda brandished a hat fashioned from wrapping paper and plonked it on Ellie's head amidst giggles from the women. If these kinds of games were typical of American baby showers, Clare could see why they hadn't crossed the ocean. Still, she laughed and clapped along with the group. If Ellie was enjoying it, she'd try, too.

After a few rounds of baby blankets, sleepsuits, and soft toys, Ellie finally selected Clare's gift. As she tore off the gift wrap, confusion settled on her face. 'Oh, it's a candle. Along with my favourite perfume, moisturiser, and bubble bath.'

'Bet I know who gave her that,' Amanda mumbled.

Ellie turned to Clare. 'Thank you! I love this perfume, and that candle smells gorgeous.' She kissed her friend on the cheek.

'You won't be able to light a candle with a baby around! And what a shame you can't wear the perfume for a while.' Amanda's hair swished as she shook her head. 'Didn't you say last week strong smells make you nauseated? If you're breastfeeding, you can't spray on scents. Sometimes it puts Baby right off its meal!' She gave a tinkling laugh.

Clare's heart dropped. Perhaps she should have bought something for the baby, after all. But she wanted Ellie to know she could be a mum and her own person; it was okay to indulge herself, too. Maybe now was the wrong time to express that sentiment. And how was she to know perfume made Ellie ill these days? Not to mention that thing about breastfeeding.

'I can still use the lovely bath bubbles,' Ellie said. 'Can't wait!'

'You'll be lucky if you have a bath in the next six months,' the woman across the table said, laughing. 'I wasn't able to get five minutes to myself, let alone a *bath*.'

And people wondered why she didn't want to have kids, Clare thought.

Panic flashed across Ellie's face before her nailed-on smile reappeared. 'Well, I'll look forward to using it when I can. Ooh, now who gave me this one . . . ' Her voice trailed off as she picked up the next gift. Clare leaned back, letting the chatter wash over her. The way these women made it sound, having a baby was the equivalent of being locked in a cave without any creature comforts, enslaving yourself to another soul, and hoping you came through the other side intact. Ellie was about to undertake an epic journey, the likes of which Clare knew nothing about.

As she watched her friend ooh and ahh over—what was it?—some kind of nipple cream, she couldn't help feeling yet again Ellie was slipping away from her. She figured it was only natural: parents were drawn to other parents whose kids could play together, just like that Amanda person had said.

She smiled vacantly as another bow was pinned to Ellie's hat after Ellie correctly guessed Amanda had given her the gorgeous hand-knit blanket. Clare would always support her best friend and the new family member; that would never change. But it was definitely time to track down some child-free friends of her own, and if she had to start a club to do it, she would.

∽

Later that evening, back in the comforting silence of her flat, Clare hauled her laptop to the kitchen table and cracked open the lid. How did one go about starting a club, anyway? She tapped her fingernails against her teeth as her brain spun. Logistically, it shouldn't be too difficult: members and a venue were really all she needed. She'd work on finding people, then worry about a meeting place later.

First things first: she needed a way to spread the word to reach potential members. She logged into her Facebook account, thinking it'd be a good place to start. But one glance at her newsfeed showing yet more toothless wonders changed her mind. There was no point putting something up on her Facebook profile; she had to reach beyond her social network to find these kindred spirits. Lord knew they certainly didn't exist in her own realm.

Clare leaned back and gazed at the screen, rolling her eyes at an advert in the corner proclaiming belly-fat loss in just five days. Yeah, right—and why were they targeting her? She glanced down at her still-flat stomach. For a thirty-nine-year-old, she was in decent shape. That was one benefit to not having a baby. Clare cringed, remembering her horror when Ellie had showed off her stretch marks, like a million wriggly worms burrowing under her skin. They'd fade eventually, but . . .

Hey, wait! Clare sat upright as an idea hit. She could create a Facebook advert for the club, targeting men and women in London and the surrounding counties. Facebook had a gazillion users, and it would be a great way to reach different contacts. Imagine all the new people she'd meet . . . and maybe a man? Edward's face flashed into her mind's eye, and a brief pang of grief speared her before she managed to push it away. They didn't want the same things, that much was evident, and the sooner she accepted that, the better.

Time to move forward, she told herself firmly as she clicked to create a Facebook page for the club. She'd advertise the link to the page, and people could contact her there by posting or messaging.

The name of the page was easy enough—The No-Kids Club was short and clear—but what should she put for the "about" section? **A club for men and women who don't want children**, she typed. Hmm, maybe not "don't want children", because that might limit the membership. There were plenty of women who couldn't have kids for a variety of reasons, and they might be looking for a refuge too. Perhaps something like "a club for men and women with a child-free life" was better. Clare quickly made the correction, and then typed out the rest.

Tired of friends who can't stay out late because they need to put the kids to bed? Bored with endless conversations about the best schools and potty training? Looking for like-minded people who won't judge your childless life? Then post here or message Clare Donoghue to be an inaugural member of The No-Kids Club. Meetings will be held weekly at a central London location.

Not bad, Clare thought as she skimmed the text, then sat back and examined the page. Still pretty bare, but at least the basic scaffolding was in place.

Now for the advert. She clicked "create ad", completed the necessary information, made a nominal payment (as much as she wanted to meet people, she wasn't about to invest her life savings—she'd wasted enough on Internet dating), and hit "place order". Done.

Padding to the bathroom for a Tums to settle her still-queasy stomach, Clare wondered what kind of people would respond. Surely there must be legions of well-adjusted, child-free individuals like her, looking to meet similar souls. Well, once the advert went live, she'd find out.

CHAPTER FOUR

'Excuse me! Miss!'

Anna Nelson glanced up from the box she was unsuccessfully trying to open with a pair of scissors and stifled a sigh. At this rate, it'd take all morning to get the stock sorted. Only 10:00 a.m. on a Monday, and already it felt like half of Muswell Hill had been into the bookshop, dragging their progeny behind them.

A customer with expensive-looking sunglasses holding back honey-coloured hair loomed over her. Beside the thirty-something woman, a curly haired boy clutching a gleaming scooter was already dismantling the display of books Anna had carefully co-ordinated first thing that morning.

Anna pasted on a smile and clambered to her feet, brushing bits of cardboard box from her tailored trousers. Days like this, she thanked her lucky stars the job was only part-time. 'Yes?'

'Milo and I are looking for the latest book in the Terrible Tom series. Milo! Get down!' The woman rolled her eyes at Anna instead of pulling Milo off the bookshelf he was attempting to scale with the determination of a Sherpa bound for the summit of Everest. 'You can't keep them under control at this age! It's a crazy time, isn't it?' She shot Anna a smile, clearly expecting Anna to share her commiserations. Why did women of a certain age always assume that similarly aged women had kids, too, Anna wondered? And even if they didn't, that they found children's bratty antics sweet and endearing?

Anna quite liked kids—well, those who didn't destroy an hour's work in ten seconds. She loved cuddling babies or even babysitting every once in a while, but she'd never thought of having one of her own. So when Michael, her husband and the love of her life (a cliché, yes, but he really was) had made it clear children weren't on his agenda, Anna had been perfectly fine with that.

Six years on, and she still was; no maternal twinges for her. Things might have been different if she'd married a man who wanted kids, but she couldn't imagine life without Michael. After watching her mum and dad rip each other apart in an acrimonious divorce, Anna knew she was lucky to have him and vowed their relationship would never hit the lows of her parents'. Giving up something she hadn't envisioned in the first place wasn't a high price to pay when she had her dream man.

'The Terrible Tom series is on that table over there.' Anna pointed to the corner of the shop where a neatly stacked pile of colourful books rested. She gave it about thirty seconds before Milo knocked them onto the floor.

The mother nodded her thanks. 'Come on, Milo!' she rang out in a high falsetto, trying to extricate her son from the bookshelf onto which he was clinging. She looked back at Anna and smiled. 'That'll keep him occupied for the rest of the afternoon.'

Anna watched them head off towards the books. How on earth did people with children have time to talk to their partners, let alone ensure the relationship was on an even keel? God knows making everything run smoothly at home on top of her job here was more than enough. Add a kid to the mix, and Anna wasn't sure she could keep it all up. Her co-workers often lamented how they made it out child-free just once a year or that they hadn't had sex for months, and she could only shudder.

Granted . . . Anna chewed the inside of her lip as she watched Milo tear a page from the book in his hands. When *was* the last time she and Michael had made love? And forget making love, when had they last gone out together? Michael worked long hours as a software engineer, and lately his idea of a fun night seemed to be a virtual assault on the population of Mars, or whatever video game he was obsessed with these days. Anna often tried to coax him away with suggestions of tickets to a West End show, a football match, and even a speed boat down the Thames. But each time, Michael had patted her back, said 'some other evening', and turned towards the telly. Anna had nodded, telling herself he just needed a good night's rest.

But a good night's rest had become a good *year's* rest! Fear ran through her. Were they turning into one of those boring couples who never did anything, never went anywhere, and had nothing to say to each other? For goodness' sake, they weren't even in their mid-thirties, yet the most exciting thing they'd done together recently was purchasing a new rubbish bin from Homebase.

Anna tapped her foot as her mind spun. Maybe she'd been trying too hard with her suggestions. Something closer to home might do the trick—a film or even a walk on nearby Hampstead Heath, like they used to. A return to simpler pleasures would be just the ticket, she was sure. Her heart lifted. She couldn't wait to get home now!

A woman dragging a scowling toddler approached, and Anna sighed. First, though, she had to face the rest of Muswell Hill's Miniature Mussolini Brigade.

⌒୨

A few hours later, back in the large semi-detached house Michael had insisted on buying for just the two of them, Anna heard the front door click closed.

'Honey, I'm home!'

She smiled from the kitchen at her husband's familiar cry. He'd started doing that not long after they'd moved in together, joking she was like a nineteen-fifties housewife when she served him his after-work whisky. Anna hadn't been offended: as far as she was concerned, those women knew how to keep a relationship going, and while she didn't agree with their lack of opportunities, she *did* think women should be able to take pride in domestic duties. Women had a choice these days, and they should be able to make a decision without being ashamed. Wanting to make your husband happy and comfortable was hardly something to feel badly about.

'Hey, babe. I'm in the kitchen!' Anna gave the risotto another vigorous stir. This was the tricky bit, where it could all go wrong and end up a sticky mess. Her last try only half an hour ago had done just that. She sighed, exhaustion creeping in after a long day on her feet in the shop. She couldn't really blame Michael for wanting to relax in the evening, but too much relaxation was the death knell for any relationship.

Michael's steps thumped down the oak corridor towards her, and then his smiling face appeared. 'There's my sweetheart.' He wrapped his arms around her waist and nuzzled her neck. 'Ummm, something smells good.'

'That's the risotto, not me.' Anna laughed, kissing him quickly before stirring the dish some more. The brush of his five o'clock shadow and his lingering scent never failed to make her heart quicken, even after all these years. They were lucky to still have that chemistry, unlike many of her workmates who complained the only chemistry they experienced these days was a handful of vitamins each night. Anna sighed, thinking she and Michael just needed to *act* on it a bit more. Well, there was no time like the present to get started on her mission to drag Michael from his self-induced cocoon.

'Go relax and I'll bring you a drink,' she said, continuing to mix the risotto with one hand while opening the fridge with the other. 'And then maybe we can check out the Odeon in Swiss Cottage? I'm sure there's a good action film on there.' Anna would have preferred a chick flick, but there wasn't a hope in hell of luring Michael from his lair to see something like that. 'Or perhaps we can take a walk? Some fresh air would be lovely. It's been ages since we've been to the park.'

'You want to go out?' Michael ran a hand over his closely cut hair.

'Well . . . yes, I thought it would be nice to spend some time together.' She tried to make her voice sound easy and relaxed despite the knot of tension she felt inside.

'I don't know, honey.' Michael glanced towards the lounge where his video games awaited. 'I'm a little tired tonight, and I've got an early start tomorrow. Maybe on the weekend?'

Anna swallowed back her disappointment, anxiety curling through her as she realised she'd never seen Michael happier than when he was firmly ensconced in front of the TV, worlds away from reality—and her. She stirred the risotto forcefully. He didn't want to go to the theatre. He didn't want to hit the pub. And he didn't want movies or a walk! Well, if Michael wasn't up for going out, she'd at least make sure they made love tonight. It had been way too long, and what man would turn down sex?

But when she entered the bedroom a couple hours later—clad in her skimpiest negligee and slathered in her yummiest-smelling moisturiser—Michael was propped up in bed, mouth open, and snoring loudly. It would have been comical if not for the sense of dread settling over her.

Enough was enough, Anna thought, tying back her wavy red hair before throwing on a robe and jamming her feet into slippers.

She'd no idea how they'd reached this point, but she was bloody well not letting it go any further. There *had* to be something that would draw Michael into the real world again and revitalize their relationship.

She padded downstairs and slid into a cold metallic chair at the kitchen table, then turned on the laptop. 'When in doubt, Google', was Michael's mantra, and it had rubbed off on her. First, though, just a quick peek at Facebook . . . Anna sighed as photo after photo of babies clogged her newsfeed. They were cute, yes, but personally, she'd much prefer a night out with her husband than a crying kid. She was about to open a new tab when an advert in the corner of the screen leapt out at her.

The No-Kids Club, it said. **A club for men and women with a child-free life**. Anna tilted her head. This was right up Michael's alley! He was always complaining how none of his old friends were free to play video games on the weekends anymore. Okay, so this was a club and not a romantic rendezvous, but they had to start somewhere. A new social circle, different activities . . . this was just what they needed to push past their slump. And she could do with some female company who didn't feel the need to play twenty reproductive questions every time they saw her.

Quickly, Anna clicked the link, devoured the information on the Facebook page, then sent a message to the founder.

If this didn't entice Michael to leave the house, Anna thought, she hadn't a clue what would.

CHAPTER FIVE

'Okay, class, now you need to trace your hand on the front of the card.' Poppy Elliot swished the pencil around her fingers, then held up her paper as an example. Thirty 7-year-olds squinted at her in concentration, and she couldn't help smiling. They were so cute at this age: they *wanted* to please you and loved learning something new . . . if they sat still long enough. As trying as being a primary school teacher was sometimes, Poppy couldn't imagine anything better—except a child of her own.

She walked around the tables, peering over the children's shoulders to make sure they were on track. Mother's Day wasn't for another week and a bit, but she'd learned from experience creating cards was a time-consuming task.

'How's this, Miss?' Faisal, one of her secret favourites, held up his card for examination.

Poppy nodded as she glanced at the shaky tracing of a hand without a thumb. 'It's fantastic, Faisal. Your mum will love it! Make sure you remember to give it to her first thing on Mother's Day.'

'I will, Miss,' he said. 'I'm going to cover it in sparkles, too.'

'Even better.' Poppy patted his shoulder.

'Will you get a card for Mother's Day?' Faisal's big brown eyes met hers, and a familiar dart of pain went through her.

'Not this year.' She kept smiling, even as grief contracted her insides. Every Mother's Day, she hoped this would be the one she could finally call herself a mother. And every year, despite the endless parade of herbal remedies, acupuncture, then doctor's visits leading to fertility drugs and even four rounds of IVF, she was still not a mum.

But she would be one day, she told herself, willing her eyes not to fill with tears. Ever since she and Alistair had married, she'd imagined a tiny baby with her curly blonde hair and Alistair's grey eyes, the perfect fusion of them both. Alistair had started making noises about investigating adoption, but Poppy wasn't ready to quit just yet. Despite countless tests and investigations, experts still couldn't explain her inability to conceive, and although Alistair had a low sperm count, she wasn't going to give up until a doctor told her getting pregnant was impossible.

She realised with a start that Faisal was staring at her expectantly. 'Sorry, sweetie, did you say something?'

'Earth to Miss!' He grinned. 'I said, maybe next year?'

Poppy nodded and crossed her fingers. 'Yes, maybe next year.' In fact, if she started another IVF cycle sooner rather than later, she could very well be cradling her baby next Mother's Day. She made a mental note to broach the subject with Alistair when the timing was right.

Poppy cleared her throat and looked up at the clock on the wall. 'Right, class, five minutes to finish up and clean your table before home time!'

The classroom erupted into chaos as kids rushed to complete their cards and tidy up. Finally, the bell rang and after all the students had been shepherded out the door and into the waiting arms of parents and nannies, Poppy sank into the chair behind her battered wooden desk and breathed in the silence. There was something about the stillness of the room at the end of the day which calmed her soul. She'd love to go home and have a huge glass of wine to relax, but with the next IVF cycle looming, it was better not to indulge.

Sighing, Poppy rounded the space, crouching to pick up scraps of paper, the odd pencil, and Pritt Sticks the children had left behind. Alistair would be at work until six, and the house they'd bought eight years ago—the house they'd hoped to fill with at least two kids by now—would be empty and quiet. Every so often she considered getting a cat for company, but she'd tell herself to give it one more year. One more year had turned into almost a decade.

Poppy plopped into her chair again and booted up the ancient computer. If she wasn't heading home, she'd do some work. But first, a bit of a browse on Facebook to see what her friends were up to tonight. With its endless stream of baby photos—each one an arrow straight to her faulty ovaries—Facebook used to be a no-go area until she'd installed an app that replaced baby pictures with generic photos of cats. Poppy often wished there was an app to replace all things baby in the real world, too.

She scrolled through the statuses of friends she hadn't seen for years, even if they did live in the same city. London had a way of doing that, of separating everyone into their neat little islands that only intersected with great difficulty. And it wasn't just the city: add children to the mix, and logistics became a nightmare. She was about to log off when an advert on the right caught her eye: **The No-Kids Club. A club for men and women with a child-free life**.

This was exactly what she'd been wishing for! A place where she could relax without being reminded every ten seconds of what she was missing. Poppy leaned back in her chair. Were these people anti-kids, though? She clicked the advert, then ran her eyes across the brief lines on the page. There was nothing to suggest the members hated children, and perhaps she'd find a few others like her—who wanted kids but had been unsuccessful so far. She'd joined online fertility groups, but they were so depressing, and anyway, this was meeting people in real life. Just what she needed.

Before she could ponder any more, she fired off a message saying she was interested and she'd love to come to the next meeting.

Done. And who knew, maybe someone there would have the magic pregnancy bullet she'd been searching for.

෨ඁ

Clare staggered through the front door Tuesday morning, then collapsed into a chair at the kitchen table. The older she got, the harder these overnight shifts became. Apparently Monday night was the new Saturday night, judging from the number of stomachs she'd pumped. As exhausted as she was, though, she was dying to check the club's Facebook page to see if any responses had come through. Less than twenty-four hours had passed since posting the ad, but social media could work quickly, right?

She pulled up the link, blinking at the screen. Wow! Already, the page had received thirty "likes". Okay, so it wasn't a huge number, but it was a start. If she could get thirty members to come out, this thing definitely had potential.

Her heart dropped as she scanned the posts. A pensioner in Tasmania was looking for company, a mystic was offering to cleanse her members' auras, and a philosopher wanted to lecture the club on the ethics of choosing not to procreate. Clare shook her head. Why did not wanting to have kids mean something was wrong with you? Why couldn't it just be a choice one made, like deciding to live in the country or the city? She quickly read the rest of the posts. There *were* a dozen or so genuine inquiries, but either the people weren't based in London or they shied away from meeting in real life. The whole point of this club was to meet up and get to know each other, to have a social circle you could actually do things with.

Maybe there was something in her message inbox? Ah, here we go: someone named Anna wanted to come with her husband. That made two . . . Clare combed through a few more nutters before coming across a message from a normal-sounding woman called Poppy, who was excited to come along to the first meeting, and that was it. She leaned back in the chair. Four members weren't bad to begin with, albeit somewhat fewer than she'd hoped. The advert had only been up for a day, though, and you had to start somewhere.

Right, onto the next challenge: where to meet. A public place would be best; no way was Clare about to invite these strangers into her home. Perhaps a pub? A central location that wasn't too noisy and that would accommodate their numbers until they grew large enough to rent a function room. Her brain ticked over as she tried to think of suitable pubs or cafés around Soho or Tottenham Court Road. God, it'd been ages since she'd left Chelsea. This club was just what she needed to get out there again.

Maybe the café inside the iconic bookshop Foyles would do, she thought, perusing Google Maps. She'd spent hours there scouring the collection of medical books and knew the place like the back of her hand. The café was large, quiet, and comfy. Plus, it closed at nine, so it was ideal for a quick getaway if these people turned out to be weirdos.

Fingers flying, Clare responded to both messages, saying she'd be waiting at 7:00 p.m. at the café in Foyles tomorrow night, her one evening off all week. It might be short notice, but what was the point of living child-free without a little spontaneity? Then she mustered up the energy to trudge to the bedroom and collapse on the downy mattress. A feeling of satisfaction ran through her as she sank into the pillow. Friends might fade away once families came into play, but soon she'd have a group of people with exactly the same mindset.

This No-Kids Club was a great idea, Clare thought as her eyes closed. She only regretted not starting it sooner.

CHAPTER SIX

Anna rushed down Charring Cross Road towards Foyles, where the No-Kids Club was meeting. It was already a few minutes past seven, and she hated being late. She'd spent a good half hour trying to convince Michael to come along. He'd sauntered through the door early for once, and her heart had lifted. But her attempts to cajole him out of his work clothes and back onto the Tube proved fruitless. Instead, he'd slumped onto the sofa, kicked off his shoes, and started playing a video game where he had to defuse a bomb before it blew up a Middle Eastern city.

Why anyone would want to go straight from work to an equally stressful game was beyond Anna, but she hadn't been able to tear Michael away from the screen. She'd tried to tempt him with the promise of dinner afterwards at Nando's, his favourite restaurant. Even that hadn't made him budge.

For a second, she'd contemplated staying in, too. She'd already told Clare to expect her, though, and Anna had been looking forward to going out. Ever since marrying Michael, her circle of female friends had shrunk dramatically. Her own doing, really, as she was constantly turning down invitations to stay in with him.

Staring at her husband as he fiddled with a bomb onscreen, Anna's unease at how dull their relationship had become crept in again. And it wasn't just their relationship. The satisfaction she'd once felt at keeping their home neat and orderly was fading, too.

They just needed a bit of variety, she told herself, something different. She'd try again to persuade him out to the club next week.

Right, better get a move on. She took a deep breath, filling her lungs with the March air: cold, but with a hint of springtime warmth. It wouldn't be long until the days were longer, if not sunnier. Hopefully by summer she'd have tempted Michael from his bubble and they'd have a whole new social circle, courtesy of the club. She couldn't wait to meet everyone.

As she threaded her way down the crowded pavement, Anna wondered what Clare Donoghue would be like. The club's Facebook profile hadn't given much away, the small photo showing an attractive woman in her thirties with dark hair. Fingers crossed the place wouldn't be so packed Anna couldn't recognise her. She hurried inside the bookshop and up to the first-floor café.

To her surprise, the space was practically empty except for a woman in the corner with long hair pulled into a sleek ponytail. A tight black polo neck made her high cheekbones look even more sculpted. That had to be Clare. Anna swallowed back the rush of intimidation that swept over her, a usual occurrence whenever she was faced with pulled-together, professional-looking women. Somehow, they had a way of making her feel inferior, as if their corporate accomplishments diminished her domestic achievements.

There were different kinds of success, Anna reminded herself, and as long as she was happy . . . She drew up her shoulders and marched towards the woman in the corner, her ballet flats making squeaking noises on the polished floorboards.

'Excuse me, are you Clare?'

The woman's head whipped up from her steaming drink. 'Yes. Poppy?'

'No, I'm Anna.' She held out a hand. 'Nice to meet you.' At least there's one other person coming, she thought, sinking onto an empty sofa. Making small talk with Clare all night appealed as much as joining Michael in his bomb defusing.

Clare's fingers closed around her palm in a firm grip, and Anna relaxed as the woman shot her a friendly smile. 'Thanks for coming out. Sorry, I thought you were bringing your husband, so I assumed you were someone else.'

Anna looked down at the floor. 'He couldn't make it tonight. Maybe next time.' She hoped. 'How many are you expecting this evening?'

'Just one other woman. I only started advertising a couple of days ago, so I'm sure loads will come in the next few weeks. Let's hope there are more people than us in this city who aren't planning to have children!' Clare shook her head. 'You don't know how lucky you are to have found a man who doesn't want kids. I've searched high and low without success.'

Anna smiled. Despite the recent lull in their relationship, Clare was right. She and Michael *were* lucky to have had found each other. 'I know. He's my everything,' she said simply, warmth flooding through her. Clare's nose twitched as if she'd smelled something bad, and Anna flushed at the cheesy-sounding words that were better suited to a song lyric. It was true, though. She couldn't imagine life without him.

'So how did you two meet?' Clare asked, draining her drink and staring over at the entrance. Anna could see she wasn't that interested, but until this Poppy person turned up, they might as well kill some time.

'It's not the world's most romantic tale,' Anna said, although personally, she thought the steady, straightforward way they'd got to know each other—with no drama or arguments—was a hundred times more romantic than her parents' whirlwind courtship. 'We met in university, up at York. I was doing a degree in literature and he was finishing his masters in engineering. We used to see each other every morning at the café in the students' union, and eventually he came over and started talking to me.' She grinned at the memory of how she'd been about to rush off to class and he'd materialized in front of her. Her coffee had splashed onto his trousers, but instead of being annoyed, he'd laughed. The spark in his eyes combined with a killer smile had instantly attracted her.

'Sounds romantic enough to me,' Clare said. 'And the best bit is that you're on the same page when it comes to children.'

Anna nodded. 'Exactly.' She and Michael rarely argued about anything. In fact, she couldn't remember the last time they'd exchanged angry words.

She glanced around the room, wondering what to say next. Funny, she'd just assumed because members had the no-kids things in common, they'd have lots to chat about, too. Thankfully, she was saved by the tentative smile of a woman hovering over them.

'Oh, hello,' Clare said. 'You must be Poppy.'

'Yes, hiya!' Poppy panted. 'Sorry I'm late. The Tube took ages.'

Anna scooted over to give Poppy room on the sofa. 'Nice to meet you. I'm Anna.' She held out a hand, wondering what this woman's story was. With delicate features and curly blonde hair, Poppy looked like she was created to have babies. Everything about her was soft and warm, a sharp contrast to Clare's no-nonsense persona. 'Right, I'm in serious need of coffee.' Anna gestured towards the counter. 'Would anyone else like one?'

'Not me, thanks.' Clare grinned as she indicated the two empty espresso cups in front of her. 'If I drink any more, I'll never get to sleep tonight! I have enough problems as it is.'

'Okay. Poppy?'

Poppy shook her head, hair flying out around her impish face. 'I wish. But no, thanks. I can't remember the last time I had a coffee, actually.'

'God, I love it. Life without caffeine isn't worth living!' Clare laughed. 'Do you not like the taste?'

'Well, no. I do.' Poppy's cheeks coloured. 'But I read that caffeine inhibits fertility.'

'Some studies have indicated higher caffeine consumption can affect fertility and the success of IVF, but there's been nothing definitive.' Clare's brow furrowed. 'But . . . ' Anna could see the wheels spin inside Clare's brain as she tried to work out why Poppy was on about fertility. Anna was having trouble working it out herself.

'Er, actually, my husband and I do want children. We've been through several IVF cycles, but it hasn't worked. Yet.' Poppy's cheeks flushed. 'I hope it's okay that I still want kids and I've come here? I just need a place to hang out where children aren't the main source of conversation.'

'Well, sure,' Clare said, smoothing back her hair. 'We want to build our membership, and the club is for anyone without kids, regardless of the reasons.'

'Don't worry, I'm won't regale anyone with tales from the fertility clinic.' Poppy smiled, but she looked more sad than happy. 'That's the last thing I want to dwell on.' She shuddered, and Anna's heart filled with sympathy.

'We're not going to give up, though.' The look of pain on Poppy's face was replaced with an expression of determination. 'I'd do anything to be a mother, you know?' She glanced at Clare and Anna as if she expected them to understand, and Anna reached out to touch her arm. She may not understand wanting children, but she *could* understand wanting something that badly. She smiled, remembering her eagerness to marry Michael and build a life together. It had eclipsed everything else—including her dream to live and work in Italy for a year after graduation.

Ever since she was young, romantic visions of Venice's canals and sun-drenched stone streets had filled her mind. Her parents had even talked about taking her there—until they'd started arguing and couldn't agree on which way to hang the loo roll, let alone holidays. In her last year at university, Anna had an interview to teach at an English language school in Venice. Then Michael proposed and wedding planning took over. She'd tried everything to convince him Venice would be the ultimate honeymoon destination, but he'd set his heart on a cosy cabin in the Lake District, and she succumbed. It was idyllic, but it wasn't Venice.

Once they'd settled into their house, Anna pushed Italy from her mind. She had another dream now: to have a marriage so strong that nothing would ever tear it apart. And until recently, she'd been happy enough with that.

A rogue dart of longing hit as she pictured the school's website, showing rows of tables underneath olive trees where outdoor classes were held. Before the vision took root, she pushed it from her mind and got to her feet.

'I'll just grab that coffee,' Anna said, leaving Clare and Poppy to chat for a moment. She breathed in the scent of roasted beans at the counter as she waited for the barista to make her Americano, wondering what Michael was up to right now. It'd been ages since she'd gone out socially without him, and part of her felt uncomfortable alone here, as if their worlds were being pulled further apart. The thought made her even more determined to find an activity they could enjoy together—or at least drag him out to the club's next meeting.

'So!' Poppy smiled as Anna plopped into her chair, and Anna couldn't help grinning back. There was something child-like and endearing about her. 'Clare's just told me all about her job as an emergency doctor.' Poppy's eyes were wide with admiration. 'What do you do, Anna?'

Anna gulped. There was nothing wrong with being house-proud, but she hated when people asked her that—and even more with people like Doctor Clare beside her. 'I work part-time in a bookshop.'

'That must be fun!' Poppy enthused. 'I adore bookshops. I'm there all the time tracking down books for my class. If I could find part-time work in one, I would, too.' She paused, and Anna jumped in before Poppy could ask what she did with the rest of her time.

'And apart from that, I make sure everything runs smoothly at home,' she said in a rush. Her cheeks coloured, and she told herself there was nothing to be so defensive about. 'My husband Michael and I have a lovely house, and I'm busy doing it up.' She didn't mention they'd moved in over six years ago, and 'doing it up' mainly included ironing shirts, washing dishes, and cooking Michael's dinner each night.

'Oh, fantastic. I've always wanted to be able to redo a house from the inside out. I loved decorating the nursery . . . ' Her voice was bright, but Anna spotted the liquid glistening in her eyes. 'So you don't want children?' she asked, tilting her head.

'No, we're happy just the two of us.' Well, they had been, and they would be again once Anna found something to inject life back into her husband.

'Ladies, I think it's time for some ground rules,' Clare said, leaning forward. 'Although we all have different reasons, we're here for the same thing: to escape from talking about kids. So from now on, can we try to find something else to discuss and enjoy the night, child-free?'

Anna nodded, thinking how funny it was that children kept sneaking into the conversation, even in a club for child-free living.

'Sorry, sorry.' Poppy's cheeks flushed again and she tucked a strand of flyaway hair behind her ear.

'Well.' Clare crossed her long legs, looking as if she was searching her mind for topics. 'What do you two like to do for fun?'

Oh, Lord. Anna took a sip of coffee. Fun? To be honest, she couldn't even remember the last time she'd done something for kicks. Usually, everything had a purpose: the windows needed washing; the floor needed polishing. It might not be fun, but the sense of accomplishment made her feel secure, like the day had strengthened some invisible shield protecting her marriage. Even back when she and Michael had gone out, the activities were usually things he'd enjoy. It was enough for her to know he was happy. Or it had been, anyway.

She shifted awkwardly, waiting for Poppy to answer. But Poppy seemed just as uncomfortable as her.

'Um, well, most of our income has gone into IVF,' Poppy responded finally, cheeks flushing, 'so we don't have a lot left over for extras.'

'How about you, Clare?' Anna asked to shift the focus away from poor Poppy. Surely their leader had a list of hobbies a mile long. Ambitious people weren't known for their relaxation skills.

'Oh, my schedule doesn't allow much time for leisure activities,' Clare said breezily, waving a hand in the air. 'It's pretty crazy.'

Silence fell again, and Anna glanced from Poppy to Clare, then cleared her throat. 'Cold out there tonight, isn't it?' She could scarcely believe they'd descended to talking about the weather, but at least it was one thing they all had in common. First meetings were always awkward, Anna told herself. They probably just needed more time to gel.

They discussed the British climate's fickleness for a few more minutes, then Anna looked at her watch. 'Wow, is that the time?' She'd better get going if she wanted to say good night to Michael before he hit the sack. It was silly, but somehow the evening didn't feel right without her good-night kiss.

'Okay, thanks for coming,' Clare said. 'Same time next Wednesday? Feel free to bring along your husband, as well as anyone else you think might like to join. And how about next week, we meet somewhere with *real* drinks?'

'Sounds good to me,' Anna responded. Maybe that would tempt Michael away from his video games. Poppy looked ready to protest—alcohol was probably on the banned list also—but she just nodded.

'Works for me, too.'

'See you then.' Anna stood and smoothed down her skirt, then weaved a scarf around her neck and waved goodbye.

As she clattered down the steps to the Tube and onto the Northern Line, she couldn't help replaying Clare's disapproving expression when she'd said Michael was her everything, and how uncomfortable she'd felt when Poppy asked what she did. It *had* been a while since she'd met new people, though. Maybe she was just out of practice making small talk.

It didn't matter what they thought, Anna told herself as the Tube rattled through the darkened tunnels. What mattered was the man waiting for her in the home they'd created together. Sure, the exterior might need a little sprucing up, but it was everything she'd wanted.

CHAPTER SEVEN

Poppy trudged up the slight rise from Ladbroke Grove Tube, her breath making clouds in the air. It was past six on Friday evening, and she'd already endured a full day of lessons plus two meetings with parents, but she wanted to get a jump-start on the weekend's pile of work. Sighing, she listed the tasks in her head: finish lesson planning for Maths, figure out what on earth to do for Music next week, and mark the week's spellings. Heading out on a weekday night was a rare thing, and the No-Kids Club had put her behind. Still, meeting Clare and Anna had been interesting, even if she was disappointed neither of them was on the same track as her.

In fact, Poppy thought as she rounded the corner to her rickety maisonette, all three women couldn't have been more different from each other: the clever career-woman Clare, who cherished her independence so much she didn't want to get married let alone have kids; Anna, who was so busy building a home for her husband she hadn't room in her life for children; and her, longing for a child. Poppy couldn't imagine marriage without a little one running around. It'd certainly be interesting getting to know the two women much better—along with any other new members sure to join in the coming weeks.

She unlocked the squeaky front gate and navigated down the stairs to the door of the maisonette, noting once again the light was burnt out. This whole place was starting to fall apart! It had been newly renovated when they'd first purchased it after the wedding, but since then, every spare drop of cash and time had gone into having a baby.

'Hey there, I'm back.' Poppy flicked on a light in the corridor, breathing in the smell of Alistair's famous homemade lasagne. Yum. Her stomach grumbled as she realised she'd missed lunch today to let the children finish up their Mother's Day cards. She stuck her head into the kitchen. 'Anything left for a hungry woman?'

Alistair turned from the sink and gave her the smile that never failed to melt her heart. He was so handsome, with long-lashed eyes and sandy-brown hair now streaked with the odd bit of grey. They'd both grown up in the Surrey village of Leatherhead, but they hadn't got together until they'd run into each other in a Notting Hill pub one night. Ever since, they'd been inseparable.

Funny how they were compatible on so many levels except the one that seemed to matter most: making a baby. People always said the two of them were perfect together. If only they knew.

'I wouldn't want to risk your wrath, now, would I?' Alistair joked, neatly hanging a tea towel on a hook. 'Of course there's some left. I was waiting for you to get home before tucking in.'

Poppy planted a kiss on his cheek. 'Oooh, you're nice and warm. Thanks.' She spotted a cheesecake on the counter. 'Yum! Maybe we can start with that.' Poppy's cheesecake fetish was a running joke ever since Alistair had challenged her to eat a whole cake in one go. To his surprise, she'd devoured it.

Alistair whacked her playfully on the bottom. 'Get changed, and I'll put dinner on the table.'

Poppy scooted from the kitchen and up to the bedroom, her tummy rumbling in anticipation. Alistair was in a good mood— maybe tonight she could bring up IVF? She'd been trying all week to find the ideal moment, but the days had flown by and the timing never seemed right.

Stripping off her typical uniform of trousers and blouse, her eye caught a pile of brochures and leaflets on the bedside table. Hmm, what were those? She pulled on jogging bottoms and a T-shirt, then drew the top one closer.

"Adoption in the UK: FAQs", the title said in big, bold lettering. Hands shaking, she flipped through the stack, each to do with the ins and outs of how to adopt a child in Britain. Panic rose as her eyes frantically scanned the words. Alistair wasn't giving up on IVF, was he? Sure, he'd been making noises about checking out other options, but she hadn't thought he was ready to actually start investigating them.

Poppy had nothing against adoption. In fact, she was all for it—just not for them. Not until she'd tried everything to carry the baby she always wanted inside her. Alistair's desire to throw in the towel so soon made her heart thud as if she'd climbed to the top of the Shard.

She scooped up the literature and plonked down the stairs, the cold floorboards searing her soles. Alistair was sitting at the kitchen table, reading today's *Guardian*. The table was set, a steaming lasagne filled the space with the heady scent of garlic and tomato, and a candle flickered. But the cosy atmosphere did nothing to diminish the impact of the leaflets burning a hole in her hand.

'What's all this?' She plonked the pamphlets on the table a little harder than intended.

Alistair's head snapped up from the paper at the slapping noise. 'Oh, those.' His voice was calm . . . almost deliberately so, as if he knew he had a battle on his hands. He folded the newspaper and gestured to her place. 'Come on, sit down before the food gets cold. We can chat while we eat.'

Poppy forced herself to slide into the chair, her toes now freezing. The lasagne looked delicious, but she couldn't imagine taking a bite. Her stomach was twisted in knots at the thought of officially giving up on pregnancy. She wouldn't do it, and that was that.

She cut off a slab of lasagne to show she was making an effort, and glanced over at Alistair. 'So?'

'So.' He leaned forward, his grey eyes serious. 'Well, we've been trying for a baby for ages, Pops. You know that. And we've done pretty much everything. You've been through the ringer with investigations, injections, IVF, the lot.'

'I'm fine—don't worry about me,' Poppy yelped. 'I'll do anything I can.'

'That's just it, Poppy.' Alistair's gaze was steady. 'I know you will. I know how much you want to get pregnant, give birth, and all of that.'

All of that? Poppy screamed inside her head. How could he trivialise what some women considered to be their purpose in life— and biologically, what women were made to do? The lucky ones, anyway.

'The thing is,' Alistair continued, 'we could go on forever, trying for a baby, and miss out on the chance to have one through other means, like adoption.' He slid the pamphlets towards her. 'We could have a child in a matter of months if we decide to go down that route.' His eyes lit up with excitement at the thought.

Poppy's heart beat even faster at the look on his face. Sure, she'd be willing to consider adoption at some point in the future—the distant future, if need be. But not now! For goodness' sake, she was only thirty-four. She still had a few good years left to try in her. 'I'm nowhere near ready to even think about that option,' she said, her voice shaking with conviction. 'I can't believe you are!'

Alistair reached out to take her fingers, and the fork she'd been holding clattered to the floor. 'Pops, listen. I'm not saying I'm ready to give up. Just that . . . it might be time to consider something else, too. Our last round of IVF took you quite hard, remember?'

'Quite hard' was a definite understatement. Poppy's mind flashed back to the failed IVF attempt in early December. On her way to the Harley Street clinic for a blood test to check for pregnancy, her heart was filled with optimism and hope. Even the day seemed to echo her spirits: the sky was a deep blue and sun streamed into Oxford Street, making the elaborate Christmas decorations sparkle. She threaded between a group of carollers and down a narrow corridor into St Christopher's Place, where café tables were packed with people wrapped up enjoying coffee in the sun.

Breathing in the crisp air, her mind drifted to how much she'd love being pregnant over Christmas. Not that she could tell many people—it would still be very early days, and doctors had drilled into her that one in five pregnancies ended in miscarriage. But just knowing a baby was growing inside her, all cosy and warm, as carols played and she and Alistair unwrapped their gifts . . . and this time next year, the baby would already be a few months old! She couldn't help smiling as she pictured a chubby cherub, face wreathed in smiles, ogling the Christmas tree.

But the idyllic vision had been shattered a few hours later when the doctor informed her, his tone businesslike and perfunctory, that the procedure hadn't been successful. Poppy had nodded, feeling dead inside, and left the clinic. The bright day now felt overcast, the sounds and decorations muted. She'd made her way home like an automaton, climbed into bed fully clothed, and lay there staring up at the ceiling for hours, her heart heavy. How could she grieve something she'd never had in the first place, she asked herself over and over.

Alistair had tried everything to cajole her out of bed, bringing her meals which lay untouched. Finally, after a few days when nothing had worked, he'd climbed the stairs, sat down beside her, and cried. He could deal with not having a child, he'd said, but he couldn't face losing her, too. She'd only seen him weep once, when his father had died, and his tears had startled her into action. There was still plenty of time ahead, Poppy had told herself, and their next attempt would work.

'Anyway.' Alistair squeezed her hand again. 'It wouldn't do you any harm to have a look at the literature, don't you think?'

Poppy stared down at his fingers entwined with hers. 'No,' she said in a numb voice, pulling away from him and getting to her feet. 'I won't look at it. There's no point.'

And with that, she padded back up the stairs, feeling Alistair's gaze following her as she walked away.

CHAPTER EIGHT

Clare's eyes snapped open at 5:00 a.m. Saturday morning. She reached out to smack off the alarm before remembering she hadn't turned it on: today was a rare weekend day off. Some medics couldn't handle an emergency doctor's' erratic schedule—fellow medical students had even gone as far as opting for the predictable timetables of GPs or dermatologists—but Clare didn't mind. She found the change invigorating, despite the near-constant sensation of jetlag. A roil of nausea went through her and she closed her eyes, willing it away. Ugh, speaking of jetlag . . .

Slowly, she poked out an arm from under the duvet, feeling the cool air of the room, then stretched. *Ahhhhhh.* She loved the silence, the freedom to come to terms with the day ahead on her own time. Sharing a bed was bothersome, really. There were too many limbs and too much movement for such a small space.

Funnily enough, though, whenever Edward stayed over, she'd slept like the dead. The memory of his broad chest rising and falling and the even sound of his breathing crept into her mind, and she shoved it forcefully away.

Clare turned on a light, as if by doing so she could banish the memories. Onwards and upwards, she told herself as she swung her legs around the bed, wiggling her bare toes against the cold floor. Okay, the No-Kids Club still had a way to go, but it *was* growing. Granted, she had been hoping for more women like her. The inaugural members weren't really what she'd envisioned:

a homemaker who'd rival Martha Stewart, and another who was desperate for children. Beggars couldn't be choosers, though, and the club had to start somewhere.

Maybe Ellie would have some ideas how to reach new members, Clare thought as she scrubbed her dark hair in the shower. Her friend's social networking ability was legendary—she'd brought in some hefty commissions because of it, propelling her straight to the top of the agency's best sellers. They hadn't spoken since the baby shower, despite Clare leaving several messages. She knew Ellie was busy, but . . . She'd try to ring her again later.

Shrugging on a robe, Clare slathered her face with moisturizer, then padded into the kitchen and made an espresso. Steaming drink in hand, she plonked down at the table with her tablet to check the Facebook page for any new messages. There were the usual enquiries from far-flung locales, along with spam and crazies. Sighing, she was about to put down the tablet and go get dressed when a post on the club page caught her eye.

Sounds very interesting. I'd love to come along to a meeting. Please message me with more details.

The name was Nicholas Hunt, and from what Clare could make out from the thumbnail-sized profile picture, he looked normal enough. She clicked on the photo, tapping her fingers on the table as she waited for the larger size to load. With blond hair, blue eyes, and an open, friendly smile, he'd seem at home on the pages of a J. Crew catalogue. Fingers flying across the keyboard, Clare messaged him with the date and time of the next meeting, saying she'd be in touch again once she confirmed a venue. God knows they needed to move on from Foyles.

She was about to log out when her messenger pinged. Could that be him, she wondered? She hadn't thought anyone would be up at 5:30 a.m. on a Saturday morning!

Shame, I'm busy this Wednesday. Would love to meet soon and learn more about the club, if you're available?

Clare bit her lip. Hmm, okay. It'd be good to see a potential member in the flesh before they came along to the meeting. She was typing a response when her messenger bleeped again.

Taking a punt here, but are you free for coffee this morning?

Her eyebrows flew up. This morning! Well, why not. She was gagging for caffeine and could do with some company. She'd planned to visit Tam and drop off her Mother's Day gift a day early, but Tam was visiting her own parents in Suffolk. And without Edward or Ellie, Clare's days off seemed to stretch forever.

I can do eight, if it's not too early for you. Carluccio's, on Fulham Road?

Clare grimaced as she glimpsed her reflection in the mirror. Wet hair hung around her face in clumps, and dark circles ringed her eyes. She'd have to do a major repair job if he did agree to meet, otherwise he'd run screaming in the other direction. She looked more lunatic than club founder.

See you there.

The response came within seconds, and Clare glanced at the clock. Yikes, she'd best get cracking. It was amazing they'd arranged a time to meet so quickly, Clare thought as she hurried into the bedroom. In her experience, finding a free night with a mutual Londoner required effort equivalent to building the Pyramids. It'd taken her and Edward forever to co-ordinate their schedules in the beginning! But the longer they'd been together, the easier it had become. Their lives had just fallen into sync. A tiny dart of sadness pinged her heart—what would he be doing right now? Probably still sleeping. He'd never been one for early mornings, always grumbling and grunting until she forced him from the bed.

Reaching into the wardrobe, Clare selected her favourite pair of skinny jeans and a turquoise jumper—her usual day-off uniform. A smile nudged her lips as she recalled how Ellie had persuaded her to buy the trousers, saying she must be the only person in the world still wearing boot cut. She'd whistled as Clare pivoted in front of the mirror, commenting how the garment made her look like she had 'junk in the trunk'. God knows where her friend had picked up that one! Sighing, Clare pulled the jeans over her hips. She missed doing things with Ellie; it had been ages since the two of them had an outing lasting longer than a brief coffee.

Eek, there *was* a little too much junk in the trunk right now, Clare thought, straining to do up the button. She felt bloated, as if someone was attempting to blow up her abdomen from the inside out. Probably PMS, she sighed, tugging a jumper over her head. It'd been a while since her last period and she must be due on any day now.

Was this all right? Her brow furrowed as she examined her reflection. Don't be silly, she told herself. It's not a date. Still, she couldn't help feeling a little nervous. She was out of practice meeting men—before Edward, she'd been on a blind date every couple of weeks. She had it down to a fine art: quick check in the mirror, quick drink at a nearby pub, and more often than not, quick getaway. Usually, she was in and out in less than thirty minutes, and by the time she was home, the date was far from her mind.

Clare tugged her hair into a ponytail, slicked on mascara and lip gloss, grabbed her bag, and was out the door. No matter what this man turned out to be like, she could murder a cup of coffee right now.

Outside, the early morning sky was dark, and Fulham Road was free from its usual traffic. As she walked to Carluccio's, she wondered if Nicholas was already there. The worst thing about blind dates was trying to figure out who the guy actually was. More than once she'd approached the wrong man—not that it was difficult to do, given how fuzzy some of the photos were! One elderly bloke had actually sent a picture of his thirty-year-old son, pretending to be him.

Oh, there he was. Even with his blond head bent over an iPad, Clare could tell straight away it was Nicholas. She smoothed her hair and scurried towards him.

'Hi, there,' she said, hovering awkwardly over his table.

He glanced up, lips lifting in a friendly smile. God, his teeth were white, Clare thought as he got to his feet. 'You must be Clare,' he said. 'Lovely to meet you. Have a seat.' He gestured to the padded banquette across from him.

'Nice to meet you.' Clare slid onto the bench, but not before noting how tall Nicholas was. Edward had been only an inch or so taller than her—she'd had to be careful her heels weren't too high whenever they'd gone out. 'You were up early this morning! It's good to meet someone else who can't sleep in on weekends.'

Nicholas nodded. 'I'm a TV producer for *Wake Up London*, and we have to be at the studio by five. Even when I'm not working, it's hard to shut off the internal clock.'

Clare grinned. 'Tell me about it.'

'So what can I get you?' Nicholas asked, sliding the menu across the table. A half-full espresso cup sat in front of him.

'I'll have the same as you.' As Nicholas beckoned over the waiter, she took the opportunity to examine him. With a high forehead and straight nose, he was actually much better looking than his Facebook photo. That must be a first, she smiled to herself. The Breton-striped jumper and jeans fit his solid body perfectly.

'So.' Turning back to face her, Nicholas caught her giving him the once-over, and Clare quickly averted her eyes. 'Thanks for meeting with me—I'm sorry I couldn't make Wednesday. But I'm really interested in learning more about the club. It's so hard to meet like-minded people, women especially. When I saw your Facebook advert pop up, I knew I had to get in touch.'

'I'm glad you did,' Clare said. 'I've had a great response to the ad, but a lot of people aren't based in London or just want to make it an online thing. I started the club to create a real-life social networking group for both men and women to meet new people. So many of my friends are housebound now with families.'

'Children do have a way of cramping your lifestyle.' Nicholas made a face, and for a second, it almost seemed as if he was speaking from experience. 'I've seen it first-hand with my brother and his wife,' he explained quickly. 'They used to be huge clubbers, and now a good night out involves heading to the off-license for wine and frozen pizza. With the energy my two nieces have, I can't say I blame them.'

Clare laughed. 'That's precisely why I formed the club. I'm hoping with time and a few more members, we can arrange some weekend getaways and other activities, too.'

'Sounds perfect.' Nicholas smiled, and again Clare was struck by how handsome he was. 'How many members do you have so far?'

'Only three, but it's early days. I've set up a Facebook page and I'm looking for other ways to spread the word. I'm sure there are loads of people in London who want a place to get together and have fun without conversations constantly being hijacked by kids. I just need a way to reach them. Any ideas?' As someone who worked in media, maybe he could suggest a strategy.

Nicholas tilted his head, a thoughtful expression on his face. 'Actually, I might be able to help with that. *Wake Up London* is always looking for new events, different trends, and the like. If you want, I can pitch your club to my boss and see what he makes of it. It'd definitely be a great way to get more members.'

'That would be fantastic!' Clare's eyes widened with enthusiasm.

'Let me talk to him and I'll get back to you.'

The waiter set an espresso in front of her, and Clare breathed in the heady scent of coffee. 'Cheers!' she grinned before lifting it to her lips for a sip.

'Cheers! Here's to the No-Kids Club . . . and to living child-free.' Nicholas raised his drink in the air, too, meeting her eyes as their cups clinked. Clare felt her cheeks flush under his intense gaze.

'Tell me a bit more about you, then,' she said, lowering her head to hide the redness of her face. 'Do you enjoy working in TV?' What a silly question, she chastised herself. God, she really was out of practice.

But Nicholas just nodded. 'I love it,' he said. 'I don't have the angst of appearing on air, and it's very satisfying to see your piece come together. You get to create something every day—even if it *is* sometimes a little frivolous, such as interviewing a fashion designer for dogs.' He laughed, and Clare joined in. It was so nice to see someone in London who, like her, actually enjoyed their job. Most of the men she'd met spoke of their work as a necessary evil. Something else we have in common, Clare thought.

'It means getting up at half-past three weekday mornings, but I don't mind,' he continued. 'I've been there for eight years now, so I'm used to it.' Nicholas took a sip of his espresso. 'Kids don't fit easily into that kind of lifestyle, you know? And the responsibility weighs you down.'

'I hear you,' Clare said. 'My job has some crazy hours, too, and I like my life and my independence too much.'

'You seem like a woman after my own heart. I tell you, it's so difficult to meet people who feel that way! I should know—I've been trying. My friends have even taken to pairing me off with post-menopausal women.' Nicholas grinned, and she felt warmth and mutual recognition pass between them.

'Sounds fun.' Clare could identify all too well. The last dinner party she'd been to, an old mate from university had made a more than obvious attempt to match her up with a man who must have been about seventy. He even had a cane, for God's sake! "But at least he didn't want kids," her friend had whispered.

Nicholas looked at his watch. 'Oh, bollocks. I'm sorry. I have to run.' He smiled at her, then a thoughtful expression came over his face. 'Look, I know this is kind of sudden and we've just met, but I got a pair of tickets through work to this evening's performance of *Madame Butterfly*. I was planning to blow them off and stay in, but would you be free to join me? I'd love to spend more time with you.'

This evening? Clare jerked in surprise. Usually, she liked taking things slowly on the dating front. And the opera? It seemed so formal . . . she'd much prefer a quiet pub dinner or somewhere they'd be able to chat.

Come on, she chided herself. The opera might not be her ideal first date, but Nicholas was exactly what she was seeking: someone to have a little fun with and enjoy life together. Plus, he was incredibly handsome, and they were definitely on the same page—not just about children, but work, too. She could sense he really *got* her, and she did want to get to know him better. Anyway, what else did she have planned? A hot date with a Chinese takeaway?

'That would be great,' Clare said, meeting his blue eyes.

'Perfect.' Nicholas got to his feet. 'I'll come by at six—just message me your address on Facebook. I'm so sorry to dash off.' He grabbed the bill from the table. 'And I'll take care of this. You sit here and enjoy your espresso.'

His cool, smooth cheek brushed against hers as he leaned down to kiss her goodbye. It was different from Edward's, which had been littered with stubble and was always warm, even in the chill of winter. She'd used to joke he was like a furnace that kept burning at all hours.

Lifting a hand to wave goodbye, she felt a flicker of hope course through her. Nicholas was exactly what she needed to forget the past few months and move on.

She'd been right to start the No-Kids Club. Already it was paying off.

CHAPTER NINE

A few hours later, Clare perched in front of the kitchen window, waiting for Nicholas to pick her up. She gave herself a quick once-over in the mirror: dark hair twisted into an elegant chignon, slim black trousers, and a tailored blouse. Not too dressy, but not too casual either. Nerves jolted through her, and she told herself not to be anxious. It wasn't as if she was looking for 'her everything', like Anna had said, and she didn't need to determine if Nicholas was the one. Clare was dubious 'the one' existed, anyway. How could you find someone who slipped perfectly into your life, and you into his? Disagreement and compromise were inevitable. Much better to keep things simple and fun.

A black BMW pulled over in front of her flat. Clare slipped her feet into court shoes, threw on a fawn-coloured mac, then hurried outside. She opened the car door, smiling at Nicholas, whose navy blazer made his eyes look even bluer. Inside the close space, the air was thick with the scent of his cologne, and Clare's stomach shifted unpleasantly as she breathed in the spicy fragrance.

Nicholas leaned over and kissed her cheek. 'Good to see you again. Thanks for coming out at the last minute. I'm glad you were free.'

'That's one advantage to not having children,' Clare said. 'No need to arrange babysitters.'

Nicholas nodded. 'You're lucky. And so am I,' he added. 'The cost of childcare these days is crazy, from what I hear.'

'It's been ages since I've been to the opera,' Clare said, eager to change the topic away from children. She tilted her head, trying to remember when she'd last seen a performance. Maybe in secondary school, on a school trip? Even then, it was only the local theatre production of *Aida*. Wincing, she recalled how the singers were more suited to scaring off wildlife than performing arias.

'Oh, really?' Nicholas gave her a sidelong glance as he pulled into the street. Fulham Road was clogged with Saturday night traffic, and Nicholas darted around a cab that had stopped to let out passengers. 'That's a shame. Well, you'll love this, I'm sure. I try to catch at least one show a season.'

'What's the story?' Clare asked, impressed to find a man interested in culture. Most of the blokes she met treated culture like a venereal disease.

'Actually, it's quite tragic.' Nicholas swerved to avoid a white van. 'A Japanese woman marries an American soldier. He leaves to go back to America, promising he'll return. In the meantime, she gives birth to his son.'

Clare nodded, admiring his clean-cut profile. He had a strong nose and jaw, she decided, just the way she liked it. 'And?'

'Well, he does come back—with his American wife.' Nicholas grinned. 'Men, eh?'

She forced a smile, thinking once again that pregnancy and children weren't beneficial for women, no matter the age or the culture. Sure, there were successful examples like Ellie, who seemed to be holding it all together. But more often, motherhood made women vulnerable, dependent on those around them.

'Anyway, the long and short of it is, Madame Butterfly kills herself.'

'Wow.' Clare raised her eyebrows at the dramatic conclusion. So much for a little levity on a Saturday night. God, even at the opera she couldn't escape from children and the inevitable tragic consequences.

'I know,' Nicholas said. 'Rather heavy going. But the music is divine, I promise, and the sets and the costumes are beautiful. I've seen the opera several times, and on each occasion I've really enjoyed it.'

'Thanks for asking me.' Despite balking at the sudden invitation, Clare was happy now she'd pushed aside her hesitation.

'My pleasure.' Nicholas squeezed her hand. 'I'm delighted you could make it.'

'Me, too,' she said, as his warm fingers intertwined with hers. 'Me, too.'

∾

Four hours later, Clare followed Nicholas down the curving stairs of the opera house, feeling like she was in a trance. The performance had been simply breathtaking; there was no other word for it. The music had swirled around her ears, transporting her to another time and place, and even though she hadn't understood everything, the emotion was palpable. She'd never thought music could have so much power.

'That was amazing,' she said when they were out on the street and the spell had dissipated.

Nicholas placed a hand gently on her back. 'I know. I told you you'd enjoy it.' He glanced at his watch, then checked his mobile phone. 'Right. Got time for dinner? I'm ravenous.'

Clare's hand slid down to her belly. Despite not eating since lunch, she wasn't the slightest bit hungry. Even though she had to be up early tomorrow morning, she wasn't ready for the evening to end. The music was wonderful, but she hadn't been able to chat much to Nicholas.

'Dinner would be great.' She smiled as he took her hand and led her to a nearby restaurant. Inside, it was crowded and warm, and a maître d' showed them to an empty table in the corner.

'So I'm interested in your take on Madame Butterfly,' Nicholas said as he settled into his chair. 'Tragic or idiotic? I know where I stand,' he continued before she could respond. 'I mean, I understand in that society, women had little power. But to kill yourself because you lost your husband? Purely idiotic in my books.'

Clare nodded. Although she had felt sorry for Madame Butterfly and her plight, ending one's life over a failed relationship was ridiculous. Her mind flipped again to Anna and her relationship with her husband. In a million years, Clare couldn't fathom making one person your all. What would happen if Michael ever left? Clare had found it hard enough when she and Edward broke up, and they'd only been together a few months.

All in all, it provided a very good case for the kind of relationship Clare was seeking now: one that wouldn't consume her emotions or her life.

'I have to agree with you there,' she said finally.

'The woman had a child, too.' Nicholas shook his head. 'At the very least, she should have stayed alive to take care of him.'

'If you make the choice to have kids, you should honour the responsibility.' As she spoke the words, Clare couldn't help thinking of her mother.

'Exactly.' Nicholas nodded emphatically, pausing to order a bottle of red from the waiter.

'So you've never wanted children?' She hated when people asked her that, but she knew Nicholas wouldn't judge her, and they were on the subject anyway . . .

Nicholas shrugged and then reached out to grab the menu. 'It's a lot of responsibility,' he said distractedly as he scanned the tiny print. 'Hmm, I think I'll get the steak and chips. How about you?'

Finally, a man who wanted to talk less about kids than she did. 'That sounds perfect,' Clare said, although the thought of food made her stomach groan in protest.

A waiter swooped in and took their orders. Nicholas reached across the table and clasped her hand again. The feel of his skin against hers was lovely, even though she felt curiously detached, as if she were watching from above. They chatted as they downed their dinner, Nicholas regaling her with humorous tales from his job. He'd just finished describing how the on-set chef had spectacularly burnt a roast lamb in the oven when Clare caught a glimpse of the clock on the wall.

'Yikes, it's after midnight. Guess we had better make a move. I've got an early start in the morning.' She pushed back her chair, rummaged through her handbag, then removed her credit card. 'Shall we split this?' Edward had always rejected her offer, but Nicholas just shrugged.

'Sure,' he said, taking her card and handing it over with his to the waiter. At last, a bloke who didn't feel obliged to pay for her, Clare thought. She hated feeling like she owed her date, and besides, Nicholas *had* given her a free ticket to tonight's performance.

Out on the street, Clare breathed in the cool night air, glad to escape from the stuffy restaurant. She'd choked down most her dinner, and her stomach was having difficulty accepting her efforts. As they climbed into the car, Nicholas kept up a running commentary about his job. Clare let the patter wash over her, trying to suppress a yawn. She'd enjoyed the evening, but exhaustion was pressing down on her, and curling up on the leather seats to snooze was becoming more and more irresistible.

'Here we are.' Nicholas pulled over in front of her flat, eyes glittering as he turned towards her. He laid a cool hand against her cheek. 'I've had a great night with you, Clare. I'd like to do it again some time.'

Clare nodded. 'Me, too. Thanks for asking me.'

He leaned in and she closed the space between them. His mouth slid against hers, and his arms encircled her. There was no awkward bumping of noses or slippery tongues; everything was smooth and slick and . . . *nice*.

She climbed from the car, waving as Nicholas pulled away. They got along well, he was fun to be with, and they agreed on all the important points. What more did she need?

There was nothing wrong with nice, Clare told herself, unlocking the front door. Nice was perfect, actually.

CHAPTER TEN

Poppy tried to ignore the sun peeping through the crack in the curtains. Usually, she was raring to go—Alistair always groaned at how she leapt from the bed with so much energy, as if she flicked a switch to 'On'. But today was different. Today was Mother's Day.

Her mind flashed back to Friday afternoon, when she'd helped the kids put the finishing touches on their Mother's Day cards. They'd been so excited, regaling her with tales of how they planned to surprise their mums on the big day. Faisal had told her all about the breakfast in bed he'd organised, so proud that his dad was letting him make French toast by himself. Poppy had forced herself to nod and smile while her gut contracted with grief and longing.

She tugged the duvet over her face and closed her eyes, trying to go back to sleep, but her buzzing mind wouldn't submit. Instead, her brain filled with images from Friday night . . . how Alistair had climbed into bed and said her name quietly, and how she'd pretended to be asleep when in reality she'd been far from it. They rarely disagreed about anything, but when they did, they were sure to make up within hours.

Not this time, though. Alistair hadn't mentioned adoption again, but he had helpfully left the literature on her bedside table, just in case she had a change of heart. She'd leafed through it, tears pooling in her eyes as she recalled his hopeful expression. He'd said he wasn't giving up on IVF, but . . .

Sighing, Poppy flopped over and stretched out an arm across the empty bed. Alistair was in Brighton on a training course for his physiotherapy clinic this weekend, and because it was so close to where his mum lived, he'd stayed there last night to be with her for today. He'd invited Poppy over, but she wasn't in the mood to play happy families. She wanted to stay home and lick her wounds in peace.

Suddenly claustrophobic in the stuffy room, Poppy sat up and threw off the cover. Outside, sun streamed from a brilliant blue sky and the first hint of green was appearing on trees and bushes. Maybe some fresh air would make her feel better about everything. She quickly pulled on her clothes and jacket, tugged on her boots, and was out the door. A wander around Portobello Road usually lifted her spirits. She loved watching the market booths being set up as the vendors bantered and laughed.

The sun was high but the air was cool, and Poppy quickened her pace to keep warm. As she scurried under the Westway, her eyes fell on a family in front of her: mum, dad and two dark-haired girls with ringlets and high, clear voices that cut through the hum of the motorway above her. The children clung onto each of the mother's hands as they chatted about where they were taking her for breakfast, making her guess and laughing with abandon as her answers became increasingly outlandish.

The smaller of the two girls turned and smiled straight at Poppy, and her heart ached as she noticed the little one was the spitting image of her mother. Unable to tear herself away from the family, she lingered several feet behind them, smiling as their voices floated back. Before she knew what she was doing, she'd followed them down a side street and right up to the door of a small restaurant called Mike's Café.

'Coming in?' The dad turned to look at her quizzically, holding the door open behind him.

Poppy froze, her cheeks flushing. 'Um, no, that's okay.' Before the man could respond, she rushed down the street, pulling her blonde hair forward to cover her flaming face.

She sagged against a concrete wall, the longing that gripped her insides making it hard to breathe. Oh, God, how she wanted that— a child whose grin resembled her husband's, whose laugh echoed her own. Desire mixed with determination as she thought of the literature littering her bedside table.

If Alistair was thinking of adoption because he was worried about her, than he needn't: she was strong enough to handle any disappointment on the road to pregnancy. Hurt and frustration wouldn't get the better of her, like it had before. They didn't need to consider other options, because someday soon, she'd carry their child inside her. She could feel it in her bones: this time, it would work.

But how could she convince her husband? He always laughed at her 'bones', asking if she could predict the weather the next day or when the Chinese takeaway would arrive. Poppy gnawed her bottom lip as her mind turned over. Perhaps she couldn't persuade him to buy into her prediction, but she could show him she was calm, in control, and able to tackle the emotional process once more.

In fact, Poppy decided as she strode home, she'd prove how ready she was to move ahead by booking an appointment next week for another IVF consultation. Alistair had always overseen all the logistical details, even giving her the hormone injections when she felt squeamish. No wonder he was getting tired of the process.

This time, she'd take on everything herself.

❧

'Thanks for coming with me to Mum's,' Anna said to her husband as she navigated the early Sunday-afternoon traffic on the way home. 'Sorry lunch didn't work—I'd no idea she'd already made plans.' Imagine, her own mother not wanting to go out for Mother's Day lunch!

Anna sighed, slowing at a red light. Ever since the divorce, Mum had built up a huge circle of friends, all single women who were determined to stay that way. Every holiday, they went out to lunch as a group, providing support to those who didn't have families. The irony was that even though Mum did have a family, she preferred to spend time with her friends. Anna and Michael had only managed to nab an hour before her mother headed off.

Not that Michael minded leaving early. Anna had barely dragged him off the sofa in the first place, and while he and her mother weren't on bad terms, tension floated in the air whenever they met. More than once, Mum had commented how Anna should look for a full-time job or get out of the house, subtly implying her daughter shouldn't dote on her husband so much. Anna gritted her teeth. As if Mum was one to give relationship advice! What she and Michael really needed was more time together, not less. If only she could think of something he couldn't turn down.

'That's all right.' Michael glanced over and smiled. 'But I'm starving! Do you think you could knock up that delicious beef stew for lunch?'

Anna shoved away the hope of heading out to eat, biting back the response that Boeuf Bourguignon, or 'that beef stew', had to simmer for ages and wasn't something she could throw together. 'Sorry, no, but I might be able to do some spag bol.' That was as much as she felt like cooking right now.

Anna pressed down on the pedal as the light changed, wishing she could swing the wheel, turn away from home, and *drive*. She didn't even care where they ended up! Just somewhere different; somewhere miles from everyday life.

As if on cue, a huge billboard reared up in front of her. "Discover Venice", the lettering said over a photo of a gondola floating down a canal. Anna swallowed hard, the image filling her eyes. *Venice!* This had to be a sign. One of the most romantic places on earth, it was sure to give their relationship a jumpstart. Not to mention she'd been wanting to go since forever. And she could even make the trip a surprise! If everything was organised already, Michael wouldn't say no.

Hope and excitement jetted through her. This was exactly what they needed to get things back on the romance track.

CHAPTER ELEVEN

Clare rubbed a hand over her face, then ogled her watch in disbelief. Six o'clock already? The last time she looked, it had only been mid-afternoon. Then an ambulance arrived bearing victims from a multi-vehicle accident on nearby Brompton Road, and everything else had disappeared. Rolling her aching shoulders, she trudged to an empty room to change before heading to the second No-Kids Club meeting at All Bar One near Oxford Circus. She'd wanted to pick somewhere quiet and more off the beaten track, but she hadn't the time. Given there were still only three members—including herself—and it was a Wednesday, not Friday, it shouldn't be too hard to get a table.

As she rushed to the Tube, she wondered if Nicholas had pitched the club idea to his boss. It'd be good to have some fresh blood. Anna and Poppy were nice, but they weren't really her kind of people. And despite the continuous messages flooding her Facebook inbox, the club had yet to pick up any more real-life members. Lots of vague 'maybe next week' and 'I'm busy Wednesdays' messages instead. It seemed London's no-kids contingent weren't exactly keen socialites.

It was still early days, Clare told herself, slapping her Oyster card on the reader and hurrying down the escalator. And if Nicholas had responded out of the blue, there were sure to be others like him.

A pang of disappointment hit at the thought of Nicholas. After he'd dropped her off on Saturday night, she'd hoped to hear from him soon. Already it was mid-week, and there hadn't been so much as a text. But that was what she wanted: plenty of space, flexibility to do her own thing. They'd meet again soon, she was sure. Anyway, she was so bloody tired these days, she'd probably fall asleep on him.

Thirty minutes later, Clare entered the packed All Bar One, scanning the crowd for Poppy's petite frame and Anna's flaming hair. Ah, there they were, hunched over a small table at the back. Anna was almost through her red wine, while Poppy was drinking—Clare squinted—*was that cranberry juice?* That woman really needed to let her hair down and have some fun. Clare wondered what her husband was like, and if he wanted a baby as much as she did. If not, well . . . there was bound to be tension there, she was sure.

Speaking of husbands, wasn't Anna supposed to bring hers tonight? By the sound of things, they were usually joined at the hip. How on earth that woman managed to make a life out of doing up a house and working part-time in a bookshop, Clare couldn't even begin to imagine.

'Hi, ladies.' Clare squeezed past a swarthy man crammed into a suit and collapsed on a chair. Ah, it felt so good to sit after the hectic day. Now all she needed was a glass of wine and she'd be set. Her heart sank as she took in the hordes at the bar. 'I'm going to grab a drink. Would either of you like something?'

'I'll have another Merlot, please,' Anna said, taking the last sip of hers. 'I've got to get my tolerance up for my Italian getaway this weekend!' Her face glowed.

'Oh, fantastic,' Clare said. 'Where are you going? The Amalfi Coast is beautiful.' Her mind flipped back to the family holiday there the year before Mum left, heart twisting as she recalled her parents clasping hands, drinking wine on the balcony overlooking the sea. In that one moment, she'd truly believed they were happy together. To this day, she still couldn't make the memory jive with her mum's departure the next year.

'We're heading to Venice,' Anna responded. 'I've always wanted to go there.'

'You've never been?' Poppy asked.

'No, it's the first time for both me and my husband.' Anna grinned excitedly. 'I'm planning the whole thing as a surprise. I can't wait to see his face!'

'Wow.' Clare raised her eyebrows, impressed with Anna's chutzpah. Given what she'd said about her husband, Clare had her pegged as the passive one in the relationship. She hoped for Anna's sake the man actually went along with the plan. Personally, she hated surprises. 'Poppy, how about you? Would you like a drink?'

Poppy shook her head. 'No, thanks. I'm fine with this.'

'Tell you what,' Clare said, making it her mission tonight to get Poppy to relax. A single drink wouldn't impede her fertility. 'Why don't I get us a bottle and three glasses.' She threaded through the crowd before Poppy could open her mouth to protest.

A torturous fifteen minutes later—ordering at an All Bar One on a weekday night was the equivalent to dodging rabid bulls in Pamplona—she returned to the table, clutching a bottle of Merlot and three glasses. Quickly, she sloshed liquid into each glass and placed it in front of the girls.

Poppy examined the wine like it was poison. 'Oh, I'm sorry, Clare. I really can't.'

Clare was about to respond that it would take a whole lot more than one glass to stop her getting pregnant, but she snapped her mouth closed. Although she couldn't understand wanting a baby so badly, she didn't want to make the woman feel worse than she already clearly did. That's not what this club was about.

'Okay,' Clare said, meeting Poppy's eyes. 'I just thought you could do with something to relax. You seem kind of tense.' She did, too. Hunched over the table with her foot jiggling away, she looked like someone who could explode any minute.

Poppy sighed. 'I am a little tense. And believe me, I'd love to have that wine. All of it.' For a second, the intensity of her gaze at the glass made Clare think she would grab the bottle and down it. Then, she pushed the drink away and shook her head. 'I have an appointment tomorrow to start another IVF cycle.'

'Wow,' Anna said. 'Good luck.'

Poppy breathed in a quivering sigh. 'Thanks. I really hope it works this time. I mean, I'd do it as many times as necessary, but my husband . . . ' The way her mouth twisted showed they might not be in agreement. 'I think he may have given up after the last round. He found the whole thing quite tough.'

'And he's willing to try again for you, despite how he feels?' Anna raised her eyebrows. 'Sounds like a great guy.'

Poppy looked down, her fair cheeks turning rosy. 'Yeah, he is. He just needs a little encouragement to keep going.'

A small pang hit Clare as she glanced from Poppy to Anna. Even though baby-making or husband-pleasing was worlds from what she wanted, these women had been able to find men they loved with the same priorities. For the millionth time, Clare cursed the fact that Edward wanted children. And, she thought as she toyed with the stem of her wine glass, it had hurt that he wanted kids more than he wanted her. Then again, she hadn't budged on her position, either. It'd been a reproductive stalemate, and neither had been willing to cave.

But that was in the past, she told herself firmly. Nicholas was the kind of man she should be with now. And even if she never heard from him again, there were bound to be others like him out there. Somewhere.

'All the more wine for us, then.' Clare grinned at Anna, who nodded and took a big gulp as if her life depended on it. 'So onto the business of the club,' she said, after sipping her own wine. Was it her imagination, or did it taste kind of strange? That's what she got for ordering the cheapest bottle. 'Still a lot of messages and interest from everywhere in the world, but only one person who might actually come along. Nicholas Hunt is his name. He's just busy this week.'

'Oh, it's a man? That's good news,' Anna said. 'If I do ever manage to get Michael to come out, it'd be great for him to have another bloke to chat with.'

Clare nodded. 'Exactly. I want this to be a place for both men and women to socialise and provide support. And the best bit is, Nicholas works as a producer for *Wake Up London* and he might be able to get the club mentioned on the show. It'd be a great way to boost numbers.'

'That's fantastic!' Poppy said enthusiastically. 'A friend of mine once got her new business onto the telly, and she sold out of everything within a few days.'

'Just what we need to help get more members,' Anna agreed. 'I could post something in the bookshop, too. We have a community bulletin board there.'

'Okay, that sounds good.' Clare thought that'd have all the efficacy of a sponge trying to dry up the Mediterranean, but she appreciated the effort.

'I'd love to do something to help, too, but I don't know what.' Poppy sipped her cranberry juice. 'I mean, I work in a school, and by default most people there are parents or other teachers, who all have children.'

'Don't worry.' Clare waved a hand in the air. Poppy would probably be pregnant in a few months anyway and fall into the same hole that had engulfed Ellie. 'Just have a think,' she added, hoping she didn't sound too dismissive, 'and if you run across anyone or a way to spread the word, let me know.'

They chatted about Anna's visit to Venice for a bit, working their way through the bottle of wine. When the conversation slowed, Anna glanced at her watch.

'I'd better make tracks. I have a few more things to finalize for our trip.' Her face lit up with anticipation again.

'You'll have to tell us all about it next week,' Clare said, although in reality, the last thing she wanted to listen to was someone else's romantic vacation. Still, Anna seemed so excited it was hard not to want to share it with her.

'Oh, I will! I'll take tons of photos, I'm sure.' She heaved a handbag over her shoulder and lifted a hand. 'See you next week!'

'I should make a move, as well,' Poppy said. 'I've got an early start in the morning.'

Clare sighed inwardly. She didn't have to work until seven tomorrow night, and while a big night out was never on the cards, she *had* hoped they'd make it past—she looked at her watch— bloody half past eight! God, this club really did need some new blood.

'Okay, well, I'll see you both next week, then.' Clare pasted on a smile as she watched them go, feeling the funny pang inside again. They were heading back to waiting husbands, and she was going home to . . . an empty flat. But silence was nice, especially after her hectic day at work. Sighing, Clare downed her glass and stood, her muscles protesting. The sooner she got home, the sooner she could crawl into bed and sleep.

CHAPTER TWELVE

'You do know your chance of conceiving falls with each unsuccessful IVF cycle, yes? And as this is your fifth attempt . . .' The doctor's voice trailed off as he sat back, regarding Poppy with serious eyes.

Poppy shifted in the chair. 'I know. But there *is* still a chance, right?'

'Well, yes. There is.' He leaned forward. 'I know you've been through the process several times already, but I'll review it again. We'll give you a hormone that will suppress your monthly cycle— you'll need to inject this every day for two weeks. Then, we'll stimulate your egg supply by giving you another hormone, again which you'll inject for another two weeks. A day or so before your eggs are due to be collected, you'll have an injection to help them mature. Finally, the eggs will be collected and mixed with your partner's sperm. We'll check after twenty hours to see if any are fertilised.'

Poppy nodded, the doctor's words washing over her. She'd studied the process so many times that it was practically tattooed on the inside of her brain. Not to mention she'd been through it already— and not just once. She tried to forget the cramping and pain (what the medical literature labelled "a little discomfort") after the eggs were harvested. It would be worth it in the long run, and that was nothing compared to what she'd experience during labour.

Anticipation rushed through her at the thought. The birthing process terrified many of her friends, but she couldn't wait to have a little human being make its way from the comfort of her womb and into the world.

Poppy had a good feeling about this cycle. It would work. It *would*.

'And your husband?' Poppy jerked upright as she realised the doctor had stopped his explanation.

'Oh, yes, my husband. He can't wait to start. He just had a meeting at work today and couldn't get away.' Poppy met the doctor's eyes, hoping her cheeks weren't flushing at the lie. It was mostly true. Alistair *did* have a meeting, and he would be on board, once she said the process was underway. She'd opened her mouth more times than a guppy fish to tell him about the appointment. At the last minute, though, the words had withered on her tongue. She was just being silly. Of course he wouldn't say no; he wanted her to get pregnant as much as she did. But the timing had never seemed right to discuss it. Anyway, the more she did on her own, the more he'd believe she could handle what was ahead.

'Okay. If you're certain you'd like to continue, we'll need the fee in full. Once you've paid—either today or whenever you're ready—the nurse will meet with you to begin the suppression injections. Oh, and we'll need your husband to sign a few updated consent forms before we begin stimulation.'

Poppy nodded. That gave her about two weeks—she'd definitely have his buy-in before then.

'Would you like to pay today, then?'

Poppy stared at the doctor, her mind ticking. She'd love to pay now and get everything underway. But although she could take care of appointments and injections, she couldn't handle the financial side on her own. As much as she enjoyed her job, the salary barely covered half the mortgage and groceries. By the end of the month, she was lucky if she had enough to splash out on a bottle of Tesco's Finest. Over the past couple months, she'd managed to save almost two thousand pounds from the sale of her car—she never used it, anyway—and by setting aside any spare cash whenever she could. But that would barely cover half the procedure's cost, and she'd already shelled out two hundred pounds for today's consultation.

When she got home, she'd sit Alistair down and tell him about the appointment. Once he saw how eager and in control she was, Poppy knew he wouldn't hesitate to start again.

'We'll pay in full the next few days, and I'll contact the nurse to begin the process.' A corner of her mouth nudged up as happiness grew inside.

'Perfect. Until then.' The doctor gave her a this-session-is-now-over smile, and Poppy hurried through the plush reception area of the Harley Street clinic, avoiding eye contact with any of the waiting women. When she'd come for her first cycle, she'd tried to have little conversations with them, embracing the feeling she wasn't alone in this battle. Soon, she'd discovered hearing how many failed attempts they'd undergone—or even their successes—made her feel like a pessimistic failure. That was part of the reason she'd joined the No-Kids Club. At least there, no one would think she was any less of a woman if she didn't have children. In fact, Clare likely thought she was mental for wanting a child in the first place, and Anna would probably consider Poppy crazy for needing kids when she already had a happy marriage.

Poppy shook her head as she strode towards the Tube. Children would make their marriage even happier! She was bursting now to tell Alistair they were good to go, to see the excitement on his face. What man didn't want his own flesh and blood? In a few days' time, they'd be on their way to parenthood.

She couldn't wait.

CHAPTER THIRTEEN

Clare slicked down a piece of Sellotape on the box of chocolates from Harrods she'd bought for her stepmum. The Mother's Day gift was almost a week overdue, but Tam had been away last weekend, and today was Clare's first free day since her date with Nicholas. Not that she was complaining—burying herself in work on Mother's Day had been a blessing. The occasion was always a harsh reminder that her own mum had chosen not to be a mother. Thank goodness for Tam, Clare thought for the millionth time.

Glancing at her watch, she noticed it was only half past ten—still plenty of time to catch the train to Berkhamsted. Despite hitting Carluccio's for coffee, strolling down Fulham Road, and reading the morning papers, the day was dragging. Maybe she'd have a quick look at the club's Facebook page before she left. Fingers crossed there'd be some new messages. Or perhaps one from Nicholas? Almost a week had passed and she'd still heard nothing. She liked that he wasn't invading her space, but it would be nice to see him again.

Sighing, Clare opened the browser on her laptop and logged into Facebook. There were the usual random enquiries and messages of support, but nothing that signalled an influx of fresh blood.

She was about to snap the lid closed and head for the door when she spotted the message icon blinking on screen. Clare scrolled to her inbox, eyes bulging and pulse quickening when she saw Edward's name. Edward? Why would he get in touch?

As she clicked the mouse, she noticed her fingers were shaking, and she took a deep breath to steady herself. Whatever the message said changed nothing. They wanted different things, and that was that.

Or was it?

Eagerly, she scanned the sentences before her on the screen, her mouth falling open in surprise. Edward wanted to talk? He missed her? Her heart squeezed with longing. God, she missed him, too. Her lips lifted in a smile as she pictured him typing away on his state-of-the-art laptop, feet tapping the scarred oak floorboards of his flat just off Spitalfields. Before meeting him, Clare had never known much about that part of London. He'd brought the area to life, and ever since their break-up, she hadn't the heart to return.

Rereading his words, a memory of their first date flashed into her head. It had been a cold December day a few weeks before Christmas, and the sky was already dark by the time Clare headed out. She always tried to meet online dates for a quick drink close to her flat—that way, when they inevitably turned out to be losers, she hadn't invested much time—but Edward had insisted on a place in East London, saying the food was incredible. Clare hadn't been thrilled with trekking all the way across town, but she had been quietly impressed with his persistence. Usually, her Internet dates would be happy to chew beef jerky. And if he wasn't her type, she told herself, she could use the long journey home as an excuse to leave early. She'd run a brush through her glossy dark hair, pulled on her skinny jeans and a soft rose cashmere jumper, then tugged on a heavy black coat and was out the door.

She'd recognised Edward straightaway. Waiting on the steps outside Liverpool Street station, his dark eyes lit up when he saw her. Right down to the tightly curled hair and tan skin, Edward had looked exactly like his photo. So far, so good.

'Hello!' He'd leant in to kiss her, and Clare had caught a whiff of his citrusy cologne. Something about the scent of him and the feel of his cheek on hers had made her face flush and her tummy flip. 'It's good to meet you.'

'Good to meet you, too,' Clare had echoed, actually meaning it for once. They'd stood there for a second, smiling at each other as commuters pushed around them. Then Edward had taken her hand and they'd dodged traffic as they crossed the street to the restaurant. Despite its no-frills interior with long tables lining the room and diners cheek to jowl, the buzz was welcoming. They'd elbowed their way to two empty seats, and with Edward so close she could feel the heat from his leg, Clare had devoured some of the best comfort food she'd ever tasted, finishing off the meal with a jam roly-poly.

Finally, when she could eat no more, Edward had led her out into the night, walking her through the deserted Spitalfields market and then over to Brick Lane past the former Huguenots houses, explaining the history of the area. She'd listened to the pleasant cadence of his voice, falling under the spell of its warm timbre. And by the time he'd deposited her back at the station, it wasn't just his neighbourhood she was familiar with; she felt like she'd known Edward forever. He'd told her where he'd grown up, how he'd wanted to be a fireman when he was young but had ended up a graphic designer, and about his secret addiction to the *Daily Mail*. Somehow, he'd managed to work his way past her barriers, drawing her out and learning all about her, too.

When they'd said good night, Edward had wrapped his arms around her, bringing her close for a kiss. She'd never forget the warmth of his lips and how their breath had made clouds in the cold night air as they pulled apart, surrounding them in a misty white haze. If she'd been a romantic, she'd have said it was magical. From that moment on, they'd been together.

Until he'd ruined it by mentioning children.

Clare scanned the message again. He wanted to meet up to see if they could hammer this thing out; he thought they were too good together to let what they had go so easily. In theory, Clare agreed, and oh, how she'd love to see him again. But there was the tiny issue of kids and the people carrier . . .

Unless he was open to changing his mind? She looked at the words in front of her. He hadn't said as much, but . . . A flicker of hope went through her. Maybe she'd give him a call when she was back from her parents'. The possibility of hearing his warm voice made her heart jump as she grabbed the shiny present from the table, threw on a coat, and slammed the door behind her.

A couple of hours later, Clare grinned into her father's cheery face as he stood at the entrance of the house where she'd grown up. Tikki curled in and out of his legs. 'Hi, Dad. Sorry I'm late. The trains were a nightmare.'

Dad shook his head, his neat grey hair still showing comb tracks. Every time she saw him, there was more and more white in his bristling beard, but his eyes were just as blue as she remembered. 'I don't know why you don't get a car. With your salary, you could certainly afford one. What's the point of all those years in medical school if you're not going to treat yourself to some creature comforts?'

Clare rolled her eyes. She'd heard this refrain a million times, on everything from the car to her rented flat. Sure, she could buy a car and her own home, too, but for some reason the thought of it made her uneasy. She liked being able to hop on the Tube or train without worrying about parking or upkeep. 'Where's Tam? I brought her something for Mother's Day.'

'She's in the kitchen baking your favourite cake.' Her father opened the door even wider and ushered Clare inside. The aroma of rich chocolate cake brought Clare back to the days when that dessert was the only thing making life bearable. For a brief instant, as she bit into the warm, spongy goodness, she could forget Mum's absence had left a gaping hole in her heart that no cake could fill, no matter how many she ate.

'Oh, yum!' Despite the heaviness in her stomach, she could always handle cake. Clare gave her dad a hug, then hurried down the narrow corridor towards the kitchen, where she could hear Tam cheerily humming away to a tune on the radio. Tam's plump, matronly figure was a sharp contrast to Clare's memory of her mum: slim body and high cheekbones like a model in a magazine. Clare drew a hand to her cheek. Dad used to say she was the spitting image of her mother, a sentiment that made Clare quiver with anxiety. She might look like Mum, but no way did she want to be anything like her. Nothing excused leaving a husband and child just because you decided they weren't for you.

Thank goodness Tam had come into her life. Soft and gentle, Tam was the only mother figure Clare wanted to remember today. She shoved all other thoughts of Mum from her head and breathed in the heady scent of cake again.

'Happy Mother's Day! Sorry I'm a little late.' Clare threw her arms around Tam, inhaling in the aroma of talcum powder mixed with vanilla and cinnamon. She drew back and held up the chocolates. 'I brought these for you.'

Tam's cheeks coloured with pleasure, and she wiped her hands on an apron before reaching out to take the gift. 'Thank you, love. Come on, sit down. I want to catch up with what's going on in your life! It's been ages since we've seen you.'

Clare sank onto a floral cushion tied to the roomy pine chair, trying to hide a smile as she noted several cushions now adorned each seat. Tam had a thing for pillows and cushions, and every time Clare came home, she noticed the number had multiplied. It was as if Tam was trying to cover the sparseness left by Clare's mum and provide a soft landing for Clare and her dad. Well, she had certainly done just that.

'Sorry I haven't been by,' Clare said, pushing back her dark hair. 'My schedule's been all over the place lately.'

Tam placed a glass of orange juice in front of Clare, and Clare grinned. Despite telling Tam over and over she'd moved into the wonderful world of caffeine, Tam still insisted on giving her the juice she'd always drunk as a child. Clare took a sip, the citrusy flavour exploding in her mouth.

'I don't know how anyone can live a normal life with such topsy-turvy hours,' Tam tutted as she poured herself a glass and slid into the chair across from Clare. 'How can they expect you to do that?'

Clare shrugged. 'It's just the way it is. You get used to it after a while.'

'And what about the men in your life?' Tam asked, her brown eyes crinkling at the corners as she smiled. 'You still with that one . . . what was his name, Edward? The one you told me about at Christmastime?'

Oh, God. Had she actually broken her cardinal rule and mentioned a man to Tam? Why, oh why had she done that? She *knew* talking to Tam about relationships in her life was like drawing a moth to a flame. Tam was desperate to pair her off and have grandchildren, despite Clare's constant refrain that she didn't want kids. She seemed to think Clare was going through a phase and kept waiting for her maternal clock to start ticking. Clare hadn't the heart to tell her she'd be waiting forever.

'Um, no.' Clare sipped her juice. 'We broke up a couple weeks ago.' The spark of hope at Edward's earlier message flared again. Was there a chance they'd work things out?

'Oh, I'm sorry, honey.' Tam reached over and squeezed Clare's hand.

'It's all right.' Clare forced a bright smile. 'There are plenty of fish in the sea.' Tam had always told her that when she'd had her heart broken in secondary school. Shame it didn't seem to be true. 'So tell me about these cushions!' She knew Tam wouldn't be able to resist filling her in on the latest additions to the collection.

But this time, Tam didn't take the bait. Her normally cheery face was serious as she fixed Clare with her big brown eyes. 'Clare, listen. There's something your dad wanted me to talk to you about.'

Clare tilted her head, wondering at her stepmum's solemn expression. 'Why can't he talk to me himself?'

'Well, he finds anything to do with your mother a little difficult,' Tam said. 'So I told him I'd mention it to you.'

'My mother?' Clare felt her throat tighten. 'What about her?'

'Well, honey, as you know, she's been in York for the past little bit, working at the university.'

Clare nodded, her eyes fixed firmly on Tam's face. Yes, she remembered Tam telling her something like that, along with the fact that Clare's mother wanted her to get in touch. Clare hadn't even considered it—Mum hadn't been in contact for years after she'd left, and Clare wasn't going to rekindle the relationship now.

Grimacing, she recalled how devastated she'd been on her sixteenth birthday when Mum failed to ring. Despite the years of silence, Clare had been convinced Mum would call—she'd always said turning sixteen was a major milestone, and she couldn't wait to celebrate with her daughter. Clare's friends had tried to persuade her to go out, but she'd made an excuse to linger by the phone.

The phone had stayed silent, and Clare had lain on her bed for hours, staring glumly at the ceiling. Finally, Tam had knocked on the door with a piece of her legendary chocolate cake and a glass of juice.

'There's more of that downstairs, along with some presents from Dad and me. Why don't you come on down and we can celebrate your sixteenth together?' She'd smiled and reached out to touch Clare's shoulder, but Clare had shrugged her off, wrapping her arms around her knees.

'I'm busy,' she'd mumbled, not even making the effort to look occupied. Tam would get the hint.

But something must have been wrong with Tam's radar, because she didn't leave the room. Instead, she'd sat down beside Clare on the bed. Clare had shifted, not wanting anyone to see the hurt and anger on her face.

'Love, I know you were hoping your mother would get in touch, and I'm sorry you haven't heard from her. I'm sure she's thinking about you and she'll call when she can. In the meantime, your father and I are all set to celebrate with you.' She'd leaned over and stroked Clare's hair, and Clare had jerked away.

'I don't want you or Dad. I want Mum!' The words burst from her in a shout, and as soon as she'd said them, she realised it was her mother she was angry with, not Tam. But it was too late; they were out.

Without saying more, Tam had got up and walked away. She'd closed the door softly behind her, and Clare had felt even worse than before. And when she'd crept downstairs and noticed the huge chocolate cake Tam had decorated for her, along with the elaborately wrapped gifts that clearly weren't the work of her father, guilt squeezed her gut like a vice.

'Your mum wasn't sure how to reach you now,' Tam continued, 'so she contacted us here. She's accepted a job in London, at King's College working in the fundraising office. She still wants to see you . . . or at least get in touch.' Tam's voice was soft and gentle, as if she knew how each word was twisting Clare's insides.

'I'd rather not,' Clare said firmly. 'My mother's involvement in my life is behind me. She wanted out, and I want to keep it that way.' London or not, proximity didn't mean they were any closer to reconnecting.

Tam reached across the table and took Clare's hand. 'It's not always that easy to separate the past from the present,' she said. 'And sometimes it's better not to. You and your mum could still have a relationship if you gave her a chance.'

Clare raised her eyebrows at Tam's words. A relationship? As if! People didn't change that easily, and if Mum had been able to choose a new life over her daughter once, she'd ditch her again, if need be. And what was Tam on about, claiming it was better not to separate the past from the present? When the past included a mother who abandoned you, Clare didn't doubt for a second she was better off keeping those memories high up on a shelf, gathering as much dust as they possibly could. The only way to look was forward—in life and relationships.

A dart of sadness hit as she pictured Edward's dark eyes, an expression of tenderness on his face as he typed this morning's message. Was he best left behind, too? Clare sighed as she realised the answer was probably yes. The issue of children was insurmountable, and opening that door again would only lead to more hurt and pain. They'd done the hard bit and broken up once. Clare wasn't keen to prolong the torture.

Anyway, she wasn't looking for a serious, committed relationship now. Nicholas, with his easy humour and hard-to-tie-down lifestyle, was the ideal fit for her. In fact, when she got home, she'd ring him up and ask him out to dinner. There was no reason she had to wait around for him to get in touch.

'Have a think about it.' Tam stood, fluffing up the pillow she'd been sitting on. 'I'll forward her number to you in case you change your mind.'

Clare nodded and smiled, although she knew the chances of her reaching out to Mum were about as likely as the Queen sporting a mullet.

'Hey, any chance of some cake?' Clare's dad stuck his head around the kitchen door, eyebrows raised hopefully.

'Sure.' Tam bustled over to the counter where the chocolate cake was standing in all its glory, and Clare breathed a sigh of relief the subject of her mother was closed.

Clare watched her father smile over at Tam as she placed a piece of cake before him. She'd never have thought it at the time, but Mum leaving was a good thing in the long run. She'd got her freedom, and Clare and Dad had got a woman for whom being a mum was a ready-made role.

Everything had turned out for the best.

CHAPTER FOURTEEN

Anna hurried home from Books on the Hill, hoping Michael wasn't back from work already. It was almost five on Friday, and she wanted to pack his case in readiness for the surprise getaway. As soon as he came in the door—and before he'd even a chance to think about booting up games—she'd hand him his bag, bundle him into the car to Heathrow, and they'd be in Venice by midnight.

Excitement coursed through her as she pictured the swank hotel she'd got a great deal on. It was minutes from Piazza San Marco, and the description had said when you opened your window, you could hear canal water lapping the building's facade. The hefty deposit was non-refundable, and with the cost of the flights the trip had pretty much wiped out the small savings she'd set aside from her job. But it was more than worth it. She couldn't believe after all this time she was finally going to her dream location.

Anna smiled at the clichéd vision that drifted into her head: the two of them, locked in a passionate embrace while floating down the canal in a gondola as accordion music echoed off buildings around them. She'd even bought some new lingerie, in racy red lace that Michael loved. If ever there was a weekend to christen it, this was it. In such a romantic venue and away from the usual daily grind, her husband was certain to regain his missing libido.

She unlocked the front door and scurried inside, heart dropping when she heard the telltale sound of explosions and gunshots. Oh, bollocks, Michael had made it home before her for once.

But that was all right, she told herself. They wouldn't have to rush as much and he could pack whatever he liked.

Her heart thumped and her grin grew bigger. She couldn't wait to tell him they were off and see his reaction! She stuck her head around the corner of the lounge.

'Guess what? We're . . . ' Her voice trailed away as she spotted not just Michael but two other men all crowded around the television, each holding a console in one hand and a beer in the other.

'Oh, hi, honey.' Michael glanced over and smiled before turning his attention back to the game. 'You know Grant and Mo, right?' The men threw her a quick hello.

Anna nodded. 'Yes, I think we've met.' Shit, she thought, her mind frantically turning over. What was she going to do now? If she and Michael didn't leave by seven, they'd miss their flight. His friends couldn't be staying too long, could they? They must have better things to do on a Friday evening than play on the Xbox. God, tonight of all nights, Michael had to be pally-pally with his workmates. He used to say he reserved Fridays for her. When had that stopped?

'Sweetie, can you grab me another beer?' Michael asked, not even averting his eyes from the screen. 'Guys, you want one, too?' The other men nodded, and Anna turned on her heel and made her way to the kitchen. For goodness' sake, she hadn't even taken off her coat yet! An unfamiliar flicker of anger rose within her, and she switched on the light, blinking as the gleaming steel appliances came into focus.

It's not Michael's fault, she told herself as she grabbed three cans from the fridge. He had no idea what she'd planned. She drew in a deep breath as she walked back to the lounge. It was only five, and if the guys left in the next hour, there'd be plenty of time to catch the plane. Maybe she'd pack Michael's case now to save a few minutes. Anna handed over the drinks to the monosyllabic men, then padded up the stairs, listening closely for the sound of the door opening and closing as she kept one eye on the clock.

Fifteen minutes passed, then half an hour, then forty-five minutes . . . Finally, when she'd folded Michael's underwear more times than necessary and she couldn't prolong the packing any longer, she perched on the side of the bed. She hated to barge in on the fun downstairs, but they couldn't afford to wait much more. Rushing turned Michael into a ball of stress, and she wanted to start their weekend on a good note.

She was about to stand when Michael appeared at the bedroom door. A whoosh of relief went through her. Oh phew, they must have finished. Now she didn't need to interrupt their fun.

Michael's gaze fell on the open case beside her on the bed. 'Aw, thanks, honey. I could have done that myself, though.'

Anna's brow furrowed. She hadn't said anything about going away. So why was he thanking her?

'Did you put in my green jumper? It's the warmest I have, I think—it gets quite cold, even at this time of year.'

Had he somehow discovered their destination, Anna wondered, confusion sweeping over her? But how? Spring nights in Venice *could* get chilly, but she was certain she'd left no trace of the getaway anywhere.

'Ah, there it is.' Michael looked up from rifling through the case. 'Thanks so much. You're a star!' He dropped a kiss on the top of her head. 'I reckon we're almost ready to set off, then.'

Anna's mouth fell open and she snapped it closed, trying to cover her surprise. He'd obviously found out . . . God knows how. But however he'd uncovered her plan, at least he seemed happy and excited. Part of her had worried he'd balk at going away. 'I guess so!' She reached up and touched his cheek, smiling at the thought of the weekend ahead. 'Just let me print off the hotel details and directions.'

'Oh, no need.' Michael waved a hand in the air. 'Mo's got everything sorted. He's a little obsessive that way.'

Anna drew back. *Mo?* What on earth was Michael talking about?

'Anyway,' Michael continued, 'Mo's been there a there a few times before, so he knows the route. Best place to golf in Scotland, he says!'

Anna's heart dropped so fast she could swear it crashed through the floor into the room below. *Best place to golf in Scotland?* The shouts and laughter of the men drifted from downstairs as she frantically tried to assimilate her husband's words.

'I didn't know you were going away this weekend,' she finally managed to croak.

Michael didn't seem to notice the choked way the words left her mouth. 'What? Really?' Now it was his turn to look puzzled. 'I'm sure I told you when we booked it a couple months ago.'

Anna shook her head. 'No, I don't think so.' Michael leaving his video games for a whole weekend was an event she'd definitely have remembered.

Michael put an arm around her, drawing her close. 'Oh, I'm sorry, hon. I was sure I'd told you. We've been talking about it at work for ages. This place is supposed to be spectacular! And we're going to visit a whisky distillery, too.' The words tumbled out of him. It was the first time she'd heard her husband so excited in ages—at least since the latest Xbox release.

Anna leaned her forehead on his shoulder so he couldn't see the tears filling her eyes. The idyllic weekend was slowly fading away, a bitter disappointment seeping in to take its place.

'We'll be back Sunday afternoon,' he said. 'So what do you have planned for the next few days? Are you working? Big night out with the girls?'

Anna swallowed hard to keep down her emotions. A big night out with the girls? As if. And she'd traded her shifts at work, thinking she'd be away all weekend. Empty space stretched before her like a desert.

'Oh, I don't know,' she responded, forcing her voice to sound bright. 'I'll find something. Have fun.'

'I will.' Michael's lips met hers, then he pulled her in for a hug. She felt numb in his arms, her head still trying to understand that she wasn't going anywhere. 'I'll give you a call tomorrow—it'll be too late by the time we arrive tonight.' He looked at his watch. 'Guess we'd better set off. I'll see you Sunday.' And with that, he zipped closed the suitcase, dropped a kiss on her cheek, and lifted a hand as he walked through the door.

Anna stayed frozen in place as she listened to his feet thumping down the stairs, the bustle and excited voices of the men as they gathered their things, then the bang of the door as it closed behind them. Silence filtered through the house, cloaking it with loneliness.

She sank onto the downy pillows of the bed. There was so much she should be doing—cancelling their flight, letting the hotel know they wouldn't be checking in—but that all made the ruin of the weekend seem real. Not only that, but the one occasion her husband did drag himself from his lair, it hadn't been to spend time with her. It'd been to pal around with his workmates, who he saw every day.

It wasn't Michael's fault, she told herself again, staring up at the ceiling. Besides, she could always rebook—if she could get the cash back. But despite her attempts to rationalise his leaving, she couldn't push aside the feeling that no matter what she did, nothing was revitalising their relationship. And on top of everything, she seemed to be the only one who noticed—or cared.

If Michael was happy, perhaps she should just leave it. He certainly didn't appear bothered by how things were going. Maybe she shouldn't be, either.

But even as she closed her eyes, Anna knew that wasn't the answer. The only problem was, she didn't know what was.

CHAPTER FIFTEEN

Clare pivoted in front of the mirror on Saturday night, raising an eyebrow at her reflection. Were the black jeans and jade-green blazer too formal or just right? Did these high heels make her look like she was trying too hard? And did she really need to be wearing the lacy lingerie? Better safe than sorry, she thought, grimacing as she pictured her usual greying cotton underwear. Nicholas would run away screaming if she sported those undergarments.

Truthfully, sex was the last thing she fancied. With all her night shifts, she was used to being exhausted, but this queasiness . . . She took a swig of Gaviscon, hoping this would do the trick, because she was really looking forward to tonight.

She'd rung Nicholas after returning from her parents' house, keen to banish the past—and Edward—from her mind, and ready to embrace the life she wanted. Nicholas had been full of enthusiasm, saying he knew just the place for dinner. He'd made no explanation for the silence since they'd last met, but Clare wasn't bothered. They were their own people; they didn't need to account for what they got up to when they weren't together. Who wanted to hear all those boring details, anyway?

Tam's words about separating different parts of her life came to mind, and Clare shook her head. She might have meant just the present and the past, but Clare saw nothing wrong with keeping other bits of your life separate, too—it certainly made things easier to deal with.

Okay, so she still hadn't succeeded in packaging up Edward's memories. She'd deleted his message, but just last night Clare had dreamed they were together again, up on his tiny rooftop. He'd been sipping the port he loved and reading one of those thick novels Clare never wanted to invest so much time in. She lay next to him, wrapped up in blankets as the lights of London glowed in the sky. When her eyes had snapped open this morning and she realised she'd never see him again, her insides squeezed painfully. She'd thrown off the covers, forcing herself to think about tonight . . . and Nicholas.

The flat buzzer sounded, and Clare glanced at her watch. Seven p.m.—right on time. She sprayed on some perfume, then hurried to the entrance.

'Hello.' Swinging open the door, she smiled at Nicholas. Clad in a slim-fitting cream jumper and a tailored pair of jeans, he was even more handsome than she remembered.

'Hello, yourself.' He grinned and leaned down to kiss her cheek. 'Ready? I've booked a fantastic place.'

Clare nodded. 'More than ready. So where are we going?' she asked as they went out into the chilly night. Drizzle hung in the air, making Clare's face feel cold and clammy.

'It's a new spot that just launched over in Camden. Top-class DJ and fantastic sushi.'

'Fabulous,' Clare managed to say, despite her stomach turning at the thought of sushi. Given her tricky tummy, raw fish was the second last thing she wanted—right after sex. And a DJ? Hopefully the music wouldn't be too loud. She'd kind of been hoping to learn a bit more about Nicholas. For God's sake, she thought, rolling her eyes at herself. When had she become so old?

Nicholas opened the door to his sleek BMW and ushered her in. The man had manners! On previous dates she'd been whipped in the face with the door when the bloke pushed through before her, failing to hold it open.

'You're going to love this place,' Nicholas said as they crossed the city. 'The food and service are fabulous, and only over-eighteens are allowed in. It's nice to enjoy eating out without sitting next to a screaming baby or watching a toddler mash a meal all over his face.'

Clare laughed, recalling the time she'd gone to Pizza Express one night with Ellie and the child at the table next to them had thrown the pepperoni like a discus. 'Very true.'

Nicholas manoeuvred the car into a vacant space on the street outside Camden Market. He cut the engine and turned to face her, eyes gleaming in the dark. 'You know, I'm so pleased I found someone who isn't in a rush to settle down.' He put a hand on her arm, and Clare glanced down at it, noting the slender fingers. An image of Edward's solid hands—and how they practically engulfed hers—swam into her head. She shoved it away. 'I'm really looking forward to tonight.' His words were weighted, leaving no doubt what he meant.

'Me, too,' Clare said, trying to mentally replace the thought of Edward's hands on her body with Nicholas's. It was time to move on, she told herself; she hadn't worn her sexy lingerie just for kicks. Given the way the bra was cutting into her, it felt more like torture.

Nicholas led her across the canal lock then up a flight of stone stairs to the restaurant. Music drifted from various pubs lining the street, and the whoop of partygoers echoed up and down the canal. It was Saturday night in Camden, and she was going to have a good time if it killed her. Her stomach flipped again and she stifled a groan. At this rate, it just might.

And when Nicholas led her inside the restaurant, it became even clearer having fun might take more effort than she could expend. House music boomed from a turnstile in the corner of the room, and purple spotlights illuminated each table as if they were on a stage. Waiters and waitresses—clad in black clothing with neon patches—looked like luminous aliens floating around the space. The whole thing was uber-cool, stylised to within an inch of itself . . . and exactly what Clare didn't want.

'Isn't this fantastic?' Nicholas yelled over the music, his face lit up with enthusiasm.

Clare forced a grin and nodded. 'Amazing.' It was amazing— just so not her thing. She gave it ten minutes before her throat was sore from shouting.

Nicholas rested his hand on the small of her back as the maître d' showed them to a table, the warmth of his palm seeping through her blazer. She slid onto the metallic banquette, squinting from the purple lights reflecting in the shiny surface.

'I'll join you here so we don't have to yell.' Nicholas scooted beside her, angling his body in her direction. 'Right,' he said after handing her the cocktail menu. 'Good news! I finally ran your pitch about the club past my boss.'

'And?' Clare raised her eyebrows.

Nicholas's eyes crinkled as he smiled. 'And they think it's a great idea. Child-free living is always a hot topic; people love to debate it, as I'm sure you know. You'd be up for an interview to explain why you set up the club, right?'

Clare nodded. 'I guess. I mean, I don't have much experience with television, but I could give it a try.'

'Don't worry, it won't be live. If you lose your train of thought, we can always start over. And I'll take it easy on you.' He grinned suggestively, and Clare returned his smile, waiting to feel a rush of attraction, of anticipation, of *something*. Right now, the two of them in bed seemed more theoretical than real.

'Sounds good. I'd love to find some new members,' she responded. 'And speaking of members, do you think you can make it out to the club one night, maybe this week? It'd be great to have you along.'

'Oh yeah, possibly. Let me check and make sure I don't have anything else on this Wednesday.' He grabbed his iPhone and punched at the screen, then tossed it on the table. 'Silly thing, I can never figure it out. I'll have a look and let you know. Ready to order some drinks?'

'Oh, I haven't even read the menu yet.' Clare scanned the long list of cocktails, wondering at his lack of response. Hadn't he got in touch because he wanted to join the club? So why wasn't he keen to come? Perhaps he was busy, but if that was the case, why didn't he just tell her? She'd have to run it by Ellie when she had a chance. God, she hadn't seen her friend in ages. The closer her due date, the harder Ellie seemed to be working.

After a very strong vodka martini, the purple lights took on a softer glow, darkness wrapping the table in a cocoon-like atmosphere. Even the music didn't seem as loud or irritating, fading into the background like a pleasant hum. Combined with a bottle of warm sake, Clare managed to stomach some blackened tuna and rice. Dinner passed in a blur and she'd no idea what they talked about, but Nicholas was as effusive and charming as ever. The tip of her nose was numb from too much drink, but at least the alcohol had taken the edge off her fatigue.

'This has been great, Clare.' Nicholas met her eyes and leaned in until his face was inches from hers. She couldn't help focusing on his lips and the little cleft in his chin.

She moved closer, too. 'I've had a really good time. Thank you.' Although this place wasn't her speed and she wouldn't be keen to do it again, she *had* enjoyed Nicholas's company.

'So . . .' He paused, then gave her a smile. 'I'd love to invite you back to my place for a nightcap, but I'm having some renovations done and it's a disaster. Maybe we can head to yours?'

Clare held his gaze, the wheels in her foggy mind turning. The night had been leading up to this, she knew, and she *did* want it—at least her brain did. She'd feel more in the mood once they were away from this place and settled back at home. She was just about to open her mouth to say that'd be wonderful when a fresh wave of nausea crashed over her and she gulped in air.

'Are you okay?' Nicholas eyed her with concern. 'You've gone a little pale.'

Clare nodded, trying to fight the sensation. 'I just—' Her stomach clenched, and she shot to her feet and stumbled down a corridor towards what she hoped was the loo. Leaning against a cubicle door, she bent over and gulped in air until her tummy righted itself. She should have known not to drink alcohol so quickly.

A knock sounded on the door. 'Clare? You all right in there?'

She gingerly lifted her head, waiting to see if she actually was okay. When her stomach stayed settled, she splashed some water on her flushed cheeks, grimacing at her dishevelled reflection in the mirror. 'I'll be fine, thanks.' She swung open the door and met Nicholas's eyes, trying not to notice how he subtly backed away as if she was about to upend the sake on his shoes—not that she blamed him.

'I should head home,' she said. 'But I definitely want to take a rain check on that nightcap.'

'I understand, and yes, for sure, when you're feeling better.' Nicholas touched her lightly on the back. 'Are you all right to get in the car now, or do you want to wait a bit?'

'I'm fine,' Clare said, wiping sweat from her brow. She still felt woozy, but she couldn't take another second of this music and the now-pulsating lights. Before Nicholas could respond, she was out the door, breathing in the fresh night air. Shouts and music reminded her the night was still young, and she turned to face her date. 'Sorry to make you head home so soon.'

Nicholas shrugged, taking her arm as he led her back down the stairs. 'That's okay. I don't usually stay up late anyway.'

'Because of your job.' Clare nodded as she climbed into the car. 'I'm the same.' Despite the differing tastes in restaurants, it was nice to find someone similar in so many ways.

Thirty minutes later, Nicholas pulled up in front of her flat. Clare turned to face him, relieved her stomach contents had stayed put. 'Thanks again. And I'm sorry.'

Nicholas waved a hand in the air. 'Please don't worry. I just hope you feel better soon.' He leaned in and kissed her on the cheek. 'Get some sleep. I'll be in touch. I'm already looking forward to the next time.'

'Night.' Clare wiggled her fingers as she climbed from the car.

As she stood on the pavement and watched him pull away, she realised that despite the few dates they'd been on now, she still didn't know much about him. The car vanished around the corner, and she dismissed the thought. She knew the important things, and hadn't she just been thinking how similar they were?

The rest of the blanks could be filled in over time.

ᘒᕲ

Poppy watched as Alistair cheerily dried the last plate after the Sunday night roast. It was a tradition in their house that every Sunday, Alistair cooked and washed-up after the meal, leaving Poppy free to finish her last-minute planning. People often thought being a primary-school teacher was all fun and games, but there was a hell of a lot of preparation involved to get thirty little ones working in tandem. Still, she'd definitely miss it when she took a year off for maternity leave.

This round of IVF *would* work—if they ever got started. Poppy sighed, thinking of the mess of the past week. She had returned home from the clinic, eager to tell Alistair she was ready to begin again. But as soon as she'd swung open the door, mayhem had met her eyes. The upstairs neighbours' bath had overflowed, and the flood of water had weighed down their plaster ceiling so much it had caved right onto the kitchen table.

The days that followed had been a nightmare of calls to the insurance company, workmen traipsing in and out, and fumes that made her dizzy. The experience had left both her and Alistair with frazzled nerves—hardly the ideal time for a serious discussion, even if it was for something as wonderful as IVF.

Now, though, calm had finally been restored—along with their ceiling—and Poppy was determined tonight would be the night to talk about it. She'd even read in the *Daily Mail* yesterday of a couple who'd been successful after seven IVF cycles! She'd clipped out the article and placed it by Alistair's bedside in a move straight from his book, thinking this would be the perfect opener to tell him about her appointment. But when she'd got up this morning, he hadn't said a word; just drank his one cup of coffee, kissed her quickly, and carried on as normal.

She swallowed hard. What if she'd been wrong, and he didn't want to try again? Poppy pushed the thought from her head. He just needed some encouragement, proof she could handle it this time.

'So.' Poppy smiled up at her husband as he plunked two cups of tea in front of them. Her heart beat fast as the words circled around her brain. Here we go, she told herself, gripping onto her mug. She was about to open her mouth to mention the appointment when he sank onto a chair next to her, rubbing his head.

'What a week, huh?' He grabbed his drink and took a sip. 'Thank God I've got some extra clients lined up next month. That repair job has pretty much wiped out our bank account. Insurance will reimburse us, but who knows how long that will take. In the meantime, we'll have to be very careful.'

Poppy's heart sank. They'd never had a big financial reserve, and they'd spent most of their savings on IVF cycles. It had been a few months since the previous attempt, though, and she'd thought— combined with the meagre amount she'd managed to put aside— they'd enough to scrape together the fee. If Alistair *was* having doubts about trying again, the cost of IVF certainly wouldn't help. And the last thing she wanted was to give him a reason to say no.

Her mind raced. Perhaps she should wait until their finances were solid once more? But Poppy was ready now: she was healthy and strong, both mentally and physically. With the consultation completed, the urge to start was unstoppable.

If only she could find the money they needed, without putting additional worry or stress on Alistair. She sipped her tea, thoughts tumbling through her brain. Her credit cards were maxed out, and a bank loan would mean paperwork, phone calls, and time.

Maybe her parents? Poppy quickly dismissed the thought. She'd never been particularly close to them, and anyway, they were unlikely to have a spare thousand or two lying around. They'd just done up the conservatory on their house and already her mother was planning a loft conversion.

'You okay, hon?' Alistair reached out and touched her fingers, and Poppy's head snapped up.

'I will be. *We* will be.' She squeezed his hand. Somehow, she'd find the funds and begin IVF. Alistair would fold her into his arms and thank her for not giving up on their family. Their story would have a happy ending, she'd make certain of that.

CHAPTER SIXTEEN

Clare hurried towards All Bar One for the next meeting of the No-Kids Club. Thank goodness *Wake Up London* had agreed to help spread the word, because at three weeks and counting, they were still no closer to gaining new members. The Facebook page was growing in likes and comments every day, but somehow that didn't translate in actual people coming out. Hopefully the story would run in the next few weeks, although she'd yet to hear from Nicholas since their date. Maybe he'd come tonight? He *had* said he'd check his schedule.

Clare heaved open the door to the bar, the noise hitting her like a wall. Once again, Anna and Poppy had beaten her here and were seated in the same corner, sipping their drinks and chatting. The two of them looked as knackered as she felt. Poppy's normally rosy face was drawn and pale, while Anna hunched over her drink as if someone was going to snatch it away. No sign of Nicholas, Clare thought, her heart dropping. Despite the less than stellar end to the evening, she'd hoped he'd get in touch sooner rather than later.

'Hi, ladies.' She pulled out a chair and sank into it, her bones aching with fatigue. God, what she wouldn't give to crawl into bed now. 'So how was your romantic getaway?' she asked Anna.

Anna's face clouded over, and Clare bit her lip. Uh-oh. Maybe she shouldn't have asked—she'd have thought Anna would be bursting to talk about it.

'What getaway?' Anna said bitterly, taking a huge swig of her wine. 'We didn't end up going. My husband forgot to tell me he'd booked a weekend golfing with his mates. So he went up to Scotland and I stayed home.'

'Shit,' Clare said, raising her eyebrows in surprise that Anna would voice any dissatisfaction with her husband. Maybe things weren't as lovey-dovey as Clare had imagined. 'Did you have a big bust-up, then?'

'Well, no.' Anna waved a hand. 'We can always visit another time. Honestly, he probably wouldn't even want to see Venice, anyway.'

'But you wanted to, right?' Clare asked.

Anna nodded.

'Why didn't you go yourself? You could have had a ball ogling all the hot Italian men.' Clare grinned to show she was joking. Somehow, she doubted Anna would even dream of winking at another man besides her husband. If Clare's partner had taken off for the weekend like that, she wouldn't have hesitated to jump on a plane.

Anna jerked her gaze towards Clare as if she'd never even considered the option. 'Oh no, I couldn't do that. We'll go another time,' she muttered, sticking her nose in the wine glass. She lifted her head. 'Doesn't matter. I had a nice relaxing weekend on my own.'

Yeah, right. Clare could see by Anna's pained expression her weekend had been anything but nice.

'Anyway, when you're married, you can't just take off to some foreign country alone without discussing it with your partner first,' Anna continued. 'You have to make decisions together. Right, Poppy?' She glanced sidelong at the other woman as if to enlist support, and Poppy jerked towards her.

'Er, right,' she responded finally. 'As long as it's something you're on the same wavelength about. You might not always agree on the best way forward.'

'True.' Anna nodded. 'But marriage is a partnership. You have to work together to make sure you're both happy.'

'Yes, but sometimes the other person might not realise what would make them happy,' Poppy shot back, 'and you need to act to help them see it. Like you booking a surprise getaway.'

Clare watched the women volley back and forth, wondering at the vehemence of their tones. It was obviously something that hit close to home—the two of them were clearly facing issues in their relationships. That's why it was a good thing she and Nicholas were starting off in exactly the same place: there'd be no need for any of this tension or complication. If she ever heard from him again!

'Anyway,' Clare said, thinking she'd better interrupt the conversation before the women came to blows. 'Guess what? You know how I told you I've been in touch with a producer from *Wake Up London*? Well, they're going to mention the club, and I might even do an interview.' A wave of nerves crashed over her. 'I don't know when exactly, but I'll keep you posted.'

'That's fantastic,' Poppy said with forced enthusiasm. 'It'll be great publicity, I'm sure.'

Anna nodded, her cheeks flushed from the exchange earlier. 'Sounds brilliant.'

The three women fell silent, and Clare peeked at her watch, noting with chagrin only thirty minutes had passed. Please God may *Wake Up London* get in touch soon, because the way things were going, she doubted the three of them would last much longer.

'Any luck posting a sign in the bookshop?' she asked Anna to make conversation.

'Oh, God.' Anna dropped her head. 'I knew there was something I was supposed to do. Sorry, I completely forgot. It's been a crazy week.'

Crazy how? Clare wondered. The woman only worked part-time and she'd been home alone all weekend, for goodness' sake. How crazy could it be? 'That's fine.'

They chatted awkwardly for the next half hour or so, then Clare looked at her watch again, feigning surprise. 'Is that the time? I'm so sorry, but I've got to go.' She wracked her brain for an excuse but could come up with nothing. 'I'll see you two later.' She lifted a hand and pushed out the door.

What was she going to do now? Despite the fatigue weighing down her muscles and the fog of her tired brain, she didn't want to go home to her empty flat. Maybe she could give Ellie a call. It was only eight o'clock, it had been ages since they'd chatted, and she could do with a good catch-up with her friend. Despite her hopes, Anna and Poppy had come nowhere close to filling the hole Ellie had left.

Clare pulled up Ellie's contact on the mobile and hit "Call".

'Hello?' Ellie's familiar raspy voice came through the line.

'Hey, stranger! You up for some company? I'm at Oxford Circus and I can be at your door in about twenty minutes.' Ellie lived in Hillgate Village, a batch of colourful houses behind Notting Hill Gate station.

'Actually, I'm at work.' Ellie sounded even more exhausted than Clare. At eight months' pregnant and working a twelve-hour day, Clare couldn't begin to imagine how she must feel.

'Why on earth are you still there?' Clare asked, pushing past a man with a battered guitar as she hurried towards the Tube. 'Go home and get some sleep, for God's sake. At this point in your pregnancy, you need to take it easy on yourself. Doctor's orders.'

She laughed to inject levity into her words, but she hoped Ellie got the message.

'Don't you think I know that?' Ellie snapped. Clare raised her eyebrows, taken aback by her friend's tone. She couldn't remember the last time she'd sounded so frazzled.

'Sorry,' Ellie said a heartbeat later. 'It's just, my boss lumped this huge property onto me and I've been working like mad to sell it before I take my maternity leave.'

'Surely they wouldn't expect you to sell it with only a few weeks left.' Clare strained to remember when exactly Ellie had said she was going to take her leave, but all she recalled was her friend laughing that as soon as she got too big to waddle through the Tube turnstile, she'd stop. Given the size of her friend's stomach when Clare had last seen her at the baby shower, she must have reached that stage by now.

'Well, my boss hasn't exactly said it in so many words, but he's made it clear. And to be honest, I really want to, too. I don't want to put in the hard work and then have someone else close the deal.'

Clare nodded. She could understand, but she hoped Ellie wouldn't push it too far.

'And besides that, the agency has told us they're looking to lay off the lowest performers.' She paused, and Clare could almost envision her friend's anxious face.

'You shouldn't have to worry. Weren't you one of their highest sellers?'

'Last year.' Ellie's voice was strained. 'This year, I had to take all those days off when I had morning sickness.' She snorted. 'Pah, most inaccurate name ever. It lasted all day!'

'God, I can relate. Well, sort of.' Clare sighed. 'I'm having PMS from hell, feeling queasy all the time—either that or I picked up a bug from the hospital. I've no idea how pregnant people deal with it.'

'Maybe you *are* pregnant.' Ellie laughed. 'Hey, wouldn't that be great if you were?' she said, clearly keen to follow through with the fantasy. 'We could be on maternity leave together. Depending on when it happened, of course. When's the last time you had sex?'

'Whoa!' Clare rolled her eyes. 'Hold on right there. I'm not going to tell you when I last had sex! I can barely remember,' she joked. 'And anyway, I have contraceptive injections. They're 99 percent effective.'

'Ninety-nine isn't one hundred, my friend.' Clare could hear Ellie tapping away at the keyboard. 'Amanda was on the pill when she conceived her twins.'

Twins! Clare cringed at the thought.

'But anyway, I'm just kidding.' Ellie sighed. 'To be honest, though, I kind of wish someone else was pregnant with me—at least here in the office. Maybe if there were two of us, we could stand up to the boss a little better.'

'You'll be fine, El.' If anyone could handle both parenthood and job, it was Ellie. She organised everything, including her husband Graham, to within an inch of its life. Clare didn't doubt she'd put Gina Ford to shame once the baby arrived.

'I'm sure you're right.' Clare smiled, pleased to hear the energy and determination back in Ellie's tone. 'Anyway, how are you? What's new? How's the club thing going?'

'Okay.' Clare thought of the two women she'd left behind, hoping they hadn't starting brawling over marriage practice. 'It's been a little slow to start with, but we're going to get a mention on a London TV station, so I'm hoping that will help pick it up.'

'That's fantastic!' Ellie said. 'How did that come about?'

'Well . . .' Clare paused. Was she was up for the inevitable twenty questions that would result from mentioning Nicholas? It was still early days, and she could do without any pressure. 'A producer got in touch through the Facebook page,' she said finally. It felt strange keeping quiet about Nicholas; with Edward, she and Ellie had dissected every last detail. But Ellie had enough on her plate, and it was kind of nice not to let Nicholas bleed over into another part of her life.

'That'll really help spread the word,' Ellie said, still typing. 'Okay, I'd better get going. Let's try to meet up soon, though—I'll give you a ring.'

'All right. Bye.' Clare hung up, wondering how long it would be before she heard from her friend again.

She put the phone back in her bag and clattered down the stairs to the Tube. As she collapsed into an empty seat, Ellie's words rang in her ear. *Maybe you are pregnant.* Clare shook her head to dislodge them, forcing herself to smile. As if! The chances of her falling into that one percent were as slim as Graham Norton playing the next James Bond.

But try as she might, she couldn't forget that her friend was right: ninety-nine percent wasn't one hundred. Fear ran through her as she recalled the nausea that had been coming and going for days, feeling bloated, and the absolute exhaustion unlike anything she'd ever known.

Clare bit her lip, trying to remember her last period. It *had* been awhile and she'd never been regular, but . . . Damn Ellie for putting the thought in her head! Her friend might have been kidding and the chances were miniscule. Even so, Clare couldn't escape the very slim possibility that this wasn't simply PMS or a virus, but something much, much worse.

❦

Poppy crawled under the covers beside Alistair, trying her best not to disturb him. Thank God he was sleeping, she thought, sliding across the mattress so the bed didn't jiggle. She'd stayed out as late as possible with Anna, despite their earlier heated discussion. Anna hadn't seemed in a hurry to head home either, downing glass after glass of wine as Poppy watched enviously.

Listening to Alistair's even breathing, Anna's words about marriage as a partnership circled around her head. Until now, she and Alistair had been partners, supporting each other as they worked towards a common goal. Now—although she was doing the best thing for both of them—she was doing it alone. Without their usual baby chats and daydreams, their relationship felt deflated, and Poppy was left holding the empty balloon. Or womb, she thought bitterly.

All the more reason to get the process underway quickly, she told herself, so she could prove Alistair's initial objections wrong and they could be a team again. Poppy chewed at her lip, trying for the millionth time to figure out how the hell she was going to conjure up almost two thousand pounds. It was a small sum for many, but for her, it was starting to seem an insurmountable mountain. For the first time ever, she wished she'd chosen a flash career in the City rather than plodding along as an inner-city school teacher. The amount of money they made was obscene. Alistair's brother Oliver was a trader, and his bonus was about the same as her yearly salary.

Poppy jerked as an idea hit: maybe she could ask Oliver for a loan! A couple of thousand would be nothing to him. Why hadn't she thought of him before?

Beside her, Alistair twitched in his sleep, like he was reading her thoughts. Poppy edged further away from him and towards the edge of the mattress, as if by putting more distance between them, he wouldn't have access to her brain. The two men weren't close, and Poppy always sensed Alistair was vaguely resentful of Oliver's money and lifestyle. She'd have to ensure Oliver didn't say anything to his brother, of course, and make sure he knew this was just a loan until she got together the funds to pay him back. If she saved half her paycheque for the next few months, it would be doable . . .

The heaviness of sleep closed in, and Poppy shut her eyes against the darkness and the tiny pinprick of guilt. It would all be worth it in the end, she reminded herself.

Tomorrow, she'd ring up Oliver and ask him for the money, then she'd make an appointment to see the nurse and be one step closer to starting their family.

Sorted.

CHAPTER SEVENTEEN

Clare's phone rang bright and early the next morning. She jerked upright, groaning as her stomach performed twirls. If possible, she felt even worse than last night. Despite her best efforts, she'd tossed and turned for hours, the bed seeming more and more like a prison as the thought of pregnancy loomed larger in her mind.

Finally, sometime around two, she'd decided to settle this whole thing by grabbing a pregnancy test at the chemist when she woke up. That settled, she'd drifted into a troubled sleep with dreams of screaming babies and piles of nappies—until the phone had jarred her awake.

'Hello?' she croaked, swinging her legs around to touch the floor and hoping solid ground would make her feel more settled. She squinted at the clock: 5:00 a.m. Who the hell would ring now?

'Clare?' Nicholas's warm tone came through the line. 'Sorry to call so early, but I figured you might be up?'

You figured wrong, Clare thought. She finally had the day off, and she'd planned to spend it celebrating not being pregnant after the negative test. Because she wasn't pregnant, she told herself firmly. 'No,' she said. 'I'm not working today.'

'Fantastic!' Nicolas's voice was energetic. 'This works out well, then. Look, we've had a last-minute cancellation to our line-up this morning and we're desperate to fill the time. I'd love to have you come into the studio for a live chat with our hosts about the No-Kids Club.'

Clare shrank back at the thought. 'But you said it wouldn't be live!' She'd be rubbish trying to answer questions, knowing each and every word she uttered was being broadcast and she couldn't stop to fix something if it went wrong.

'It's even better live,' Nicholas said encouragingly. 'More fun and fresh. And besides, Dennis and Debs are fantastic. They'll put you at ease.'

Clare paused, turning the idea over in her head. It would be a great way to get new members, but . . . she was dying to do that test. Don't be silly, she told herself. She couldn't pass up the opportunity to spread the word about the No-Kids Club just because she wanted to prove she wasn't pregnant. She could do that anytime.

'We'll do your hair and make-up, really pamper you,' he continued. 'And I'd love to spend some time with you when we're done. Maybe finally cash that rain check?' His voice was low and sensual. 'I'm sorry I haven't got in touch. It's been a hectic week.'

'That's okay,' Clare said quickly. 'I've been busy, too.' The thought crossed her mind that it might have been nice if he'd taken the time to fire her off a text, then she pushed it away. She didn't need an explanation, and he didn't expect any from her, either.

'All right.' She rubbed her eyes as she stood. 'Is there anything particular I should wear? And where do I go?'

'Oh, brill, thanks so much for agreeing to do this.' She could hear the relief in his voice. 'Don't worry—we'll sort out your wardrobe when you're at the studio. Just throw on some clothes and I'll send a car around to pick you up in thirty minutes.'

'Okay,' Clare said, raising her eyebrows. *Wardrobe?* What the hell had she let herself in for? Then again, she thought, eying her meagre clothing selection, that was probably a good thing.

'I'll see you soon.' Nicholas hung up, and Clare padded to the loo and washed her face, feeling her stomach slide back into place. Fingers crossed it stayed there. She cleaned her teeth and ran a brush through her hair, then went into the bedroom and stood in front of the mirror. Turning to the side, she ran a hand over her still-flat belly. She didn't *look* pregnant, but that didn't mean anything. Women often didn't start showing until the fourth month. God, she couldn't wait to take that test and put these doubts to rest. Every minute that passed, they burrowed deeper into her brain.

Sighing, Clare pulled on a pair of jeans and a loose-fitting T-shirt. Outside her window, the sky was still dark, and she brewed a very strong espresso and downed it as she watched the quiet road outside. A few minutes later, the glowing headlights of a sedan lit her narrow street, and she slipped on a pair of ballet flats, threw on a coat, and headed out into the foggy morning.

After a quick journey through the quiet roads of central London, the car pulled up to a large building situated on the Thames. The driver pointed to a door.

'Right in there, madam,' he said in a gruff voice. 'Reception will take care of you. Good luck.'

Clare nodded, her cold fingers trembling now at what lay ahead: facing down the cameras on a live show. A little more preparation might have been nice, she thought, rubbing sweaty palms on her jeans. But then again, what did she need to prepare? She was the club's founder, she knew all there was to know about it, and everything would be fine.

She pulled open the heavy door, squinting against the bright light of the reception area. Behind a curved silver desk sat a woman wearing an earpiece, tapping busily away on a computer.

'Hi,' Clare said, clearing her throat of its early-morning rasp. 'I'm here for the show?'

The woman rolled her eyes. 'Which one?'

'Er, *Wake Up London*. Nicholas Hunt is a producer.'

'Give me a sec and I'll get someone to come out and meet you.' She punched some numbers into a phone, then looked up at Clare. 'Name?'

'Clare Donoghue.'

'Have a seat.'

Clare sank onto a very uncomfortable chair made from glossy plastic, shifting from one buttock to the other to find a position where she didn't risk sliding off.

'Clare?'

She glanced up with a smile, anticipating Nicholas's friendly face. Instead, her eyes met a boy almost half her age with a quiff so high it added a good five inches to his height. 'Oh,' she said. 'I was expecting Nicholas.'

'He's backstage getting everything ready,' the boy responded, attempting to run a hand through his hair but repelled by the gel. 'If you'd like to follow me, I'll take you to the green room, and hair and make-up will come get you. We're on tight timeline, since your piece is due to run in about an hour. Nick wanted to make sure you get prime-time wake-up viewing.'

Well, that was nice of him, Clare thought as she followed the boy down a narrow corridor, trying not to notice the waistband of his boxers peeping out from his jeans. Her stomach shifted again and she popped two Tums, furiously crunching down on them.

The boy shot her a quizzical look at the sound. 'Everything okay?'

Clare nodded shakily. 'Fine, fine.' Just too much caffeine on an empty stomach, she told herself—nothing else. Despite the horror circling inside at the other possibility, she couldn't help smiling at how ironic it would be if she *was* pregnant. The founder of the No-Kids Club, live on television arguing for the rights of the childless, knocked up herself.

All the irony in the world couldn't make up for being pregnant, though, she thought grimly. God, she couldn't wait to get back home and take that test!

'Right, here we are.' The boy ushered her into a room with plump sofas and chairs. A table in the corner was heaving with pastries, and the smell of coffee drifted from metallic canisters in the far end. Clare tried not to breathe in any of the scents. 'Just chill out here for a few minutes, and Jenna will be by soon.' He gave her a quick once-over, lip curling slightly. 'Don't worry, she's a miracle worker.'

The nerve! Clare had to laugh as she sank into a brown leather chair. Not that she could blame him, though—her jeans, baggy T-shirt, and pale face weren't exactly doing her any favours. Hair and make-up would have to work a miracle to make her presentable.

Half an hour later, Clare glanced in the mirror at her altered reflection. Jenna had transported her to the land of the living, that much was true . . . although the result wasn't *quite* what she'd have chosen. Even when she went out, Clare always chose the natural-but-slightly-enhanced style, with mascara, a little mineral powder, a swoosh of taupe eye-shadow to accent her eyes, and lip gloss.

Now, though, she looked like she'd collided with a make-up truck. Her lips were a glossy crimson that would rival any vampire movie, masterful streaks of blush made her cheekbones look razor-sharp, and her lids sparkled with thick eye shadow. It wasn't bad, just . . . different. And—Clare tilted her head as she examined her reflection again—rather intimidating. With her hair scraped back into a high ponytail, the only thing missing was a whip. Obviously they were trying to transform her into the stereotypical image of a career-driven woman who put her own desires and ambitions over children.

She blinked, a surge of anger running through her. Why did people always think that was the face of today's childless women? Anna and Poppy certainly weren't focused on careers, and they didn't have kids. There was a myriad of reasons why people were child-free. She'd try her best to get that across, despite her corporate-meets-dominatrix facade.

'Hiya!' The chipper voice of a woman about her age with cropped dark hair cut into Clare's thoughts. 'I'm Liz, from Wardrobe. If you'd like to come this way, we'll get you kitted out.'

Clare nodded and clambered to her feet, then followed the woman through yet more corridors and into a room where rails and rails of clothes lined the wall. 'Um, have you seen Nicholas anywhere? I'd love to have a quick chat with him before I go on.'

Liz shook her head as she delved into one of the huge racks. 'Not since earlier this morning,' she said, her voice muffled by the clothes. 'I'll see if I can grab him once we're done here, but we don't have much time. He told me he already briefed you.'

'Well, yes.' Nicholas *had* told her what to expect, but somehow she'd thought he'd be here to shepherd her through this whole process, too. But he was a busy producer managing a top show; he obviously had other things to do than holding her hand. Besides, she was more than capable of doing this on her own. Hopefully.

'Okay.' Liz's flushed face emerged from the depths of the rack, clutching a pencil skirt, sky-high stilettos, and a wrap-around blouse with a plunging neckline. 'Here we are. You're a size ten, right?'

Clare nodded, forcing the thought from her mind that lately her trousers felt a little snug—despite the fact she hadn't been eating more.

Her heart sank as she eyed the clothing. They *were* doing her up to be selfish-corporate-woman. A thrill of righteous indignation went through her. Why didn't they treat males the same way?

No one interrogated ambitious single men about why they didn't want kids.

'I don't think that's for me,' Clare said, shaking her head at the ensemble. 'Do you have anything a bit more, er, *comfortable*?' And something that didn't scream corporate bitch.

Annoyance flashed across Liz's face. 'Sorry, hon, we don't have much time here. You're lucky we could pull this together last minute.' She glanced at her watch. 'Look, you'd be doing me a huge favour if you put this on. I've got to sort out the next guest.'

Clare ran her eyes over the outfit again. Maybe it wouldn't be that bad on—at least they hadn't handed her a whip. Yet. 'Fine,' she said. 'Just show me where to change.'

'Right here, please.' Liz's tone was brisk and efficient. 'Hang your jeans and T-shirt on this rail. You can collect them after the show.'

'Okay.' Clare shrugged as she peeled off her clothes, stepped into the skin-coloured tights Liz handed her, then shimmied into the pencil skirt, noting with satisfaction it slid easily over her curves. She shoved her arms into the sleeves of the wraparound blouse.

'Christ, that bra looks about to give up the ghost,' Liz said, arching an eyebrow at Clare's bust. 'Let me see if I have a tank to put over that. We can't risk you flashing a nipple on the morning show. I'd be burnt at the stake.'

What the hell was Liz on about, Clare thought, glancing down at her chest? She'd only just bought this bra a couple months ago . . . her eyebrows rose in surprise. Shit, her breasts did seem to be making a break for freedom, spilling over the sides of the cups. She must have shrunk it in the wash or something. But then, the lingerie she'd worn last week had also seemed a little tight. *Christ.*

Now's not the time to think about all that, she told herself, cursing Ellie and her ridiculous fantasy for planting the thought in her head. Liz handed her a tank top, which Clare carefully manoeuvred over her head in an effort not to dislodge make-up or hair. Then Liz tied the wraparound shirt as tightly as possible, manhandled Clare's cleavage into place, slid her feet into the stilettos, and declared her ready to go with minutes to spare.

'Have a look.' Liz shoved aside a rack to reveal a dusty mirror, and Clare squinted at the woman in the glass. Wow. Was that really her? She looked like a contestant on *The Apprentice*—all tightly tailored business attire with killer heels and a face so full of make-up it was a wonder her cheekbones could support it. She'd never dressed this way a day in her life. In fact, if she turned up at the hospital sporting this get-up, her colleagues would fall about laughing.

'Um, I'm not sure—'

'No time to change now!' Liz said in a falsely upbeat tone. 'I've got to take you to the green room. You're on in ten! Come on.' Without looking back, she rushed down the corridor, and Clare had no choice but to hobble after her on the four-inch stilettos. How on earth did women wear these things to work, she wondered, attempting not to topple over. Finally, she made it to the green room and collapsed into a chair. She'd barely caught her breath when Nicholas appeared.

'Clare! You look absolutely gorgeous.' His blue eyes sparkled as he took in her outfit.

Clare struggled to her feet, tugging down the pencil skirt. Oh, shit. Her breasts were nearly hanging out of the blouse despite the tank top. She tried to adjust it, but Nicholas was already leaning forward to kiss her cheek.

'Come on, follow me. We can chat on the way.' He took her arm as they walked towards the door. 'I'm sorry I couldn't see you sooner,' he said as they navigated through the maze again. 'It's been a crazy morning, what with the last-minute cancellation and everything. I can't tell you how much I appreciate you stepping in to fill the gap.'

'No problem,' Clare huffed, trying to keep up with him. She'd thought running around hospital corridors had kept her in shape, but that was nothing compared to the pace he was setting—not to mention her challenging footwear.

'So as I said, you'll be chatting about the club and how you think it meets a need in today's society,' Nicholas said as he led her through a series of swinging doors towards the set. 'I've also managed to get Mary Crowley to join us—just to add a bit of balance to the segment.'

'Mary Crowley?' Clare croaked, her mouth going dry. Mary Crowley was Britain's best-loved expert on all things domestic. A former nanny to the royals, she'd had a popular show embracing traditional family values—featuring everything from keeping kids entertained on rainy days to children's importance to the economy—and had been featured as a pundit ever since.

'Yes, we managed to reach her last minute.' Nicholas put a hand on her back. 'Relax, take a deep breath, and forget all about the cameras. You'll be fantastic, I know it.'

Clare felt her stomach shift again and she swallowed back the rising nerves. Talking about the club was one thing, but engaging in a debate with Mary Crowley live on camera was another! Maybe it'd be good, she told herself. It would give her a chance to combat the image she'd been forced into and explain there were many reasons why women choose not to have kids. Poppy's sad face filtered into her mind. For some, it wasn't even a choice.

They pushed through another set of swinging doors, and Clare could see the darkness of the set. Bright lights illuminated a huge, semicircular jade-green sofa, with three hulking cameras pointed at the two presenters who were confidently bantering and smiling.

'And we're out!' A man with a headset motioned to the present-ers. 'Back in three minutes.'

'Break for adverts,' Nicholas said in Clare's ear as they watched from the side. He turned towards her. 'Ready? I'll take you over to meet Dennis and Debs and we'll get you settled on the sofa.'

Clare took in another breath. 'Ready.'

CHAPTER EIGHTEEN

Clare pasted on what she hoped resembled a confident smile as she followed Nicholas over several thick cables and onto the raised platform of the set.

'Dennis and Debs, this is Clare Donoghue,' Nicholas said when they reached the sofa.

Dennis grinned, showing off his trademark crooked teeth. 'Nice to meet you, Clare. Thanks for coming.' He took her hand in his meaty one, and she prayed he wouldn't remark on the clamminess of her palm. Nerves were swimming through her stomach with the ferocity of a killer whale, and already she could feel damp patches forming under her arms. God, those lights were strong.

'Yes, thank you for making it at the last minute.' Debs smiled with all the warmth of a snake. 'So you're against children, then?' She narrowed her eyes and crossed her arms.

'Well, I'm not really against—'

'Don't mind her,' Dennis broke in. 'Debs just hasn't had her vodka breakfast yet. Ah, here she is!'

Clare turned to see Nicholas coming back in with Mary Crowley at his side. Clare's heart dropped as she took in the older woman's neat blonde bob and periwinkle suit. Grimacing, she tried in vain to adjust the neckline of her blouse. Next to Mary, she'd look like the Whore of Corporate Babylon.

'Hello, Dennis, Debs.' Mary smiled warmly at the two presenters. 'How are little Dolly and Lucas doing?' she asked Dennis. 'It's been way too long since I've seen them.'

Clare gulped. Oh, God. Mary knew Dennis's kids? This was going from bad to worse.

Dennis grinned. 'Not so little anymore. Dolly is twelve and Lucas just finished his GCSEs.'

Mary shook her head incredulously. 'My, my. How time flies. It must be wonderful watching them grow into the fine young adults I'm sure they are. Children are such a blessing.'

Even though the comment wasn't directed at Clare, she couldn't help stiffening at Mary's words. She was going *down*—Mary was everything people loved about mothers: warm, kind, and nurturing. Maybe Debs would back her up? She hadn't seemed supportive initially, but the woman was more apt to have pet tiger cubs than children.

But her hope deflated with Mary's next few words.

'And you, Debs? How's your little princess? It was such a privilege to be her maternity nurse for her first months in this world.'

Debs's face shone with a warmth Clare hadn't seen until now. 'Isla's fantastic, thank you. You'll have to come by and see her soon.'

'Back in thirty seconds! Please take your places, everyone.' The floor manager cut in before Clare had the chance to introduce herself to the older woman, and the two of them took a seat on the curved sofa directly across from the presenters. Mary nodded at her briefly as she crossed her legs, and before Clare knew it, the floor manager was counting them in. She wiped the beads of sweat from under her nose, feeling her cheeks flush from the heat of the lights. What on earth had she got herself into?

'Hello again.' Dennis shot a toothy grin at the camera and put an arm on the back on the sofa. 'Well, nowadays, more and more young people seem to be making the decision not to have children. Are we witnessing the decline of the family unit and society's traditional values, or quite simply a rise in the importance of the individual?'

'Sounds philosophical for so early in the morning,' Debs interjected, smiling.

'That's not something I've ever been accused of.' Dennis laughed heartily as he leaned forward. 'Let's cut the mumbo jumbo and get right to our guests. With us today, we have Mary Crowley, a former nanny, a mother herself, and an expert on families. And alongside her, Clare Donoghue, the founder of a new organisation to celebrate child-free living, the No-Kids Club. Welcome, ladies.'

Clare managed a nod, a trickle of sweat sliding down her spine. Beside her, Mary looked cool and collected, as if she'd done this a million times before. She probably had.

'So, Clare, we'll start with you. Tell us, what is there to celebrate about a life without kids?' All three heads swivelled to stare intensely at Clare.

She paused, wondering how to answer in a way that wouldn't antagonise this trio clearly in favour of children. 'Well'—her voice came out quavery and uncertain, and she cleared her throat—'it's not so much to celebrate that way of living, but to provide a social network for people who don't have kids.' There. That was innocuous enough, surely.

'And you yourself have decided not to have children?' Debs's eyes lasered onto Clare, and Clare shifted on the sofa.

'Er, yes, that's right. I'm child-free.' And please God, may she not have to deal with any unexpected turn of events to stay that way. 'But back to the club, we're—'

'Mary, you've been working in the childcare field for many years,' Dennis interrupted, turning to the older woman. 'What do you think about this new dynamic: young women who are choosing not to have children?'

Mary smiled playfully. 'I haven't been working in the field for that long, Dennis. You've made me sound ancient!'

Dennis touched her arm with a murmured apology, and Clare almost rolled her eyes. Were they actually flirting?

'But anyway, I'd like to point out this isn't a new dynamic. There has always been a certain segment of women who decide to focus on themselves and not fulfil their given role as mothers.'

Clare blinked. Wow, *fulfil their given role as mothers*? What were they, back in the eighteen-hundreds?

'And why do you think that is?' Debs asked. 'Speaking as a mother myself, I can't imagine a greater joy nor a more satisfying job than raising my daughter.'

Yeah, right, Clare wanted to interrupt. That's exactly why you hired a maternity nurse to take the load off. And hadn't she heard something about Debs going back to work after only two weeks?

Mary shook her head. 'Well, I suspect these women are too embroiled in their present lives to consider making a change for children. And I can tell you that the women I've spoken to—those who make a conscious choice not to have kids—always regret the decision when they're older. Of course, by that time, it's too late to experience the joys of motherhood.'

Clare couldn't hold back any longer. 'I'm sorry,' she cut in, 'but I don't think having a child on the off chance you might regret it when you're older is a good reason. And by the way, the club is open to both women *and* men who don't have children, all for a variety of reasons.' Hopefully that would send the conversation in a different direction than the same old 'selfish woman who doesn't want kids' refrain.

Mary turned to her. 'Yes, of course, everyone has their own reason not to have children.' She tilted her head. 'You say you choose not to. Why?'

Clare fidgeted on the sofa. Was it just her, or were those lights becoming brighter? 'Um, well . . . ' Her mind flipped through what to say without getting too personal. 'It's not in my life plan,' she responded finally, giving the pat answer as usual.

'And why is that?' Debs asked as all three leaned in towards her.

Clare met their gaze, her brain whirling with responses. She could say her career—that had always been her default response if people probed more—but she didn't want to play into the stereotype they'd created. And anyway, when it came right down to it, she wasn't even sure it *was* work. In today's career-driven society, pregnancy did put women in a very precarious position, like Ellie was unfortunately experiencing. Babies could impact career prospects, no one would argue with that. But there were ways around that—like Debs and her maternity nurse—and Clare knew that if she wanted a baby badly enough, she'd find a way to make it work.

So what was the reason? Now that she really thought about it, Clare couldn't remember actually making the decision not to have kids. It just wasn't her thing; never had been, and that was that. And anyway, why did she need to justify her choice to the nation?

'Just because you *can* get pregnant doesn't mean you should have a child,' she said finally, steering the conversation away from her own decision. Clare thought of her mother and how she'd abandoned the family to pursue a separate life. No one could argue that every woman was fit to be a mother, that was for sure.

'That's true,' Mary said. 'And I've seen some shocking examples of bad parenting in my time. But mothering is a learned skill. Society today would have us believe if women don't feel the maternal instinct or urge, they shouldn't have children. Bonding comes from care, from the hours and days spent with your newborn.'

'And that's great for people who want to,' Clare countered. 'But not wanting to—or not being able to—doesn't automatically make you a bad person.'

Mary raised an eyebrow. 'I never said anything about being a bad person, my dear.'

Clare's cheeks flushed as she realised the older woman had scored a point against her. But before she could respond, Dennis grinned broadly into the camera.

'Ladies, as much as I'd love to continue this debate—clearly an emotional issue—we're running out of time.' He turned to face Clare. 'Before we go, can you quickly tell us about the club in case any of our listeners would like to join?'

'Of course,' she said, forcing her voice to remain steady and calm. 'We meet every Wednesday night at seven at All Bar One, just off Oxford Circus. Once our numbers are big enough, we'll move to a more permanent venue. If you'd like to get in touch, search for the No-Kids Club on Facebook and you'll find our page.'

'Sounds great,' Debs said, although her tone suggested the opposite. 'Thank you for joining us, ladies.' She smiled into the camera. 'As always, please feel free to text or email any comments to us. We'll be back after this short break.'

'And we're out!' the floor manager called.

'Well done, well done,' Dennis said, shaking Clare's hand then leaning over to pat Mary's dimpled knee. 'I'm sorry we didn't have more time. Normally we'd give this kind of topic a few more minutes, but since we were filling a shorter segment I'm afraid that's all we could squeeze in.'

'Don't you worry for a second,' Mary said. 'You know I'm always happy to come along and see you and Debs.' The way the two of them were beaming up at the older woman, Clare almost expected to see her pat them on the head and throw them a biscuit.

'Fantastic job, ladies, just excellent!' A smiling Nicholas swooped down on them, and Clare shook her head. It might have made great television, but she hadn't done much to advance the cause of child-free living. 'And you should see the Twitter feed!' he said, touching her lightly on the back. 'You've sparked off a very lively debate.'

Clare gritted her teeth. She could only imagine.

'Let me take you both to the green room.' He turned to Mary. 'Thank you for coming.'

'My pleasure,' Mary responded as they walked through the dark wings and the maze of corridors once again, then into the welcome calm of the green room. For a second, the space swam in front of Clare's eyes and her legs felt like they might give way.

'Are you all right? Here, have a seat.' Nicholas manoeuvred her towards a nearby sofa and Clare collapsed onto it gratefully. The heat and lights of the set had really taken it out of her.

'Drink this.' He put a cup of cold water into her hand, and she shakily brought it to her mouth, sipping the liquid as the room stopped spinning.

'Thanks,' she said, dizziness draining away as exhaustion swept through her.

'Rest and take it easy for a few minutes. I'll finish up here, and then we can head for lunch.' He turned to face Mary, who was smoothing down her bob in the mirror. 'You all right to find your way back to reception? Let them know when you're ready to leave and they'll get a car to take you home.'

'Perfect.' She gave her hair a final pat then smiled at Nicholas. 'Thank you, my dear.'

Nicholas nodded, then hurried out the door. Silence fell, and Clare shifted uneasily on the sofa.

'Well.' Mary sank onto the sofa across from her. 'I'm knackered. The older I get, the harder these things become.'

Clare nodded, unsure what to say. The woman was sharp as a tack and Clare doubted she felt anywhere near as tired as she'd said.

'I hope you didn't find it too tough in there.'

Clare's head snapped up. 'What?' She waved a hand in the air. 'Oh, don't worry. I've been through much worse than that.'

Mary sipped her tea, then delicately set the cup on the saucer. 'I just want to say, I know people are quick to judge. And childlessness isn't a choice for everyone, like you said. It certainly wasn't for me.'

'But . . . ' Clare met the woman's gaze, noticing for the first time that despite the upbeat demeanour, sadness lurked in her eyes. 'I thought Dennis said you're a mother?'

Mary smiled gently. 'I was. My son died of a rare kidney defect shortly after birth.'

Clare winced. Despite not wanting children herself, she couldn't even imagine the pain of losing one. 'I'm so sorry.'

'Thank you. It was a very long time ago, of course, but the pain never leaves you.' Mary paused, patting her lips with a napkin. 'My husband and I tried very hard to have another, but it wasn't to be. Maybe that's why I became a nanny. Although I was a mother, I never had the chance to raise a child. And that's why I urge young women to seriously consider their decision not to become a mother, too. It's a gift, if you're lucky enough to receive it.'

Clare couldn't help but think of her own situation. Supposing if—on the very very *very* off chance she was pregnant—could she ever consider it a gift? Not bloody likely. She'd very swiftly return the gift to sender, if that was biologically possible. She felt for Mary, she really did—and for Poppy, and for all those women who wanted kids but couldn't. But that didn't mean she was anywhere near ready. She didn't even have a serious boyfriend!

She'd go home, take that silly test, and put these thoughts back on the shelf where they belonged.

'Clare?' Nicholas's voice broke into her reverie. For a second, she'd almost forgotten he was returning. 'Oh, Mary, you're still here. Is there a problem with the car?'

'No, no.' Mary smiled, slowly standing. 'I was just having a chat with Clare. Lovely to speak to you, dear. I'd better go now before I fall asleep on my feet.'

She was almost to the door when she turned to face Clare. 'Have a think about what I've said. Before it's too late.'

'I will,' Clare responded, although her stance on the subject was engraved in concrete. And what did Mary mean, 'before it's too late'? For goodness' sake, Clare was only thirty-nine. Okay, so that might be pushing it a little when it came to fertility, but she wasn't exactly menopausal just yet.

The two of them watched as Mary glided out the door.

'What was all that about?' Nicholas asked, eyes twinkling. 'Trying to bring you around to babies?'

Clare laughed. 'She's trying! I'm afraid she's got a long way to go.' The grief in the older woman's eyes flashed through her mind, and Clare shook her head. She couldn't blame Mary for wanting to stop others from experiencing her pain of childlessness. But as Clare had said earlier, not every woman—or man—should have a child.

Enough of all this, she told herself. Time to focus on something else. Christ, she'd never thought so much about pregnancy or kids until starting this club.

'You wouldn't believe all the tweets, texts, and emails streaming in since the segment aired!' Nicholas poured himself a glass of water. 'There are loads of people interested in joining the club.'

'That's great,' Clare said, thankful she hadn't put off potential members. 'You ready for lunch?' Her stomach rumbled with an odd combination of hunger and protestation.

'I'm so sorry, but I'm afraid something's just come up.' Nicholas sighed. 'I'll have to take a rain check from the rain check.'

Clare laughed, despite her dismay. Their dinner in Camden seemed ages ago, and she'd been looking forward to spending more time with him. 'No problem,' she said. 'I'll get changed and I'll see you later.'

'Thanks for being such a good sport about all of this.' Nicholas waved a hand at her attire. 'You look great, but I know it's not your usual style.'

'It's fine.' Clare leaned in and kissed him on the cheek.

'I'll call you next week to arrange something,' Nicholas said. 'Thanks again for today.'

Clare lifted a hand as she walked out the door, wondering if he actually would ring. For a second, she missed the easygoing security and warmth of Edward. He was always there, solid and dependable, whenever she'd wanted.

Flexibility was critical for two busy people, Clare told herself. They'd find a way to cash in that rain check sooner or later. She hurried to Wardrobe, anxious now to get home. With all this talk of children, the urge to banish the uncertainty from her mind was unbearable. Then, she'd have a huge glass of wine regardless of what her stomach told her, and finally, she'd be able to relax.

Any other alternative didn't bear thinking about.

⁓

Anna turned down the television, draining the last of her coffee. Well, that had been a shocker! She'd only just snapped on *Wake*

Up London when Clare's voice boomed from the telly. Setting the sputtering iron down on the board, Anna's eyebrows had risen even further at Clare's outfit: far from her normal casual get-up, her clothes were practically painted on her and her face was slathered with make-up.

Anna plopped onto the sofa, leaving a huge pile of shirts to be done. A sour-faced presenter was reading out tweets and texts from viewers who'd watched Clare's segment. 'Kids have brought so much joy to my life,' one text said. 'I can't imagine life without them,' another read. 'What do those people do with all their time?'

Anna shook her head. Iron their husband's shirts? Ever since Michael's weekend away, life had felt emptier than ever. She'd hoped her husband might return from his trip happier and full of energy. Instead, he'd come through the door and kissed her quickly, then flopped on the sofa, drifting off to sleep while Anna made dinner. After spending the weekend alone, Anna had been dying for a chat and cuddle, but she hadn't even been able to rouse him to come to the table. And ever since, it had been more of the same. The vague feeling of dissatisfaction was growing every day.

Her brow furrowed as a thought crossed her mind: would their lives be any different if they did have kids? Not likely—in fact, there'd probably be even more monotony and early nights. No, children weren't the answer, of that she was sure.

Sighing, she got to her feet and picked up the iron. Her words to Poppy about marriage being a partnership came to mind again. Lately, it felt less of a partnership and more of a one-woman show. Michael loved her, of that she had no doubt. But what she really needed was an affirmation he cared about their relationship; something small to see he could still make an effort. That wasn't too much to ask, was it? True, she usually jumped on things before he even moved, but maybe she needed to give him a chance.

She swished the iron down a sleeve, nodding as an idea hit. Their anniversary was a week from tomorrow, and although she'd a list of possible shows and concerts, along with the number to a great new restaurant in the Shard, she'd yet to book anything. This year, she'd sit back and let Michael plan the annual celebration of their matrimony.

A smile crossed her face as she attacked a particularly troublesome collar. She couldn't wait to see what he came up with.

CHAPTER NINETEEN

Clare sank back against the leather seat of the car as it jostled through daytime traffic from the studio towards Chelsea. It was only eleven, but every inch of her throbbed with fatigue and her brain felt full of static. The closer she got to home, the larger her fear grew, as if just by taking the test she was acknowledging the possibility she could indeed be pregnant.

Don't be ridiculous, Clare chided herself as the car lurched down busy Piccadilly. The test was a way to ease her fears and put an end to the wondering—nothing else. She envisioned her future self laughing and shaking her head at the negative result, pouring a glass of wine, then luxuriously napping with the knowledge that life would go on unchanged. But then a competing image filtered into her mind: crouching on the cold toilet seat, staring in horror as the stick slowly displayed the sign she was pregnant.

Clare tried to push it away, but the vision was now implanted in her brain. Taking a deep breath, she forced herself to face the scenario head-on. Okay, so what if she *was* pregnant? What next? She was thirty-nine, single, with an extremely busy and demanding job—and apart from that, she was not mother material, no matter what Mary said about bonding through care. The solution was obvious.

'Can you let me out here?' she asked the cabbie as they turned onto the street where the chemist was located, just a few doors down from her flat. She quickly paid the driver, then tumbled into the cool morning mist.

Pushing open the door to the chemist, she blinked against the harsh neon light. Where on earth did they keep the pregnancy tests? She'd been here a million times and never once noticed. She'd never imagined there'd be a need!

'Good morning.' Mr Rabinovich, the owner of the shop, greeted her with his customary smile, and her heart sank. Oh, Lord. Why hadn't she thought to go to some anonymous place in Soho? For a brief instant, she considered heading down to King's Road to see what she could find there, but exhaustion and impatience got the better of her. Mr Rabinovich must have seen everything by now; surely he was more professional than to comment.

But when she finally located the dusty tests in a dim corner and brought one to the counter, he proved her wrong.

'Well, well.' His thick eyebrows rose above his specs as she handed him the test. 'So you might be expecting! How exciting, my dear.' He ran his eyes over her face. 'About time, I'd say. You don't want to leave it too long! Mrs R was pregnant with our first at seventeen.' He nodded approvingly.

There was so much wrong with what he'd just said, Clare didn't even know where to begin. She forced the corners of her mouth up, hoping it looked more like a smile than grimace. Nosy old man!

'Good luck,' he said as they waited for her debit card to go through. 'Let me know how it turns out.'

As if, Clare thought as she took the bag from him. Funny how people assumed if you were a certain age, pregnancy was something to celebrate. Right now, it felt like she was holding a ticking time bomb, set to explode her future. She took another deep breath, reminding herself the possibility was very slim and she'd cope with whatever the outcome was.

Forcing herself not to run home, she let herself in slowly and methodically as usual. Finally, when she'd kicked off her shoes and tied back her hair, Clare grabbed the plastic bag from the kitchen table and removed the packet, helpfully containing two tests in case she didn't believe the first. Fingers crossed she wouldn't need both.

With shaking hands, she removed the plastic and peeled back the foil package of one stick, then scanned the directions. One line was fine; two was disastrous. Okay, now she just needed to pee on the bloody thing, and that would be that. She padded to the loo, tipped up the toilet seat, and tried to position herself so she'd hit the target. Thank goodness she'd had all that coffee and water earlier! Her bladder was full to busting.

Right, snap on the cap and wait two minutes. She positioned the stick on the sink counter, willing herself not to look until the two minutes were up. God, she really was being ridiculous, wasn't she? In—she glanced at the clock—just one more minute, she could look back and laugh.

Ready! Clare pulled herself up off the toilet seat and walked the few short steps to the counter. Holding her breath, she slowly leaned over the stick, almost afraid to look.

She blinked, then shook her head.

There was one line, yes. And right beside it—as clear and undeniable as the first—was another.

She was pregnant.

❧

'Hiya, Pops.' Oliver grinned cheekily as he slid into a chair at a café in the City, just steps from the gleaming skyscraper where he worked.

'Hi.' Poppy leaned over to kiss his cheek, marvelling again at how, despite similar features, he was so different from Alistair. Freshly shaven with hair neatly trimmed and sporting a black suit and paisley silk tie (Hermès', probably, since Alistair said Oliver wore nothing else), he was worlds away from Alistair's comfortable wardrobe. Their mum always joked that Alistair looked like he'd crawled rumpled from bed, while Oliver wouldn't even sleep on sheets that weren't ironed.

And the differences didn't stop at wardrobe. Ambitious and driven, Oliver had launched himself straight to the top of London's financial world, named as one of the UK's star market traders in his first year. Alistair, on the other hand, was content to work in a small practice as a physiotherapist, never aspiring to his own business. The differences meant that although the two brothers weren't on bad terms, they weren't close. She and Oliver had always got on, though, and without any siblings of her own, she considered him a brother.

Even so, this was a big ask. And as much as she hated keeping secrets from Alistair, if he discovered what she was doing, he wouldn't be happy. But there was no reason he had to find out, she reassured herself. And once she had the IVF and they held their own child in their arms, everything else would fade away.

'So.' Oliver met her eyes. 'What did you want to see me about? Everything okay with Al?'

Poppy grinned—he knew Alistair hated that nickname. 'Oh, yes. Everything's fine. It's just . . . ' Her voice trailed off, and she cleared her throat. 'Well, I was wondering if I could borrow some money.' She shifted awkwardly. 'For, um, a gift for Alistair.' It *was* a gift, she told herself to cover the discomfort at keeping secret the real reason for the funds. Alistair was a private sort of person, and although she was sure his family wondered at their lack of kids, they'd never in a million years dream of asking. The less she told Oliver, the better.

'Well, of course, Pops. You know I'm always here for you.' Oliver leaned back in the chair. 'So what's the occasion? I haven't missed a birthday or anniversary, have I?'

Poppy bit her lip. 'No, no. It's just, er, one of those things. Something I've wanted to get him for a very long time.' That much was true, anyway.

'What is it?' Oliver cocked his head. 'Al's always going on about non-material things and being happy with what you have. I'd love to hear what my brother's been longing for!'

Oh, bollocks. Maybe she should have thought this through more. Poppy's mind whirled as she struggled to think of a large item requiring thousands of pounds. 'A fridge,' she said lamely, jumping on the first thing that came into her head. Internally, she rolled her eyes. A bloody *fridge*? Surely she could have done better than that.

Oliver raised an eyebrow. 'Really? What, like one of those fancy Smeg ones with a freezer and all that?'

Poppy nodded. 'Exactly.' She crossed her fingers Oliver wouldn't remember his brother crowing how they'd bought a second-hand Smeg off Gumtree for a bargain price just last month.

'I've been thinking about getting one myself. But I eat out so much, I don't even have enough food to fill my mini-fridge,' Oliver said. 'I'm happy to help. Whatever you need, just let me know.'

A whoosh of relief washed over her. 'Oh, that's fantastic. Thank you! I hated to ask, but of course I'll pay you back as soon as I can. I just need a couple thousand. I should be able to save it up within the next few months.'

Oliver waved a hand as he got out his cheque book. 'No worries. Like I said, I'm happy to help.' He looked up at her. 'What if Al finds out, though? He usually treats my money as the root of all evil.'

Poppy felt a flush creeping over her face. 'Er, well, there's no reason he needs to find out, is there? I mean, I'll pay you back quickly.'

Oliver met her eyes, pausing as his hand hovered over the cheque. 'Well, okay, if you're sure.'

Poppy nodded. Everything would work out all right, she told herself again, pushing aside the flash of fear that shot through her. It had to, because she couldn't bear to think of the alternative.

Oliver wrote out the cheque, then carefully tore it out and handed it over. 'There you are. You know, I'm really pleased you felt comfortable enough to ask. I've told Alistair loads of times that I'm always here if he needs money, but I think he's too proud to take anything from his little brother. And don't worry—this is strictly between you and me.'

Thank goodness, Poppy thought as she tucked the cheque into the back pocket of her jeans for safekeeping. She felt terrible lying about what she needed the money for, but it was bad enough she'd asked Oliver, let alone sharing the issues she and Alistair had been having.

Onwards and upwards, she told herself, shoving away discomfort at her deception. Alistair hadn't wanted stress or strain—emotionally or financially. And whatever she was doing, she was doing for him.

CHAPTER TWENTY

Clare threaded her way down busy Oxford Street in a daze. Rush-hour commuters moved like blobs in front of her, snapping into focus when she blinked then fading away again. She rubbed her eyes, trying hard to muster up energy for the No-Kids Club meeting tonight. Ever since discovering she was pregnant almost a week ago, it was an effort to concentrate on anything outside of work. The emergency department was so rammed with human tragedy it made her own fade away.

Shame she couldn't hole up there and forget everything else, she thought now as she trudged to All Bar One. The second she left the hospital, the fact she was pregnant hit her with as much force as a blow to the head, resulting in a curious inertia. It was as if she was frozen, unable to accept the reality of her situation enough to even start thinking about changing it.

After seeing the test, Clare had sat on the toilet seat for what felt like hours, staring at those two pink lines until the image was practically burned into her retina—if she closed her eyes, she'd probably see it again. She'd told herself so many times she wasn't pregnant that she couldn't connect the test with *her*. That there was a baby growing and developing inside her body right now seemed like something from science fiction.

Clare had set the test on the counter and backed away from it slowly, as if it was a hand grenade. Then she'd promptly downed five glasses of water, waited, and taken the second test. Again, the same result. She'd collapsed on the toilet seat, mind spinning. Morning sickness didn't usually occur until four weeks at the very earliest, and she'd started feeling nauseous maybe . . . a few weeks ago, around the time of Ellie's baby shower? That would make the foetus somewhere around seven weeks old, assuming her queasiness had appeared straight after conception. *Conception*! She shuddered.

Unable to process the information, she'd crawled into bed and pulled the duvet around her. Maybe when she woke up she'd find the whole thing had been a terrible nightmare.

But when her eyes snapped open and she crept towards the loo, the two tests were still there, both pink lines as visible as ever. She'd picked them up and thrown them in a drawer, then slammed the drawer closed and crawled into bed again. And ever since, she'd been unable to think of anything else while curiously unable to act. She hadn't even told Ellie—keeping the knowledge locked inside made it seem less real somehow. Anyway, even if she did want to tell her friend, God knows she probably wouldn't be able to track her down. Clare had left a message telling her all about the stint on telly, but she'd still heard nothing in return. The distance between them was growing with each passing day.

The last place Clare wanted to be tonight was the No-Kids Club, but this was the first meeting since the piece had run on *Wake Up London*. The Facebook page had been flooded with supportive posts, and her inbox was overflowing with messages from potential members looking forward to tonight. At least there'd be more people besides Poppy and Anna. After last week's debate, she wouldn't have been surprised to see them come to blows without others around.

Taking a deep breath, Clare opened the door of All Bar One, the noise hitting her like a slap in the face. Although the space was normally busy, this was a whole new level. Punters were packed into every corner of the room, and the queue for the bar was five people deep. Everywhere she looked, people were laughing, chatting and sipping their drinks. Clare's eyes bulged—were they all here for the club? She swung her head from left to right, trying to figure out a way to penetrate the crowd.

'Miss?' A harried-looking woman appeared at her side. 'You're Clare Donoghue, aren't you?'

Clare nodded. 'Yes.'

'I thought so. Saw you on telly last week. I'm the manager here, and as much as we appreciate your custom, if you want to hold club meetings for this number of people, you'll have to book the bar for a private event.'

Clare's eyebrows flew up. So all these people *were* here for the club! She knew there were more people like her in London—people without kids, who wanted a place to come out and celebrate that lifestyle. She wasn't alone.

Except, of course, they weren't like her, she realised a heartbeat later. She was the only one in this room who was pregnant. Sighing, she pushed the thought into a back corner of her mind.

'I'm sorry,' Clare answered, her eyes still roaming the space in astonishment. 'Of course. I had no idea so many people would turn out tonight.'

'We'll let it go this time,' the woman said, 'as it looks like our bar is certainly going to turn a healthy profit.' She grinned. 'And good luck with your club. When I heard about it on telly last week, I thought it was a great idea.'

'Thanks,' Clare said, eyebrows rising even further. She was so used to negative reactions from women around her, it was strange to hear a positive one.

The crowd of faces turned towards her, and she caught sight of Poppy's blonde head in the corner. Clare was about to make her way over when a smattering of applause broke out. The noise swelled until the whole café resounded with the patter of hands.

Her mouth dropped open. Were they actually applauding her?

Anna appeared through the crowd, pushing her way to Clare's side. 'Can you believe this?' she asked, a grin splitting her normally sombre face.

Clare shook her head. 'No. I really can't.'

'Maybe you should give a little welcome speech,' Anna prodded gently. 'I think they're waiting for you to say something.'

Clare nodded. 'Okay.' She cleared her throat, her head still swimming with disbelief that all these people had come out tonight. The buzzing room fell silent when she clapped her hands.

'Um, I just want to welcome you to the No-Kids Club,' she started hesitantly. 'I'm Clare Donoghue, the founder.' Applause broke out again, and Clare's cheeks flushed with pleasure. 'I'm thrilled you could all make it tonight. I want this to be a place where we can have fun without fear or judgment. We'll be planning trips and outings in the future, but for now, please relax and enjoy yourself. Oh, and make sure we have your contact information, either by posting on our Facebook page or messaging me. We'll be moving to a new venue for the next meeting.'

She paused, looking at the smiling, supportive faces. The group was a real cross section, from women in their twenties to men in their sixties. Business suits mixed with hipsters, and couples chatted to singles. 'Thanks for coming, and I hope I get a chance to chat to everyone. Have fun!' She stepped back and the hum of the crowd started up again.

'Was that all right?' she mumbled to Anna.

'It was great,' Anna said, touching her arm. 'Listen, why don't we divide and conquer? That way, we can try to reach each one and give them a personal welcome to the club. I'll get everyone to put their names and numbers on a sign-up sheet too, in case they forget to message you. I'd hate for us to lose this momentum.'

'That would be fantastic. Thanks, Anna.' For the first time since they'd met, Clare felt a flash of warmth towards the woman.

'Can you two believe all these people?' Poppy's face shone with delight as she reached their sides. 'It's fantastic! I've already met a couple who couldn't conceive but are about to undergo another IVF cycle, just like me. Clare, this club was such a good idea.'

'But you're not meant to be talking about children,' Clare reminded her gently, a twinge of sympathy stirring inside. There was something child-like about Poppy and her determined belief that everything would be all right. Clare had learned long ago that wasn't true—she'd tried to convince herself for months her mum would return.

'Oh, I know, I know, and we won't again,' Poppy said hastily, a guilty expression sliding over her face. 'Anyway, we're going to have dinner together sometime next week. I can't wait.'

'Right, I'd better get circulating and try to say hi to everyone,' Clare said, drawing in a big breath to prepare herself. Small talk had never been her forte, and the crowd before her looked daunting.

A few hours later, she was stunned to see the bartenders taking last orders. Clare looked at her watch incredulously—yes, it was almost eleven. Where on earth had the night gone? She'd had a fantastic time meeting everyone.

It was too bad Nicholas hadn't made it out—again. It would have been nice for him to see the outcome of her *Wake Up London* appearance, if nothing else. She couldn't believe the wide array of people who had come, each with their own unique reason for not having children—it was never as simple as black and white. Every one of them said they were tired of justifying their reasons to friends and family, and how they couldn't wait to join a club that actually understood. There had been the odd one or two like Poppy, still desperate to conceive, but even they'd been interesting to chat with. Clare sensed they were happy to have found a refuge where baby envy didn't exist. This kind of group was exactly what she'd envisioned when she'd started the club. Finally, it had come true.

Shame she wasn't in a more celebratory mood. The weight of the secret inside dragged on her consciousness like a cement block. She leaned back against the wall, smiling vacantly as a woman across the room raised a glass in Clare's direction. Despite her swirling thoughts, she couldn't escape the irony that the club had blossomed only days after learning she was pregnant.

If it wasn't so tragic, she'd almost have laughed.

CHAPTER TWENTY-ONE

'And then you inject yourself right here with the needle.' The nurse pinched the skin around Poppy's belly button. 'You can also do your thigh, if you prefer.' Poppy nodded obligingly, even though she'd undergone the same process four times and was likely more experienced with injections than a heroin addict.

A flutter of excitement went through her at the thought of finally starting this IVF cycle. As soon as she'd left Oliver at the café, she'd rung up the clinic and booked an appointment. She had planned to tell Alistair before starting the injections, but then she'd met Marta and Luis at the No-Kids Club and invited them over for dinner next week. Marta was about to begin her fifth IVF cycle, too, and her hope had lifted Poppy's spirits. She was sure meeting the couple would go a long way towards rekindling Alistair's enthusiasm.

'So you're clear on everything?' The nurse shot her a quizzical look, and Poppy jerked.

'Oh yes, absolutely.' She smiled. 'I can't wait to get started. Fifth try lucky!'

The nurse's face remained neutral, and Poppy told herself they were probably trained to stay impartial. 'We'll see you back here in fourteen days to start the stimulation injections. Make an appointment at the reception, and please contact us with any questions or worries.' She sounded like she was reading off a cue card.

Poppy gathered up her things, then turned and headed out the door. Despite the unease at acting without Alistair's knowledge—first asking his brother for money and now starting the process without his approval—happiness spurted through her.

This time it would work, and in ten months or so, she'd be holding her child in her arms.

That was all that mattered.

∞

Anna dashed home from the bookshop, quivering with excitement. Happy anniversary, happy anniversary . . . the refrain rang through her mind as she rushed up the steps of the house. The timing was perfect: she'd worked until five, giving her time to relax and freshen up before Michael came back and whisked her off to whatever he'd planned. Luckily, their anniversary fell on a Friday, so he didn't even have to worry about an early start the next day.

She couldn't wait to see what her husband had up his sleeve! Just to be sure he remembered the date—although she knew he would—she'd mentioned several times their anniversary was approaching, making a point to say she hadn't planned anything this year. He'd nodded and turned back to his video games, but she was sure he'd taken it in.

So what would he have organised, Anna wondered as she unlocked the front door and slipped inside the silent house? A romantic dinner at that cosy restaurant in Soho he knew she liked? Maybe a night at the theatre? Actually, it really didn't matter what he'd planned. She'd be happy with a meal at the neighbourhood gastropub, then a little lovemaking. She hurried upstairs to the bedroom as desire rushed through her. This time, she'd make extra-certain Michael stayed awake.

Right, what to wear? Sighing, she examined her wardrobe: all blacks and greys, serviceable clothing for crawling around floors at the bookshop or at home. Surely she must have one special outfit! A flash of jade green caught her eye, and Anna pawed through the garments at the back of the wardrobe. She grabbed a corner of fabric and pulled, revealing a dress she'd bought to wear on honeymoon.

As she touched the silky material, memories slid into her mind. She and Michael, at that tiny restaurant on the lake during their honeymoon, listening to the hush of waves breaking on the pebbly shore. The wind had whipped around them, and the night sky was carpeted with pinpricks of light. The dress had rippled in the breeze, and Michael had reached out and touched her arm, sending shivers through her. His eyes had been so intense, and—just like in the movies—they'd asked for the bill and gone up to their room, where they'd made love. She'd felt like the luckiest woman in the world, vowing then and there she'd never let anything split them apart.

It seemed fitting she wear this dress tonight, she thought, pulling the garment from the hanger and holding it against her body. It might be a little tighter than when she'd worn it all those years ago—and the weather a little chillier—but she could wear a wrap. She couldn't wait to see Michael's eyes when he saw her in it again.

Excitedly, she showered, blow-dried her hair straight, then shimmied into the dress, easing the fabric over her hips. Fastening the diamond earrings Michael had bought her for their first anniversary, she carefully did her make-up then glanced at her reflection. Pretty good, if she did say so herself.

The door clicked closed and Anna pivoted towards it. He was home! Heart beating fast with anticipation, she eased down the staircase, taking care not to trip on the hem of the dress. Maybe he'd even have flowers, she thought, before telling herself not to get too worked up. Michael had never been much of a flower man, and that was fine. It was enough that he arranged the evening for them.

'Wow!' Michael's eyes widened when he saw her. 'You look fantastic.'

'Why, thank you.' Anna glowed as she spun in front of him. That look in his eyes was reward enough for freezing her arse off.

'So, where are you going, then? Got a hot date?' Michael took off his jacket, rubbing his chin. 'I'm exhausted. Long day.'

Anna blinked. He must be joking. 'A very hot date,' she said, smiling as she wrapped her arms around him.

'Oh, really?' Michael padded over to the kitchen. 'Should I be jealous?' he called over his shoulder. She heard him open the fridge. 'Sweetie, where's that leftover hummus? I could really use a snack before dinner.'

She shook her head, hoping the movement could bring clarity. He must have remembered this was their anniversary. For goodness' sake, she'd given him enough reminders! If this was a joke, he was starting to take it a little far.

Anna stepped into the kitchen. Michael had his head stuck in the fridge and was rummaging through the jars like a bear in a compost heap. 'If you're heading out, what's the plan for dinner? And where are you going, anyway?'

His words made her freeze with the knowledge that he had forgotten what tonight was—despite her carefully placed reminders. Even if he hadn't planned anything, she'd never thought he'd actually forget.

Anger swirled inside as she watched her husband dip a finger into the hummus and bring it to his mouth. Suddenly, she felt the urge to get away—away from the house, away from the dreaded task of cooking dinner, away from *him*. It didn't matter that she had no plans and was dressed for the opera. She needed to leave.

Without answering his questions, Anna grabbed her handbag, threw her trusty old black coat over her shoulders, shoved her feet into serviceable flats, and pushed out into the cold night air. Smog made halos in the streetlights as she scurried down the empty street, tears stinging her eyes. So much for showing he cared, she thought. Michael probably wouldn't even notice she was gone until his stomach started rumbling.

It hadn't always been this way, had it?

She cast her mind back through the years, but all she could see were images of herself doing things for him, day after day after day. But she'd wanted to live that way, and it had never bothered her in the slightest . . . until now.

The bright lights of the little café on the corner beckoned, and Anna swung open the door. Inside, the warm air was scented with tomato and garlic, and narrow tables packed the dimly lit space. Anna sank into one of them, easing off her coat and thanking God the restaurant was empty. She felt ridiculous in this dress now.

'Good evening.' A dark man about her age with an accent appeared, setting a laminated menu before her on the table. 'I am Christos and I'll be serving you tonight. What would you like to drink?'

'Something strong.' She usually didn't like anything more potent than wine, but tonight definitely called for it.

Christos's eyes crinkled as he smiled. 'I have just the thing. One moment, please.' He scurried away, returning with a small glass of clear liquid. The distinct smell of anise rose into Anna's nostrils.

'What is it?' she asked, tipping her head up to meet his eyes.

'It is called ouzo. We have an old Greek saying: ouzo makes the spirit.' He paused, scanning her face. 'You look like you could use a bit of that tonight.'

'Could I ever,' Anna said fervently, drawing the glass towards her.

'Would you like me to add a little water to dilute it for you?' he asked before she could lift it to her lips. 'It's what we do in Greece.'

Anna shook her head. 'No.' She touched the glass to her mouth and took a sip of the liquid, feeling it burn down her throat and into her stomach. *Wow.* But once the burning had passed, a pleasantly warm sensation lingered. She smiled up at the waiter. 'It's delicious.'

'I know.' He nodded. 'Go slowly, though—it can creep up on you.'

Anna took another sip. Forget creeping, she wanted to dive right in.

'Can I get you something to eat?'

She scanned the menu. Despite the anger inside, she was a little hungry. In anticipation of a big meal out tonight, she hadn't eaten since this morning. 'I'll have whatever's being cooked right now,' she said, sniffing the air as her stomach rumbled. 'It smells delicious.'

'It is delicious,' Christos said. 'It's called moussaka, and it's my mother's recipe. She was kind enough to share it with me when I opened this restaurant.'

Anna's eyebrows rose. She'd taken him as a waiter, not the owner. 'This is your restaurant? You do the cooking, too?'

Christos nodded. 'And the cleaning, and the accounting, and, well, pretty much everything. We are not busy enough yet for me to hire others, as you can see.' He grimaced as he glanced around the space.

'I'm sure it'll pick up,' Anna said, wanting to reassure him despite her misgivings. It certainly didn't seem to be flourishing, and with the recession on, it was a terrible time to open a restaurant. 'Maybe you need to spread the word a little.'

'Anyway.' Christos waved a hand in the air. 'Let me get your food, and then you must tell me what a beautiful woman like you is doing all alone in such a gorgeous dress.'

Anna flushed, covering her discomfort by taking another sip of ouzo. It slid down nicely now without the accompanying burning. When was the last time anyone had called her beautiful? She couldn't remember, but it felt nice. And she *was* looking good tonight—completely wasted on her husband, she thought as another wave of anger hit.

She smiled as Christos hummed away in the kitchen, then sipped her drink again. Sneaks up on you, pah. She was more than halfway through and she felt fine. Leaning back in her chair, she glanced around the tiny dining area. The walls were painted a dark blue and tiny fairy lights were strung along the ceiling. It was kitsch, yes, but also very welcoming. And in a way, Anna felt like she'd been transported from grey London to sunny Greece. Her dark mood lifted slightly.

'Here you are.' Christos set a plate of moussaka in front of her, and her mouth started watering at the delicious scent.

'Looks divine,' she said. 'What's in this, exactly?' She prodded the food with her fork.

Christos tilted his head. 'You've never heard of moussaka?'

'No. But I've obviously been missing out!'

'Well . . . ' Christos slid onto the banquette beside her, the heat from his body caressing her bare arms. He smelled of pepper and onion mixed with some kind of musky cologne. 'This is lamb in a tomato sauce with aubergine. Have a bite and let me know what you think.' He watched eagerly as Anna took a forkful and inserted it into her mouth as neatly as she could, feeling somewhat self-conscious under his watchful gaze.

The flavours exploded as she chewed. 'It's delicious,' she said once she'd swallowed. 'You made this?'

Christos grinned. 'Yes. Why? Don't think men can cook?' he joked.

Anna almost responded that her husband certainly couldn't before clamping her lips closed. Right now, she didn't want to think about Michael. It seemed all she'd done for the past six years was think of him. Here, in this restaurant away from the reality of the life she'd built with her husband, she just wanted to be Anna. 'Of course they can. It's fantastic.'

'Thank you.' Christos got to his feet. 'Let me get you more ouzo. I'll be right back.'

Anna nodded, continuing to shovel the casserole into her mouth. The alcohol had taken the edge off her anger, and the food was making her muscles pleasantly heavy. She felt like she could melt into the banquette and stay here forever.

'Here you go.' Christos's voice cut into her reverie, and she forced her eyes wide open then took another sip of the drink. God, this was really good. She'd have to get some for Mi—no! Anna pushed aside the thought, irritation swirling inside. For goodness' sake, couldn't she have one night without him invading her thoughts?

Christos eased onto the banquette again, so close now she could feel his leg against hers.

'Tell me, what are you doing here alone in that gorgeous dress?' His eyes met hers, and desire went through her. God, he was handsome. With tightly curled hair, aquiline features, and an olive complexion, he could have stepped straight off the cover of a Mills & Boon.

Anna took another sip of her drink. Yum. Why had she never tried this before? And how on earth had she never had moussaka?

'It's a long story,' she said, not wanting to go into details. She wasn't sure she could articulate it, anyway. Her lips were starting to feel numb.

'I've got all night.'

Anna flushed at the words. Christos probably didn't mean them suggestively, but she couldn't help picturing his solid body up against hers, those dark eyes staring down. She shoved away the image, twisting her wedding band back and forth. Her fingers were swollen from the heat of the place and it cut into her skin.

'Let's just say I made a mistake.' A mistake to think Michael would remember something so important. She still couldn't believe he'd forgotten. A cold sense of dread washed over her and she shivered. What would happen to their marriage if she stopped putting everything she had into it? The question whirled through Anna's muddled mind, and she held it there for a second.

Oh, whatever. Anna forced it from her head. Right now, she didn't want to think of anything to do with Michael, home, or even her life. She just wanted to soak up the atmosphere in this place with a strange man who knew nothing about her and enjoy the pleasant fuzziness taking over.

Christos raised an eyebrow. 'Very mysterious.' He pointed to her plate. 'Well done, you've finished.'

'My compliments to the chef,' Anna said, glancing down in surprise. She'd polished off the huge portion! At least it would soak up the drink. She took another sip. Might as well indulge a bit more, then. 'It really was delicious.' The words came out slurry despite her effort.

'Let me get you some dessert. And more ouzo.' Before Anna could protest, Christos had disappeared into the kitchen.

'Here we are.' He set a plate of small golden squares in front of her, and Anna squinted up at him.

'What's this?'

Christos's mouth fell open. 'Now don't tell me you've never had these, either! These are baklava.'

It sounded familiar, but as Anna bit into the juicy sweetness, she knew she'd never tasted anything like it. 'Amazing.'

'Just like you.' Christos settled onto the banquette and slung his arm over the back so he wasn't quite touching her, but almost. Anna knew she should move away; Christos was pulling out the clichéd charm, and she should at least say she was married. But what was the harm?

As she devoured the baklava and sipped back the ouzo—it was disappearing at an alarming rate—Christos told her all about the small island he'd come from, and how cold and dark he'd found London when he first arrived.

'In Greece, the whole place is full of light and colour. Everything is intense. Here, it's like the city is on mute. The colours, the noise, the people. Very different to back home.' He paused, turning to face her. 'So when I saw you in your lovely dress'—he reached out and stroked the short sleeve, and the hairs on her arms stood up—'the colour of the Greek ocean, I knew I had to do everything I could to keep you here as long as possible.'

'You definitely did that with the ouzo,' Anna joked, trying to inject a bit of levity into the moment. The way Christos was staring at her, she didn't doubt the Greek people were intense. But she couldn't say she wasn't enjoying it. It was lovely to have someone pay attention to her for once.

Christos laughed. 'I warned you about that! You're doing very well, by the way. Some people would be under the table by now.'

'I'm not sure I can stand! You might have to carry me home.' She glanced at her watch, the numbers swimming before her eyes. She'd no idea what the hour was, but it was definitely time to get out of here. Anna fumbled in her handbag, trying to focus enough to find her debit card. 'How much do I owe you?'

Christos was shaking his head. 'No, no. You owe me nothing—you have given me the pleasure of spending a wonderful evening with a beautiful woman.'

Even in her drunken state, Anna knew his words were cheesy, but she still couldn't help smiling. 'Please. I've had at least half a bottle of ouzo.'

'There's plenty more where that came from.' Christos shrugged.

'I'd better head home.' Anna struggled to her feet, the restaurant doing a wild samba around her as she stood. *Whoa.*

'I told you it creeps up on you!' Christos grinned as he watched her sway. He stood, then took her arm to steady her. 'Here. Just lean on me a second.'

Anna clutched his arm, inhaling air until the room finally righted itself. She turned to face him, noticing her lips were almost level with his. With Michael, she usually got a crick in her neck from looking up. 'Thank you, and good night.' Her voice was unsteady as her heart started to beat faster.

Christos stared into her eyes. 'Night. Please come again. It would be lovely to see you.'

Outside, the cold air was like a slap in the face and she breathed it in, trying to clear the fog from her head. She took a few quick steps and forced herself to keep walking, afraid she'd topple over if she stopped.

Several minutes later, she unlocked her front door, listening for any sign of movement. Inside, it was still and dark—Michael must have gone to bed; no surprise there. Not wanting to disturb him, Anna kicked off her shoes, propped herself up with a cushion on the sofa, and waited for sleep to claim her from this strange, surreal night.

CHAPTER TWENTY-TWO

Clare rubbed her eyes at the sound of the buzzer, then squinted at the clock on the wall. It was just past nine on a Saturday night, and she'd been drifting off to sleep to the dulcet tones of Tony Robinson and his bearded compatriots on the world's most boring episode of *Time Team*.

Who on earth could that be? Maybe Ellie? She'd love to catch up with her friend; almost three weeks had passed since the baby shower. Her heart sunk as she realised 'catching up' would entail hearing all the latest pregnancy news—and that was the last thing she wanted to think about.

Chatting to her best friend while keeping her own condition hidden would feel wrong, but discussing what she needed to do with a woman about to give birth seemed equally wrong, too. Maybe she'd plead she still wasn't feeling well and go back to sleep. Clare shook her head, annoyed at herself. Usually, she could tackle a problem head-on, solving it quickly. That's what made her such a good emergency doctor—she could almost always fix the patient's ailment, and fast.

So why couldn't she do that now? Each time she picked up the phone to call the family planning clinic, she promptly put it down, busying herself with some inconsequential task.

The buzzer sounded again, and Clare drew her bathrobe even closer around her body. 'Coming!' she yelled, padding to the door.

'Oh!' She jerked back in surprise at the sight of Nicholas leaning against the doorjamb. They hadn't spoken since the studio—not that she was surprised, given his track record.

'Hiya.' Nicholas's eyes twinkled as he smiled. 'I was in the neighbourhood. Thought I'd drop by and see what you were up to.' He raised an eyebrow as he took in her ratty robe and tousled hair, and Clare flushed. 'Hope I didn't get you out of bed?'

'Er . . . ' Clare met his steady gaze, her mind whirling with how to respond. She could invite him in, but then he'd expect . . . what? That nightcap and the rain check they'd been trying to get around to for weeks? *When a man turns up late at night, there's only one thing he wants . . . and it isn't warm milk.* Ellie's voice from her university days drifted into Clare's mind. This was most definitely a booty call, and God knows booty was not on the agenda right now.

'No, but actually, I was about to go to bed. Sorry,' she said finally.

'Oh.' Nicholas's face fell. 'That's too bad. Okay, then. Sorry to drop by like this.' He shrugged. 'Just thought I'd give it a shot. Well, have a good sleep and I'll see you soon.'

Clare nodded, thinking that she'd almost prefer *not* seeing him soon. This whole thing with Nicholas—whatever it was—was starting to be more bother than it was worth. The comings and goings, the booty calls and rain checks that were never endorsed, the uncertainty about next dates . . . She had enough on her mind without adding him and his random appearances to the mix. He probably wouldn't be in touch for a few more weeks anyway, she'd plead busy, and then they could let whatever had happened between them die naturally. Given their relationship had barely left the starting gate, it wouldn't take long to fade.

Nicholas got out his keys and climbed back into the car, and Clare watched it pull away into the dark night. Mouth stretching in an enormous yawn, she was about to swing closed the door when she noticed something contrasting against the whitewash of her step. What was that? Tiptoeing gingerly in her bare feet on the cold cement, she picked up the object, turning it over in her hands. The black leather wallet was smooth and heavy, and she scurried back into the warmth of the lounge, closing the door behind her. Her eyes widened as she spotted Nicholas's driver's license through the front plastic pocket. Shit! He must have dropped it when he got out his keys.

Clare stood for a second, wallet in hand, trying to decide what to do. Actually, she knew what she wanted to do—go to bed. But if Nicholas discovered the wallet missing and needed it straight away, he might be by at some ungodly hour later tonight to pick it up. She'd never be able to sleep knowing that could happen at any moment. No, as exhausted as she was, it was best to ring now and wait for him to come round again.

But five phone calls, two voicemails, and several texts later, Clare was still waiting. She snuck a peek at her watch: almost eleven. For God's sake, the least he could do was text her back and say he didn't need his wallet now! She tapped a finger against her mouth. If he didn't come by tonight, that would probably mean another rendezvous tomorrow. And he'd definitely expect to cash in that bloody rain check then, wouldn't he?

Clare let out a huge sigh.

She glanced at his driver's license again, noticing he lived in Belgravia. That wasn't too far from here. She could grab a cab to his flat, put the wallet through the letter box, and that would be that. After padding into the bedroom, she tugged on a pair of jeans and a thick jacket. Then she hurried out into the night and down to busy Fulham Road to hail a taxi, eager now to put all this behind her. If traffic didn't conspire against her, she could be home again in half an hour.

A few minutes later, the cab pulled up to a row of white terraces similar to her own. After asking the driver to wait, Clare tumbled out into the street. She checked the license again: Nicholas lived at number 10a in the garden flat. Lucky man, she thought as she walked towards the house. She'd give anything to have outdoor space—as long as there was someone to take care of it. Funny, she'd expected a slick penthouse rather than a homely place like this. And—she glanced around the clean and tidy exterior—hadn't he said something about major renovations? Usually that entailed scaffolding or at least a skip, but there wasn't even a ladder in sight.

Clare opened the gate and made her way up the path. Lights blazed from the window and the sound of cartoons drifted from inside. Nicholas was either home or a group of child thieves were having a party in his flat. And if he was home, why hadn't he answered her texts? Shrugging, she pressed the buzzer. She couldn't drop off his wallet and run if he was there.

'Oh, hello.' Nicholas's eyebrows flew up as he swung open the door. His normally crisp shirt was replaced with a well-worn grey T-shirt, and bizarrely, a gold clip perched in his short hair. What was that all about?

'Nice look.' Clare smiled. 'Is the clip a new fashion accessory?'

'Oh, God.' He coloured and swiped it from his hair. 'Yeah, well.' Without further explanation, he shoved the clip in his pocket.

That was strange, Clare thought. And he didn't seem in much of a hurry to invite her in, judging by the way he was blocking the door and darting little glances over his shoulder. What was going on? Maybe he was a transvestite or something in his spare time, she giggled to herself. No wonder he'd been so hard to contact.

'You dropped your wallet right outside my flat earlier.' She held it up.

'Oh, God, thanks.' Nicholas reached out to take it, slipping it into the back pocket of his jeans. 'Can't believe I did that. I didn't even notice it was gone.'

'I thought you might not. I left a few messages, but . . . '

'Oh, sorry. I didn't get them.' He paused, twisting around to look behind him. 'Well, thanks again. I would have been lost tomorrow morning without my wallet.'

'I figured as much.' The silence stretched between them, growing more and more awkward with each passing second. Finally, just as Clare was about to head back to the cab, she heard the unmistakeable sound of children laughing.

'Oh, I didn't realise your nieces were visiting,' she said. 'No wonder you were busy. Sorry—hope the buzzer didn't wake them up.' Her mind spun, trying to make sense of it all. If Nicholas had his nieces over, why had he appeared on her doorstep a few hours earlier? Surely they wouldn't be dropped off so late?

'Yes, er, no, that's okay,' he said, looking flustered for the first time since she'd known him. 'We were playing beauty salon—hence the clip.' He grimaced. 'I'd better get back to it.'

'Of course, of course.' Clare leaned in to kiss his cheek. 'Well, the cab's still waiting, so—'

'Dad! Dad!' A little girl with curly blonde hair burst into the room, and Nicholas turned towards her. 'Come on! Lena and I have to try to plait your hair.'

Clare's mouth dropped open. *Dad?*

'Sorry, Mr Hunt.' The smiling face of a twenty-something Aussie girl appeared behind the child. 'They've already done mine and they insist on doing yours before going back to bed.' She rolled her eyes at Clare in irritation. 'Better make a quick getaway before they try to shave your head or something. At this rate, it'll be morning before they settle.'

'Yes, yes!' the little girl said, beaming up at Clare. 'We can do yours as well!'

'Lucy,' Nicholas said in a warning tone. 'It's way past your bedtime. I want you and Lena to go upstairs. I'll be there in a second.'

Clare was listening to the exchange, her mouth hanging open as she tried to absorb the scene before her. Nicholas had *children*?

When Lucy and the nanny had disappeared, Nicholas turned to meet Clare's incredulous gaze. 'Right. Well.'

Clare could only stare. Why on earth had he got in touch with the club when he wasn't child-free? And all that talk about finding someone who was like him . . . Sure, she hadn't wanted to know every little detail of his private life, but having children was hardly one little detail, especially when the *lack* of children was the foundation of their relationship, or whatever it was.

'So . . . I have kids,' Nicholas said finally. 'Two children, Lena and Lucy. Lena is four and Lucy's six.'

Clare nodded, half-expecting him to whip out a series of photos on his iPhone. 'And do you have a wife, too?' she asked. There didn't seem to be one in the picture, but if a man could keep quiet about his children, goodness knows what else he could keep hidden.

'Good God, no. We've been divorced for two years now. We share custody and we both have crazy schedules, which is why I'm often here, there, and everywhere. There always seems to be some emergency or disaster.' He sighed. 'I wanted to meet a woman who's not keen to get tied down; someone not interested in having more children.' He shook his head. 'I get enough of kids and responsibility here. When I saw the advert for the club, I thought it might be just the place to find what I'm looking for. And then I met you.' He smiled. 'You're independent, you don't want to know my every thought or what I had for breakfast, and you don't need to see me each hour of the day. Perfect.'

'Were you ever planning to tell me you have children?' Clare asked, refusing to be moved by his compliments.

'Well, no. Not really.'

Clare jerked at his words. 'Why not?'

Nicholas shrugged. 'It wasn't important, was it? You'd never want to be their stepmum—and I wasn't looking for a candidate for that. Neither one of us wants a committed relationship. It's not like you volunteered much about your personal life, either. And that's more than fine by me. In fact, I like it. No complication, no fuss or mess.'

Clare stared into Nicholas's blue eyes, his explanation sinking in. He was right: every date had been on a nice, safe level, with fun banter and surface conversations. That's what made him so enjoyable to be with. No fuss or mess, like he'd said. But there was also no *emotion*.

The problem wasn't Nicholas, she realised now. The problem was her. She'd thought they wanted the same things, but she'd been wrong. The easy-come, easy-go type relationship that fit around everything else didn't make her happy—there was an emptiness about that kind of surface attachment. She wanted someone who'd miss her, who'd make time to see her.

'I'm sorry for any misunderstanding,' Nicholas was saying now. 'Do you think we can pick up where we left off? I'd really like to see more of you.'

Clare stared into his handsome face, his choice of words not going missed. He'd like to see more of her—not learn more about her or get to know her better. 'No.' She took a deep breath. 'No, I'm sorry. It was lovely meeting you and I've enjoyed our time together, but I have to go.'

She kissed him quickly on the cheek, then ducked into the waiting cab. Leaning back against the seat as the car pulled away,

Clare closed her eyes and sighed. She'd been so certain that was the kind of relationship she wanted, but she'd been wrong.

Her hand slid down to her belly, Mary's words about considering children before it was too late echoing in her mind. Could she be wrong about kids, too? Her eyes snapped open at the thought. Of course not, she told herself. Having a baby was a huge deal, and she was nowhere near ready.

So why wasn't she doing something about it?

CHAPTER TWENTY-THREE

'Who are these people again?' Alistair asked early Sunday evening as he traded his usual black tee for a wrinkled cotton shirt. 'Do I need to iron this?'

Poppy laughed as she examined her rumpled husband. 'Um, yes. You do.' She watched him strip off the shirt and exchange it for another, only marginally less creased. At least it was an improvement. 'Their names are Marta and Luis,' she said. 'I met them at the No-Kids Club.'

'Ah.' Alistair attempted to smooth down the fabric. 'They're not fanatics who don't want to have children, are they? I can't stand those people. They're so self-righteous.'

Poppy thought of Clare, who was definitely against having kids. She wasn't self-righteous about it, though, was she? In fact, Poppy felt a little sorry for her. Despite her strong words, she looked lonely. 'No, no. Actually, they're starting their fifth IVF cycle.'

'Oh, God.' Alistair groaned. 'That's not why you invited them round, is it, Pops?' He swung to face her. 'Because I really don't want to discuss the ins and outs of all that. I'm so tired of talking about it.'

'I just thought they were a lovely couple,' Poppy said vaguely, a tiny jab of fear poking her gut. What if he really didn't want to do IVF again? But no, she reassured herself, he wasn't against it—it was more the financial worries and stress. He'd be fine. Because if he wasn't . . .

'Okay, good.' Alistair interrupted her thoughts. He turned and put his arms around her, and Poppy let herself relax against his chest despite the tension inside. 'Look, I know all this hasn't been easy for you. But I promise that whatever child comes to us, it will be our own. We'll love him or her whether it's ours biologically or not.'

Poppy nodded, her head grazing his chin. She didn't doubt they would love any child. But that wasn't the point. It wasn't time to give up on their own baby—not just yet. A spurt of determination flowed through her. She'd get Alistair excited about this round of IVF if it killed her.

Three hours later, she was beginning to think it *would* kill her. Marta and Luis were nice enough, but the only thing they spoke of was IVF, IVF, and IVF, detailing everything from their first four cycles, and Poppy meant everything. Seriously, learning how quickly Luis was able to provide a sample for their second attempt was way too much information.

She swallowed more water as Marta outlined yet again their plan of action for cycle number five, noticing Alistair twitching beside her. She really couldn't blame him. Even with her own IVF underway, she was getting uber-bored herself.

'So are you off on holiday anywhere nice this year?' she asked inanely, hoping to change the subject before Alistair started to convulse.

'Oh no.' Luis shook his head solemnly. 'If Marta conceives, we want to stick around here. No flying. We're not going to take any risks.' She caught Alistair rolling his eyes as Luis reached over to pat Marta's still-empty abdomen. 'In fact, Marta will go on bed rest as soon as we find out she's pregnant.'

Marta nodded. 'That's right. I'll be leaving my job straight away. Having a healthy pregnancy is the most important thing to us.'

Wow. She and Alistair had been desperate for her to get pregnant, but they were nothing compared to these two. Were they? Doubt fluttered through her. Like Luis and Marta, they hadn't been on holiday for years, and pregnancy had dominated almost every conversation—well, until recently.

Poppy stared as Marta and Luis's monologue on egg harvesting washed over her. She didn't want to be like these people, not for a second. But now that she'd started down the IVF road, she wasn't about to give up. If her 'bones' were right and this attempt was successful, they wouldn't need to do the procedure again, anyway.

'That was fun,' Alistair said wryly a few hours later as they cleared the plates from dinner. He paused to gulp from a glass of wine she'd almost served before Luis mentioned he was off all alcohol in 'fertility solidarity'. After the night they'd had, she was tempted to have a swig herself. He turned to face her. 'Look . . . I know the adoption thing came as a shock. I've been trying to give you time and space, but do you think you might consider it now?'

Poppy forced a smile, cursing bloody Marta and Luis and their one-track mind. Far from softening Alistair towards IVF, Mr & Mrs Procreation had done the exact opposite. For goodness' sake, they could put the Virgin Mary off Baby Jesus!

Maybe the couple could work in her favour, though, to show how different her approach was this time, that the IVF attempts didn't have to be all-consuming. From injections to financing, she'd done it all on her own so far—and, apart from Alistair's sample, she could do the rest, too. Hopefully that would be enough to convince him. She drew in a deep breath, heart racing as she geared up to finally tell him her plan.

'So, um, yes, well. I *have* been doing a lot of thinking,' Poppy began, her voice thready with nerves, 'and . . . ' She gripped Alistair's hand and smiled at him, trying to convey how excited she was at the possibility of getting pregnant.

Alistair's eyes lit up. 'Yes? You'll consider it? That's fantastic news, honey.' He squeezed her fingers and Poppy's heart dropped. *Shit.*

'I didn't want to influence you too much, but it's definitely the best way forward for us,' he continued, oblivious to the expression on her face. He drew her close. 'I'm so glad we're finally moving in the right direction.'

Poppy's mouth flopped open. *What?* She'd no idea he felt so strongly about adoption. He'd made it sound an option for consideration, not something he was set on. Panic closed her throat and she floundered for a response.

She pulled back, regarding his animated face. He had more life now than she'd seen in the past few months, as if the possibility of having a child in the next year had lit him up from the inside out.

Just tell him, a voice in her head bleated. Tell him now about the IVF, before he really does think you're on board with adoption. But the words stayed stuck inside, and as Alistair pulled her close again, she hadn't the heart to force them out.

❦

'Honey, I'm home!'

Anna jerked awake at Michael's voice. Was it evening already? She'd plopped on the sofa mid-afternoon, falling asleep to the sound of property hunters cooing over a ramshackle shed in Spain. Yawning, she rubbed her eyes and sat up.

'Hey, babe.' Michael dropped a kiss on her nose, then sank down next to her and took off his shoes. 'Good day? What did you get up to?'

'Oh, you know. The usual.' Anna forced a grin, thinking of the pile of laundry still waiting to be washed, the carpets needing Hoovering, and the layers of dust gathering on every surface. Ever since their anniversary a few days ago, she couldn't rally the energy to care. After an exhausting weekend pretending everything was fine, she'd been only too happy when Monday rolled around. But once Michael had left for work this morning, she'd moved from room to room within the silent building, looking at the space she'd created for them and feeling empty. The only thing that made her feel even slightly alive was the memory of sitting next to Christos in the tiny restaurant, the warmth of his body cloaking her like a blanket, his dark eyes on her. A dart of guilt would hit until she reminded herself Michael had forgotten their anniversary.

'What's for dinner tonight?' he asked, shrugging off his jacket. 'I'm ravenous. No time for lunch.'

'Oh, I don't know. I haven't even thought about it.' That wasn't exactly true. She had thought about it—several times—but she hadn't been able to muster up the motivation to do anything.

'Shall we order a takeaway?' Michael's face lit up with excitement. 'I'd love some pizza. It's been ages since we've ordered in.'

'Sure,' Anna replied in a voice that sounded dead. 'The menus are in the kitchen, second drawer to the right.'

She watched Michael trundle off, waiting for him to comment on the unwashed dishes in the sink, but—like all the other undone chores piling up in the house—he didn't seem to notice. Frustration rose inside, pressing against her lungs until she almost couldn't breathe. She'd worked so hard every day of the past six years to make everything perfect, to create the ideal home. To keep the relationship going and be the model wife so that nothing would ever come between them, like she'd promised herself way back when.

But now it seemed her husband couldn't care less about any of it. He'd probably be happy with a takeaway every night, and as for their relationship . . . Anna lay down again on the sofa, pulling a pillow under her head. If he wasn't bothered, then neither was she.

CHAPTER TWENTY-FOUR

Poppy jabbed the needle into her leg, biting her lip to keep from crying out. This was the bit she hated. Only another week or so, she told herself, then the stimulation shots, and then they'd be ready to harvest the eggs. She had to tell Alistair about the IVF— and soon.

Easier said than done. Ever since Sunday night, he'd been excitedly babbling on about adoption as she attempted to work up the courage to say that, actually, she'd never agreed to adopt in the first place. The more time that passed, the harder it was becoming.

The doorbell sounded, and Poppy neatly discarded the needle into a plastic bag—she'd dump it later in the special bin the clinic had given her. Shoved under the kitchen sink and covered with clutter, there was no way Alistair would find it. She hated the subterfuge, but she couldn't risk him finding out before she had a chance to say anything. After jamming the bag up under her jumper, Poppy rushed into the bedroom and then pushed it into her handbag. She glanced at the clock. Ten past eight on a Tuesday night—who could that be? A deep male voice drifted up the stairs, and her heart lurched as she realised exactly who that voice belonged to.

Alistair's brother.

Shit. Not even bothering to brush her hair or take off the ratty jumper and shapeless jogging bottoms she'd thrown on after school, Poppy raced downstairs and into the kitchen, where the two men were standing. Why on earth was Oliver here? He never dropped by—in fact, Poppy couldn't remember the last time he'd come round. It'll be okay, she told herself as she huffed into the kitchen. He knows to keep his mouth shut about the loan, and anyway, it wasn't like he knew the real reason. Thank goodness.

'Oh, hi, Poppy.' Oliver smiled broadly at her as she crossed the room. Dressed in his typical black suit with expensive tie, he was a sharp contrast to Alistair's baggy khakis and worn-in polo.

'Hey there. This is a surprise!' She tried to make it sound a welcome one.

'I know. It's been ages since I've come over, and I happened to be in Notting Hill with a client for dinner, so I thought I'd pop by.' Oliver settled into a chair at the table. 'How are you two?'

'Fine, fine,' Poppy said. 'Would you like a drink? Something to eat, maybe? We have some leftover lemon fairy cakes I made for my class yesterday.' Maybe with food filling his mouth, he wouldn't be able to talk much.

Oliver grinned. 'Fairy cakes? It's been a while since I've had one of those. Sure, that would be great.' He watched as Poppy hurried to the fridge and placed two cakes in front of him. Oliver took a big bite of one, his face lighting up. 'Delicious.' He looked around the kitchen as he chewed. 'Hey, nice fridge.'

Oh, God. Poppy could feel the sweat breaking out on her brow. She willed him not to say any more, widening her eyes and sending an imploring message.

Alistair shot his brother a funny look. 'Thanks.'

'It's new, right?' Oliver winked at Poppy from the corner of his eye, and her heart started beating fast. Please Lord, may this conversation not continue.

Alistair tilted his head. 'Well, relatively new. Don't you remember me telling you about it last month? How we got it off Gumtree for such a great deal?'

Oliver raised his eyebrows, then glanced at Poppy with a look of confusion. She gave a slight shake of her head, catching Alistair staring back and forth between her and Oliver. This was going from bad to worse.

'Right, right.' Oliver snapped his fingers. 'Yes, of course. Sorry, I forgot.' He took another bite of the fairy cake as silence descended. Poppy knew she should say something to lighten the mood, but what? She could barely breathe with the tension circling inside. Finally, after what felt like hours, Oliver finished his treats and looked up at them. Poppy's expression must have signalled her desperation for him to leave, because he started shrugging on his jacket.

'Well, I'd better push off, then. Good to see you again, Pops. You, too, Al. Take care.' And with that, he lifted a hand and turned to go. The door slammed shut, and silence fell.

'What on earth was all that was about?' Alistair asked, shaking his head. 'Oliver hardly ever drops by, and when he does, he stays to eat a cake, then leaves?'

'Er . . . ' Poppy picked up the tray of fairy cakes, trying to decide if she should say anything. It was one thing to tell Alistair about the IVF, and another to confess she'd borrowed money from his brother. She'd focused so much on how to soften Alistair towards the procedure that she hadn't fully thought of how to sort things out if he did discover how she'd paid for it. 'Just let me put these back in the fridge first!' She kept her tone light and cheery, but it sounded forced even to her own ears.

'Ah, yes, the fridge. What was up with that?' Alistair's voice floated over her head as she bent down to shove the cakes on the bottom shelf. 'I swear to God, I'll never understand my brother. And what was with the Morse code between you two?'

Poppy grabbed a washcloth from the counter and pretended to wipe the surface clean. It was as if the more frantically she scrubbed, the faster the right thing to say would come to mind. Maybe she should just tell him now, she thought. Oliver dropping by had nearly given her a heart attack, and it would only complicate matters more if Alistair found out about the money from his brother, not her. He wouldn't be happy, but surely he'd appreciate her intentions. She'd only wanted to save him stress, after all. 'Um . . . '

'Stop.' Alistair put a hand on her shoulder, and Poppy turned towards him. 'Look, forget my brother. There's something I've been meaning to talk to you about for the past few days.' His face was deadly serious. 'Pops, you know you can tell me anything, right?'

Poppy nodded slowly, despite the conflicting emotions inside. Until recently, she *had* felt she could tell him anything. These past few weeks had been like a wedge driving them apart, and she'd hated the distance despite knowing her actions were for them both.

'This adoption thing, we're in it together, you and me.' He took her hands. 'We're a team, we always have been. And I can't help feeling that you might not be as excited about this as I am. If you're not, that's okay. We can wait, we can discuss it more and give you time to think, if you need it. I don't want to do anything unless you're one hundred percent behind it.'

Oh, God. Poppy met her husband's eyes, guilt sweeping through her. Here he was, willing to take a step back from something he wanted. And here she was, driving forward with hers. Suddenly, she knew she had to tell him. The timing wasn't perfect, but she'd done enough now to show she was fit and ready, and she wanted to share her hope with him.

'Look, Alistair.' She gulped in air, struggling to keep her voice level. 'I know you were hesitant about more IVF.'

His brow furrowed. 'Yes. But what does this have to do with adoption?'

'Well . . . ' Poppy squeezed the washcloth, feeling it turn damp from her clammy hands. 'I never actually said I wanted to move on with adoption. In fact'—she tried to ignore Alistair's raised eyebrows—'I want to do another IVF cycle. I know you're worried about me and my stamina,' she carried on before he could say anything. 'But you needn't worry at all! Because I've been going to the clinic, taking the first round of shots, and it's been absolutely fine.'

Alistair sank into a chair, his gaze fixed on her face as if he was trying to absorb her words. 'Let me get this straight. You decided to start IVF without even telling me?'

Poppy sat down beside him. Stay calm, she told herself. Of course he'd be surprised at first. 'Well, yes. I wanted to show you I could handle everything on my own. I was going to tell you soon.'

'Soon?' Alistair shook his head incredulously. He was silent for a moment, staring down at the table. 'I can't believe you'd do that, Poppy. I really can't.' He snorted. 'And I was actually worried I came on too strong about adoption. Guess I wasted my time thinking about that!'

He lifted his head to meet her eyes again, and Poppy flinched at the coldness of his face. 'So how did you pay for everything?'

'Um . . . ' Poppy took a deep breath. 'I had a little cash of my own, and I borrowed the rest from your brother.' She paused, biting her lip at his stunned expression. 'Don't worry, I didn't tell him what it was for. He thought we needed a new fridge.'

'Ah, the fridge.' Alistair let out a strangled laugh. 'So it wasn't enough to go behind my back for IVF—you had to secretly ask my brother for money, too. Were you planning to use his sperm, as well? Might have a better chance.' His face twisted.

'Of course not!' Poppy reached out to take his hand. 'I'm sorry I didn't tell you, but I wanted to show you how easy the whole thing could be. Look, I know this isn't the ideal way for you to find out,' she admitted. 'But once you see that it works—'

'Stop!'

Alistair slammed a hand down on the table and Poppy jerked in surprise. 'Just *stop*, Poppy. You know this won't work, the doctor knows it won't work, I know it won't work. We've tried everything, and nothing is working.'

'Please.' She tried to inject every bit of emotion and yearning into one word.

Alistair pushed to his feet. 'Don't do this to me, Pops. Don't make me out to be the one who's stopping you. It's not me, it's us.' He turned towards her, and Poppy was stunned to see the emotion on his face. 'It's our biology that doesn't work together, for a reason we may never know. How many times do we need to fail for you to finally see that?' He slumped back into the chair, as if the life had drained from him. 'The thing is, you're always going to want to do one more round. A new technique, new research, another tabloid article showing success after ten cycles . . . '

He took her hand again. 'You'll never want to stop, so, well, I'm just going to say it as clearly as I can, so there's no chance for confusion.' He took a breath in and fixed her with a steady gaze. 'I'm done. I'm done with the tests, with everything involved in trying to get you—us—pregnant. I want a child with you, and there are other ways to do it.' His eyes held hers, and she could read in them his desperation for her to agree. But she couldn't.

'Just this one last time, Alistair. We have to try. We have to.'

Silence swirled around them for what felt like ages. Finally, Alistair pulled his hand from hers and stood. 'I can't, Poppy. You need to accept that now, or . . . '

Poppy froze. Or what? Seconds ticked by as she struggled to find something to say.

Alistair shook his head. 'The Poppy I married never would have gone behind my back for anything, let alone *IVF*. You've put having a baby over me—over us. In fact, I don't know if there is an "us" anymore. We've spent so much time and energy these past few years on everything else *but* us.' He lowered his gaze. 'I'm going to pack a bag and stay at Mum's for a bit. I think we both need some space.' Before she could open her mouth, he left the kitchen and without looking back went up to the room. She could hear him opening drawers, zipping his suitcase, and finally, thumping down the stairs.

Poppy waited for him to come say he loved her, he understood even if he didn't agree, and there'd always be an *us*, no matter what hardship they faced. But all that met her ears was the thud of the front door closing as Alistair walked away.

CHAPTER TWENTY-FIVE

Anna grunted as she unpacked what must be the fiftieth box of stock. Despite the seemingly endless inventory, she was happy to be at work and out of the house. Without the usual routine of chores, she felt anchorless, like she was drifting through time. To fill the hours, she'd taken to napping for as long as possible in the afternoon. Next thing she knew, she'd be playing video games! Fifteen minutes left in her shift, and then she'd be back in the empty, dark house until Michael came home in a few hours. To be honest, she'd prefer to stay here and count books.

Maybe she could pop into Christos's restaurant on the way home? The thought sneaked into her mind like it had a million times in the past few days. But instead of pushing it away, she let it linger. If the business wasn't doing well, the least she could do was pay him for her meal the other night. If she hadn't drunk so much, she would have insisted on it at the time. Judging by the empty restaurant, Christos could use every penny. And he *had* invited her to come again. There was nothing wrong with having a chat, she told herself to placate the guilt gently stirring in her stomach.

A few minutes later, Anna was out the door, breathing in the balmy air. London in the spring could go two ways: slanting rain complete with blustery wind that made your cheeks turn red, or gentle sun and soft air that felt like a caress. Right now, thankfully, it was the latter. The scent of fresh green grass and wet earth hung in the air, and Anna couldn't help smiling as she hurried down the hill towards the restaurant.

The building looked different in the day, Anna thought, tilting her head as she took in the greying paintwork and scuffed lettering in the dusty window. The whole thing could do with a good clean to make it more inviting—people needed to know how wonderful the food was! Inside, it looked dark and still. Maybe Christos wasn't there yet? But the sign on the door said "Open". She paused, unsure what to do.

'Anna!'

Christos's friendly face appeared in the window, and he waved wildly with a huge smile. Anna couldn't help grinning in return. She loved his enthusiasm for everything. He obviously embraced life with a passion.

'Hi,' she said, glancing around the empty restaurant. Her cheeks flushed slightly. 'I was just, er, passing by, and I thought I'd check if you were here. I really want to pay you for last week's dinner.'

'No, no, I told you, it was my pleasure.' Christos leaned forward and kissed her cheek, and Anna's stomach flipped at his scent. 'Come into the kitchen.' He gestured towards an area at the back. 'I'm just doing some dinner prep.'

Anna followed him into a tiny galley kitchen, eyebrows rising at its immaculate state. Metallic surfaces gleamed and ingredients were neatly laid out. Vegetables had been chopped and set aside in white plastic boxes.

'Wow,' she said, surveying the scene. 'Looks like everything is ready.'

'Almost.' Christos handed her a few tomatoes dripping with water. 'I just need to finish chopping these. Would you like to help?'

'Sure, but I'm no expert.' Her method of chopping tomatoes basically involved whichever way did it the fastest. Although she cooked every night for Michael—well, she used to, anyway—it was more about getting the meal over with and less about enjoying the process.

'Here, let me show you.' Christos grabbed a sharp knife and deftly sliced the vegetable. 'There.' He turned and flashed his white teeth at her, and Anna felt her cheeks flush again. Must be the heat of the oven, she told herself.

'Okay, I'll give it a try.' She picked up the same knife and tried to imitate his movements. Unfortunately, the tomato didn't comply, and by the time she was done, it looked like someone had mashed the unfortunate vegetable. 'Oops,' she laughed.

'Well, okay, this might not be your calling.' Christos smiled, little lines springing out from his eyes. He took the knife from her and continued chopping his way through the remaining tomatoes.

'How did you know cooking was *your* calling?' Anna asked, curious. He seemed like such a man's man, she couldn't imagine him in the kitchen back in Greece.

'I couldn't *not* cook,' he said, shaking his head as he chopped. 'Even as a boy, I loved helping Mama make food. I just knew one day I'd open my own restaurant. And I have.' His face lit up with pride.

'So what do you like to do? What's your passion?' he asked. 'A woman like you, I'm sure you're very passionate.'

Anna hid a grin, thinking he'd probably meant to say *impassioned*. She had been passionate about building a strong relationship, but . . . Sighing, she thought again of Italy and her desire to teach there. The longing that had stirred a few weeks ago swelled inside now. 'I've always wanted to visit Italy, to learn the language, the culture, everything.' She cast a glance at the ruined tomatoes. 'Well, maybe not the cuisine.'

'Italy? Not Greece?' Christos pulled a mock-hurt face, then grinned. 'So what's stopping you? Why don't you go?'

Anna tilted her head as she considered his question. It seemed pathetic to say Michael was stopping her, because he wasn't. He wouldn't dream of telling her she couldn't go if she explained how important it was. And until the past few weeks, she wouldn't have wanted to take off without him, anyway. For goodness' sake, she didn't feel right if he went to bed without a good-night kiss!

'I've just been busy,' she muttered finally. 'So can I help with anything else?'

'Here. Why don't you give this another try?' Christos smiled as he handed over the knife. 'Your victims await,' he said, gesturing to a pile of unsuspecting peppers.

'All right.' She'd rather chop peppers than analyse her life any day. 'Ouch!' The knife sliced into the soft skin of one of her fingers, and Anna backed away from the vegetables, clasping her bleeding finger. 'Oh, shit.' Crimson liquid trickled from the wound, and Christos sprang into action, running cold water over the injury then gripping it tightly as he rummaged in the corner for the first-aid kit.

'Just keep holding it,' he instructed, opening the kit and uncovering a bandage. He took her finger and examined it quickly. 'Doesn't look too deep, thank goodness.' He wrapped the plaster around her finger. 'There. All done.'

I'm such an idiot, Anna thought as the cut throbbed. Leave it to her to nearly chop off a finger.

'You okay?' Christos's concerned eyes met hers, and she nodded. 'I'm fine, I'm fine. Sorry!'

'No, I am the one who is sorry,' he said, moving closer. 'You come to say hello, and I put you to work in the kitchen. What kind of friend is that?' He moved in even more until his warm, solid body was flush against hers. Anna knew she should back away, but every muscle felt like it was melting with his closeness. Her cheeks were flaming now.

'It's fine,' she managed to breathe, cursing her trembling voice. Christos slid an arm around her waist and her legs started to shake, too.

'I can kiss you better, if you like.'

Anna almost corrected him by saying the expression was kiss *it* better, but she couldn't get the words out. She felt like she was watching from another place as Christos slowly leaned closer and closer until she could feel his breath on her face, and then—

'Stop!' She jerked away just as his lips were about to touch hers. As much as she wanted to—and God knows, every inch of her was straining towards him—she couldn't.

'I have to go,' she said, rushing out the door and into the dining area. Fear scuttled through her, reaching every corner of her heart. Had she really almost kissed another man? Sure, she craved a bit of excitement . . . but not that kind. She and Michael may not have the perfect marriage she'd dreamed of, but she loved him. Despite all the hurt and confusion of the past little while, that much she knew.

So what kind of excitement did she want, then? Anna pushed outside, breathing in fresh air as her legs churned towards home. What she really needed was something for her; something away from Michael and their relationship. Marriage *was* a partnership, and although she'd been pulling more than her weight, she hadn't behaved as an equal. She'd been so determined to keep them together, she hadn't trusted they were strong enough to stand as individuals, too.

'Michael?' she called as she opened the door, praying he wouldn't be in bed yet. 'We need to talk.'

CHAPTER TWENTY-SIX

Clare glanced around the top floor of the pub, the new venue for the rapidly expanding No-Kids Club. Yes, this would do fine. It was a little small, but better to have a crowded space than an empty room. Anyway, this place was all she could unearth at such short notice. She'd rung up almost fifty venues to find something to accommodate the group's growing numbers— everything from a room overlooking the Thames at the Royal Festival Hall to an old converted brewery that reeked of yeast—but most had been too expensive, already booked, or too far from the beaten track. Just off Marylebone High Street, this pub was still central, and they'd agreed to rent the upstairs for free each Wednesday if the group ordered enough food. Clare sniffed the air, heavily scented with garlic. Normally she'd be eager to eat, but lately . . .

The thump of feet on the stairs heralded the club's first arrivals. She glanced up, spotting Anna and a man holding hands. Was that the notorious Michael?

'Hi there.' Clare crossed the room towards them, kissing Anna on the cheek then extending a hand. 'You must be Michael.'

'Guilty.' He gave a big, friendly smile and took her palm, his grip firm and strong.

'I'm glad you could make it. We've heard so much about you.' A pang of envy shot through her as Michael wrapped an arm around Anna's waist and she leaned cozily against his chest.

'Anna finally managed to drag me into the real world.' He rubbed his belly. 'And I have to say, I'm pleased she did! I'm starving and everything here smells delicious.'

Clare gestured towards a table she'd set up with stickered name-tags and Sharpies. 'Grab a name tag then take a seat and order some food, if you like. The others should be arriving shortly.'

Michael nodded. 'Will do. Nice meeting you, Clare.'

Michael wasn't what she'd expected, Clare thought as they walked away. In her mind, she'd pictured a bloke who needed everything done for him, a babyish figure who commanded Anna around. But this man was confident, friendly, and clearly smitten with his wife. She watched their easy banter as they completed the name tags, then settled into places at the table, laughing and smiling. All those years together and there was still a spark between them.

If only she could find something like that, Clare sighed. How could she have imagined a surface relationship would make her happy? Sure, it had been easy, and she'd enjoyed the time with Nicholas. But she wanted more. Edward's face swam into her mind, and for a brief instant she allowed herself to indulge in the fantasy of ringing him up, saying she loved him . . . and by the way, she was having his baby. Problem solved!

As if it was that simple, she snorted, sinking into a chair. They'd only known each other for a short time and while they'd got on wonderfully, add a kid to the mix and who knows what might happen. Not to mention she didn't *want* to have a baby.

She'd find someone once her life settled back to normal, Clare told herself, making a mental note for the millionth time to get started down that path tomorrow. Voices echoed in the stairwell, and Clare stood and pasted on a smile.

'Welcome,' she said to the gaggle of five men who'd arrived. 'Come on in and grab a name tag along with some food and drink, if you like.'

The group nodded and headed to the table as more members came in the door. Soon, the whole place was filled with the chatter and laughter of like-minded people here to celebrate the child-free lifestyle. After mingling for a bit, Clare collapsed back onto the chair, exhaustion overtaking her. Her mobile buzzed, and she drew it out, eyes widening at the name on the screen. Ellie—she could barely believe it.

'Hey!' A genuine smile crossed her face for the first time that day.

'Hey, there.' Ellie's cheerful voice rang through the handset. 'What are you up to? Do you want to come over? I'd love a good chat. I miss you!'

Clare glanced at her watch. Eight o'clock and the club was in full swing. She could duck out and no one would notice. Right now, she really wanted to be with someone who knew her, even if that did involve listening to a stream of non-stop pregnancy updates.

Half an hour later, Clare was at Ellie's doorstep.

'Come in, come in.' Ellie swung open the door and led Clare into the lounge, then slumped onto the sofa as if the effort had worn her out. Clare eyed her friend's puffy ankles and scooted over to grab a small stool.

'Here, put your feet up on this,' she said, sliding it over. Ellie groaned with relief as she lifted her legs onto it. 'I can't believe you're still working! You should have stopped by now. That baby looks like it could come at any time.'

'I know, I know.' Ellie sighed. 'It feels like it could come at any time, too. It's kicking and rolling all night, and I can barely get any sleep. Not that I'd sleep anyway—the heartburn is bloody killing me.' She rubbed her swollen stomach. 'But enough about me. I'm so tired of talking about it!' She gave Clare a hard look. 'What's up with you? You okay? You don't look the greatest, my friend.'

'I know.' Clare swallowed, wondering if she should tell Ellie why she looked so terrible.

'What is it?' Ellie tilted her head as she examined her friend. 'Are you, like, really ill? Oh my God, you are, aren't you? That's why you look so serious.' The colour drained from her face.

'No, no,' Clare said hastily. 'I'm not ill. I'm . . . ' Maybe saying it aloud would help make the pregnancy real, she thought, and give her a kick in the arse to do something about it. She opened her mouth, trying to move her lips to form the words.

'Yes? You're . . . come on, Clare! Anaemic? Under the weather? Exhausted? God's gift to the medical profession?' Ellie grinned.

Clare shook her head. 'I'm pregnant.'

Ellie's mouth dropped open, her eyebrows nearly shooting off her face. Her lips moved furiously, but no sound emerged. Despite herself, Clare smiled. She'd never seen her friend so lost for words.

'Want some water?' Clare asked.

Still unable to speak, Ellie nodded. Clare padded to the kitchen and filled two glasses, hoping this would give her friend time to recover. Back in the lounge, Clare handed Ellie the water. After a long sip, Ellie glanced up.

'Sorry,' she said, still looking flabbergasted. 'I mean, I know I was joking about it earlier, but for it to be true . . . So . . . What . . . How . . . Tell me *everything.*'

'There really isn't much to tell,' Clare said, leaning back against the cushions. 'It must have happened sometime in the last month I was with Edward.'

'Does he know? Have you spoken to him about it? Because this is bloody perfect! You broke up since you didn't want kids and he did. And now you're having his baby!' She hit her knee lightly. 'Problem solved.'

Her words so closely echoed Clare's earlier thoughts at the No-Kids Club that Clare couldn't help laughing. 'If only. I haven't told Edward, and I don't plan to, either.' Even as she said the words, a twinge went through her.

'Oh. Why?'

'Well . . . ' Clare bit her lip, wondering what to say. 'You know how I feel about having a child.'

To Clare's surprise, Ellie didn't do her usual nod-and-keep-mum routine like she always did whenever Clare mentioned her lack of desire to have kids. Instead, she leaned forward as much as her belly would allow, as if proximity would impart importance to her words.

'Look, Clare. I've always kept quiet about you not wanting children because I thought, well, if that's how you feel, then go with it.' She paused. 'But things have changed now. You *are* pregnant; it's not a hypothetical any longer.'

Clare nodded, Ellie's words sinking in. Until now, before actually voicing it aloud, it had felt hypothetical. 'And?'

'And . . . ' Ellie paused, and Clare shifted under her friend's intense gaze. In all the years she'd known Ellie, she'd never seen her so serious. And that included the time Ellie accidentally dyed her hair purple before the Year 11 leaving do, an experience Ellie still cited as the most traumatic of her life. 'You know I'll support you no matter what you decide. And if you decide you don't want children, and that's what will make you happy, then I'm one hundred percent behind you. But just tell me, what's the real reason you don't want children? And don't give me any of that "I want to do what I want, when I want" malarkey. Everyone wants that, kids or not. And none of the career excuses, either, because there are ways around that—nannies, night nurses . . . it's doable. Difficult, but doable.'

Clare held her friend's gaze, her mind flashing to the moment on *Wake Up London*, when the whole of the nation had been awaiting her answer. She hadn't been able to pinpoint a reason then, either. It was just a vague uneasiness, a feeling that motherhood was wrong for her.

'Are you afraid?' Ellie pressed.

Clare jerked back. 'Afraid? Of what?'

'Well . . . ' Ellie paused again, like she was deciding how best to put it. 'Afraid that you can't do it?' She rubbed her belly. 'Just because your mother made a bad choice doesn't mean you will. I bet you'd be a brilliant mum.'

Clare tilted her head. Was her mother the reason she didn't want kids? A psychologist would likely think so, but Clare didn't agree. She couldn't remember ever wanting children, before or after her mum left. 'The one thing Mum did teach me was not to even consider kids until I'm ready,' she said. 'And I'm anything but ready. I doubt I'll ever be.'

'No one is ever fully ready, Clare,' Ellie responded. 'For God's sake, do you think I know exactly what I'm getting into?' She shook her head. 'It's impossible to be ready. You do everything you can, but ultimately you close your eyes and leap.'

Clare swung towards her friend in surprise. She'd thought if anyone was ready for a baby, it'd be Ellie, with her endless classes and spreadsheets. To hear her express hesitation was a definite shocker. She fluffed the pillow behind her, trying to hide her expression. Ellie was probably hormonal; she likely didn't even know what she was saying.

Maybe talking to her friend wasn't such a good idea, after all. Clare had hoped telling Ellie would help her move on, deal with the situation. Instead, Ellie seemed determined to stir up doubts.

'So when *are* you going to stop working?' Clare asked, attempting to bring the conversation back to her friend again. Stretching out her legs, she looked over at the mound of her friend's belly. A jolt of fear went through her at the thought that if she didn't act soon, that would be her in about seven months' time.

Clare sat upright, recalling Ellie's question if she was afraid. *Was* she scared? Of course she was—as Ellie had said, who wouldn't be fearful at the unknown? But Clare had been afraid of many things in the past, and that had never stopped her conquering them. So why was this different?

She ran a hand over her face. She was so, so tired of all of this, and Ellie wasn't making it any easier.

Ellie reached out and touched her arm. 'Just have a think about it,' she said, ignoring Clare's question. 'And ask yourself this: If you really can't answer why you don't want children, don't you think you should find out before making any decision? I'd hate for you to do something you might regret later.'

Clare met her best friend's eyes, wondering if she was right. Was her hesitation to deal with the situation because she couldn't figure out why having kids didn't appeal? Perhaps uncovering the answer was just what she needed to propel her forward.

But how on earth was she supposed to do that?

❦

'That was fun.' Michael smiled up at Anna, taking her hand as they exited the Tube on the way back from the No-Kids Club. She slowed her step, squeezing his fingers. For once, she didn't want to rush home. She wanted to savour the walk and enjoy being with the man she loved. Less than twenty-four hours had passed since their chat last night, but Anna was sure their marriage would be stronger than ever. Thank God she'd finally been honest with her husband.

After returning from Christos's restaurant, she'd stridden into the lounge and switched off the video game. Michael had turned to her in surprise.

'Anna? Are you okay?'

She shook her head, sinking onto the sofa beside him.

'No. I'm not.' Anna took Michael's warm hand in hers, then drew in a deep breath. 'For the past few years, I've put my all into our marriage. The cooking, the cleaning, everything.'

'I know.' Michael's brow furrowed and he tilted his head. 'But you want to do those things, right?'

A tiny bit of guilt stirred inside her as she stared into her husband's eyes. She couldn't blame him for being confused—she *had* wanted to be the domestic glue holding them together. She'd only realised recently it wasn't enough.

'It's not just chores. You . . . ' Anna glanced down, toying with a loose thread on a pillow. 'You don't seem like you care anymore,' she said finally, meeting his eyes again. 'You're always busy with video games, we haven't gone out for ages, and we don't even make love anymore.' The words tumbled out and her voice trembled with fear. She'd kept her emotions hidden for so long, hoping she could somehow find a way to make their relationship better. Was it too late now to turn things around? Maybe if she'd spoken up sooner . . .

'Oh, Anna. Of course I care. I love you.' Michael put his arms around her, pulling her close. For a minute, Anna allowed herself to enjoy the embrace before leaning back.

'Then why . . . ' She gulped in air. 'Why haven't you made more of an effort? For the past few months, I've felt as if I'm the only one invested in our marriage.' She held her breath, awaiting his response.

After what seemed like forever, Michael nodded, gripping her hand again. 'You know, you're right—I haven't been doing much for us lately. I hadn't realised it until now, but I guess I got a little lazy, or complacent. You're always so keen to take care of everything, and it was easy to sit back and let you get on with it. I figured you'd let me know if you wanted something more.'

'But I did!' Anna said, her voice ringing out. 'What about the films I asked you to, or the speedboat, or . . . '

Michael's eyebrows rose. 'But all those were activities for me, right? I didn't think *you* actually wanted to do them.' He shook his head. 'I have to say, though, I was surprised when you disappeared the night of our anniversary.'

Anna's mouth dropped open. 'You remembered our anniversary? I thought you'd forgotten.'

'Of course I remembered. I was waiting for you to whisk me away for another epic night! I know how much you love planning our outings.'

'But I told you I hadn't organised anything,' Anna said, shifting on the sofa as memories of how she'd almost kissed another man ran through her head.

Michael shrugged. 'I thought you were trying to put me off track, surprise me like you did a few years ago. And then when you left . . . ' His face sank into a serious, almost vulnerable expression. 'You do still want to be with me, right?'

'Of course. I love you.' She'd never been surer of that, especially after the near miss with Christos. 'But I can't make our marriage work on my own anymore. I don't *want* to make it work on my

own. I need the time—the space—to do something for me, too.'
Anna shook her head, recalling her assertion to Clare that Michael
was her everything. That was the problem—no one should be your
whole world. If she'd had something else, something for *her*, maybe
she wouldn't have fallen down the rabbit hole of insecurity.

'Anna, do what makes you happy,' Michael said. 'And from
now on, things will be fifty-fifty around here, although you may
have to teach me to work the washing machine.' He grinned. 'Tell
you what, why don't we have a weekend getaway soon at the Lake
District? Celebrate our anniversary properly and mark a new start
to our marriage.'

Anna tilted her head. She loved the Lake District, but . . . 'Sure,
we could, but maybe we could go somewhere a bit more exotic.
Like Venice?' She held her breath.

Michael had nodded. 'Venice sounds brilliant.'

Now Anna squeezed Michael's hand, thankful for his presence
by her side in the London night—and in her life. He'd surprised
her by getting ready to go out tonight without her even asking if
he wanted to come along, and it had been wonderful to show up at
the meeting with him. Gazing down the small side street towards
Christos's restaurant, a mixture of emotions tumbled inside. She
couldn't believe she'd almost ruined her marriage, all because she
hadn't realised she needed something of her own, too. In a way,
though, Anna was thankful for the fiasco with Christos. At least it
had helped her reach that conclusion sooner rather than later.

They neared the door of their house, and Michael reached for
the handle. 'You know, that club has really made me think about
the future. I'll never be keen on kids. But you do still feel the same,
right? That wasn't what you were missing?'

Anna looked up at him. Children would demand even more
from her—they weren't the answer she'd been seeking. 'No. I'm

with you on that.' She put a hand on his back as he fitted the key in the lock. 'You know what? I'm looking forward to our new future together . . . and to finding something for me. I think life will be perfect, just the two of us.'

Michael swung open the door of their home. 'Me too, Anna. Me too.'

CHAPTER TWENTY-SEVEN

Poppy made a face at her reflection in the Tube window. Her wavy hair was lifeless and flat, her cheeks pale and hollowed out in the dim light of the Underground. She felt worse than she looked, if that was possible. She'd barely slept since Alistair had left over a week ago, and even though she'd tried to ring his mobile several times—to say what, she didn't know, but she was desperate to hear his voice—he hadn't answered. Finally, he'd sent a text. She cringed, remembering the brief words saying he'd get in touch when he was ready. There hadn't even been one single, solitary "x" at the end.

She wasn't really in the mood for the No-Kids Club tonight, but she'd missed last week to stay home in case Alistair returned, and at least it was better than kicking around the flat on her own. She'd lingered at school as long as possible the past few days until the caretaker kicked her out, and she hadn't the heart to face his pitying stare again. She could guzzle a few (non-alcoholic) drinks and indulge in some brainless chatter without a reminder of what was driving her and Alistair apart: kids.

Sighing, Poppy dragged herself up the Tube stairs and down Marylebone Road. She'd been so sure she could talk her husband round once she proved her ability to deal with it all, no problem. How had she got it so wrong?

Because you were only listening to yourself, a voice peeped up inside. Because you let what you wanted overtake everything else—even your marriage.

But how could you compromise on something as important as having your own child? She shook her head, opening the door to the pub. Enough! She'd been going in circles ever since Alistair had left and getting more and more confused.

The noise swelled as she neared the top floor of the pub, and Poppy let it drown out the voices inside. As she trudged to the bar in the corner, she spotted Anna with a man by her side. Must be her husband, Poppy thought with surprise, remembering Anna last telling her the man wouldn't leave his video games for love or money. Anna caught her eye and raised a hand, threading through the crowd towards her.

'Hey there!' she said when she reached Poppy's side. She turned to look up at the man beside her. 'This is Michael.'

'Nice to meet you,' Poppy said, extending a hand.

'You, too.' Michael grasped her palm, then slid an arm around Anna's waist, and Anna smiled up at him. God, she missed Alistair, Poppy thought as she watched the two of them. Whatever the problem had been, they'd evidently worked it out and were much happier for it. She'd never seen Anna so radiant.

'I'm glad we caught you tonight,' Anna said, sipping her wine. 'We're not going to be here for the next little while.'

'No?' Poppy took a long gulp of water she'd been handed. 'What are you up to? Anything fun?'

Anna nodded. 'We're off to Venice! Michael's coming for two weeks, and then I'll stay on and take some Italian classes. I can't wait.'

Michael pulled her even closer. 'I'm going to miss her.'

'I bet you will.' Poppy smiled, the longing inside growing until she could hardly draw a breath. When was the last time she and Alistair had been so lovey-dovey? She couldn't even recall. Everything—from their conversations to what they ate to when they made love—had been focused on one thing. They might not have hit Marta and Luis's level, but they'd been well on their way.

Had they gone too far to turn back? Had *she* gone too far?

She said goodbye to Anna and Michael, promising to keep in touch, then pushed through the crowd to a table in the corner. Collapsing onto a chair, the buzz washed over her as the wheels spun in her head. She loved Alistair, that much she did know, and weighed up against the theoretical possibility of having their own child . . .

Poppy shook her head. She didn't want to risk what she had with Alistair to chase the slim chance of carrying a baby inside her. Whether the doctors identified the cause of her infertility or not, pregnancy was unlikely. As much as she wanted a baby, she wanted one *with* Alistair.

Cringing, she recalled Alistair's stunned reaction when she told him she'd started the process without his knowledge. Her cheeks flushed with shame. She'd been so desperate to get pregnant, she'd convinced herself he would be happy to see she could do it on her own. Deep down, though, she'd known her actions were wrong.

'Hey there.' Poppy glanced up to see Clare slumping onto a chair beside her. The woman looked as pale and exhausted as she felt. Poppy raised an eyebrow at Clare's bust, which appeared to have magically inflated. Wow! Either she'd had a boob job or she was pregnant—and neither seemed likely options. Poppy let her eyes drop to Clare's midsection, as flat as ever. Not that it meant anything. She'd read enough books to know that some women didn't show until later in the pregnancy. But surely the founder of the No-Kids Club couldn't be pregnant. Could she?

'Hi,' Poppy said finally. 'How are you?'

'Okay.' Clare took a sip of water, and Poppy raised an eyebrow. Where was the customary glass of wine?

It wouldn't surprise her if Clare *was* pregnant, Poppy thought bitterly. Everyone but her seemed able to get knocked up—even those who were staunchly against it. Grief clenched her insides so strongly it was almost a physical ache.

'Are you pregnant?' she asked, before she could stop herself.

Clare's mouth dropped open. 'What?'

Poppy repeated the question. 'Are you pregnant?' It was none of her business, but she was too tired and drained to care.

Clare stared down at the floor, then slowly raised her head to meet Poppy's eyes. 'How did you know?'

Poppy shrugged. 'You look tired and your boobs are bigger, plus you're drinking water. Doesn't take Sherlock Holmes to put the pieces together.' She smiled to take away the bluntness of the words.

A look of horror passed over Clare's face. 'You don't think anyone else has noticed, do you?'

'I wouldn't worry.' Poppy gazed out at the crowd. 'They're not exactly thinking of pregnancy all the time like I am.' She shook her head, trying to imagine the group's stunned reaction if they discovered their founder was pregnant. 'How far along are you?'

'About nine or ten weeks,' Clare answered, sliding her hand down to her belly before jerking it away.

'And so . . . ' Poppy let her voice trail off, unsure whether to ask Clare what was ahead. After everything she'd been through, it would be almost unbearable if Clare said she didn't plan to have the baby.

Clare shook her head. 'I'm not mother material and I never have been.'

'You learn. At least that's what everyone tells me.' Poppy couldn't keep the note of longing from her voice.

'Yeah, I've heard that, too.' Clare's face twisted. 'But I'm not sure it's true. My own mother certainly didn't. She left when I was ten.'

'Wow.' Poppy couldn't imagine someone leaving their child behind. She reached out and touched Clare's arm, thinking she'd never seen her look so vulnerable. 'That must have been tough.'

Clare shrugged, tracing her finger down the dewy glass. 'It was, at least for a little while. But then my father remarried, and to be honest, Tam was a better mother than my own. I'm so lucky to have her in my life—she's my *real* mother.'

Clare's words hit Poppy squarely in the heart. That was exactly what Alistair had been telling her—that by caring and nurturing a child, it would become their own. They'd be parents through the sheer act of parenting, and the child would love them like no other. She stared out the window, thoughts tumbling through her head. Why had she dismissed adoption so quickly? She'd wanted to carry a child within her, sure, but that wasn't what made a mother. Poppy had said it herself: you learnt to be a mum by doing it.

Poppy got to her feet, energy surging through her. For the first time since Alistair had left, her head—and her heart—were clear. She knew with certainty what she wanted the future to hold.

'Right.' She gathered up her coat and handbag, pulse racing. 'Right. I have to go.' She put a hand on Clare's arm. 'Let me know if there's anything I can do to help.'

Clare nodded. 'Please keep our conversation a secret, okay?'

'Of course,' Poppy said. 'Bye.' And with that, she clattered down the stairs and out into the night, hoping—praying—it wasn't too late to tell Alistair she was ready to have a child with him.

As she rushed to the Tube, she texted him saying she knew he wanted space, but she really needed to talk. She kept the phone in her hand, ears cocked for the answering ping. But when she reached the steps of the station, the mobile remained resolutely silent. Maybe she should try ringing? Eagerly, Poppy punched in Alistair's number, listening to the tinny ring before it clicked through to voicemail.

'Hey, babe, it's me. Listen, we really need to talk—I'm ready now to look at adoption.' She paused, wondering what to say next. 'I'm sorry. Please call me back . . . I love you.'

Poppy clicked off, a slight smile on her face as she scurried down the Tube steps. He had to call back. He had to! When she got off the train in thirty minutes, she'd put money on the fact that there'd be a voicemail waiting. Bloody Underground and its lack of signal. It was like living in the Dark Ages.

A balloon of hope grew as the Tube raced through the darkened tunnels. Maybe he'd even come over tonight. They could crack open a bottle—oh, how she'd missed wine!—and talk about their plans for the future. Imagine, in just a few months, their empty nursery could finally have an occupant. Her grin grew wider as she pictured herself and Alistair leaning over the cot, watching their baby in its peaceful slumber.

Finally, her stop. Poppy raced from the carriage and up the escalator, eyes fixed on the phone and the signal bar. No, no . . . ah, here we go, connected to the world once again! Leaning against the grimy wall of the station, she waited for the phone to bleep, signalling a voicemail or text.

But there was nothing, and when she could stare at the mobile no longer—or take the watchful gaze of the station's resident homeless man—she pushed off the wall and trudged home. Maybe Alistair was out, she told herself, or he was asleep, or he just hadn't seen her messages.

As she unlocked the door to the empty flat, though, she knew none of those possibilities was likely. No matter the time, her husband had always called her back when she'd rung; sometimes, within a second of her hanging up. He wanted to be at her beck and call—literally—he'd joke.

Until now.

Poppy turned on every lamp, banishing the shadows from each room until the flat glowed. But even with the blazing light, she still felt cold and dark inside.

∽

'Clare? Oh, how lucky I've caught you.'

Clare smiled into the phone at her father's warm tone the next morning. No matter how complicated life was right now, his voice was like being submerged in a delicious bubble bath: pure comfort, and that was exactly what she needed. Her conversation with Ellie had sparked off a furious storm of questions, and for the past week, she'd been trying in vain to understand exactly why she didn't want kids. Although it had never seemed important before, with her current situation, she needed to act from a point of clarity. If she didn't, whatever decision she made might haunt her, and that was the last thing she wanted.

'Hey, Dad,' she said now. 'That was lucky, actually. I've just started my break.' Breaks in her department were rare, and it was even rarer they lasted longer than thirty seconds. Usually, she'd barely have sat down before the next emergency arrived. 'What's up?'

'I'm in London for the day, running some errands for Tam. I'll be swinging by her favourite cushion shop on King's Road. Are you free for coffee this evening? There's a café right next to the shop. I think I've tried every one of the items on the menu waiting for your stepmum.'

Clare grinned, picturing her father munching his way through all the dishes while Tam lusted after cushions. 'I should be out of here by six. Give me a few minutes to change, and I'll meet you at the café.'

'Perfect.' Clare could hear the smile in her dad's voice. 'See you soon.'

'Bye.' She clicked off, then shoved the phone in her pocket. It'd been ages since she'd spent some alone time with her father. Usually Tam was there, and although her stepmum had many good qualities, she was a bit of a chatterbox. Dad rarely got a word in edgewise, not that he was much of a talker. Even when her mum had been around, she'd taken the lead on everything, including conversation. It was why they'd really struggled after she'd left. Grimacing, Clare recalled the piles of unwashed dishes in the sink, how it'd taken weeks for her father to organise her new school uniform, and the silence that hung heavy in the dusty air.

A few hours later, Clare pulled open the door to the café on King's Road. Amidst the fashionable chrome and white interior, her father looked distinctly out of place in his checked shirt, jeans, and comfortable loafers. Not that he'd notice—as long as there was food, a newspaper, and a cup of tea, he was comfortable anywhere.

'Hey, Dad.' Clare put her arms around his solid form and gave him a squeeze, breathing in the familiar scent of cinnamon and spicy cologne.

'Hey, yourself.' He pulled back and ran his eyes over her. 'You're looking good, if a little tired. Are you getting enough to eat?'

The thought of food still made her nauseated, but Clare just nodded. 'I had a big lunch in the hospital caf today. I'm full from that.' Thank goodness her father had never eaten at the hospital so he wouldn't know the unlikelihood of that statement. Nobody ever got full from hospital food—unless you were unlucky enough to sample the bread pudding, the equivalent of ingesting concrete.

'Just tea for me, please,' Clare said to the waitress hovering over them.

'So how have you been?' her dad asked, taking a sip of his drink.

Clare met his gaze, wondering what he'd do if she said she was pregnant. Probably fall off his chair after spurting hot tea all over the table. 'I'm fine,' she said finally. 'Busy. The usual.' She tried to make her voice sound happy, but instead it came out kind of . . . flat. Life right now was anything but usual.

'Think you can come for a weekend sometime soon? Tam was just saying she'd love to have you over for a night or two—she's redecorated the guest bedroom and is absolutely gagging for some visitors. And, of course, we'd love if you spent more time than a few hours here and there. Seems forever since you've stayed longer than an afternoon.'

'That sounds nice,' Clare said, attempting to remember when she'd last stayed overnight. Maybe Christmas? No, she'd been with Edward then, and they'd holed up in his flat. She tried not to recall how they'd made love just after midnight Christmas Eve, then opened their gifts by candlelight in the first minutes of Christmas Day.

'I'll check my schedule and let you know when my next weekend off is. I'd love to come stay.' She reached out and squeezed her father's hand. Even though she was all grown up now, his palm still seemed huge to her. Despite the constant tension hanging over her, something inside eased slightly at the thought of getting away from everything. Of course, she reminded herself, by that time the situation would be resolved. It would have to be.

Her father squeezed back. 'There's my girl. You know how much Tam loves you. And me too, of course.' He waggled his bushy eyebrows, and Clare resisted the urge to remind him to pluck them.

'I love you too, Dad.' She longed to crawl onto his lap, safe in the knowledge he'd make everything all right, just like when she was a little.

'Have you given any more thought to seeing your mother?' The words came from nowhere, and Clare jerked in surprise.

'What? Um, no.' And she didn't plan to anytime soon. She fiddled with the side of the menu. 'Why? Is Tam asking?'

Her dad grinned. 'You know your stepmum. She's like a dog with a bone when she gets something into her head.' He bent over, rifled through a rucksack at his feet, then drew out a yellowed scroll. 'I brought this for you.'

Clare squinted, trying to figure out what it was. 'What's that?' she asked finally.

Her father used his teacup to anchor down the top end, then unfurled the scroll part way. 'It's your family tree. I don't know if you recall, but back in Year Five, your teacher made every pupil put one together. You near drove us mad with all the questions about your relatives!'

Clare smiled as she examined her shaky handwriting and the uneven lines. She could sort of remember creating this, but the memory was hazy.

'Look.' Dad pointed to the box containing his name. 'There's me, and there's your mum, and there's'—he moved his finger down the paper—'you.' Clare followed his finger, taking in her name hanging by a tenuous thread underneath her father and her mother.

Her dad grinned. 'You insisted on using our full names, even mister and missus, and by the end, you'd run out of room!'

'Why did you want to show me this?' she asked, meeting her father's gentle gaze.

He took her hand again. 'Clare, no matter how much you might try to forget, your mother is a part of you, and she always will be. The sooner you make peace with that, the better.'

Anger leapt inside, and Clare scraped back her chair. 'How can you say that? She left us; she turned her back on this family. She's no more a part of me than, say . . . Bon Jovi,' she finished lamely, unable to think of a better example.

'Oh, but she is.' Her father nodded gravely. 'I see her in your eyes, in the way you tilt your head. She's the snap in your voice when you're angry, and the way you curl your hair round your fist. And Clare, you may have forgotten she was a brilliant mother, actually. And a good wife, too.' His shoulder heaved in a sigh. 'But in the end . . . '

'In the end, she abandoned me. *Us*. End of story.' Clare shook her head so hard her ponytail whipped her in the face.

'Oh, Clare.' Dad's eyes were sad. 'It's not that easy. It's never that easy. I made mistakes, too. I wasn't the world's best husband— or father.'

'But you were!' Clare cried. 'You were always there.'

'I was there after Mum left,' he nodded. 'Because I had to be. But many times your mother asked me to look after you in the evenings so she could take courses at uni—she wanted to learn accounting, to do something to get back to work eventually—and I wasn't keen. I didn't say no, but I certainly wasn't supportive.' His shoulders sagged. 'What can I say, I was a selfish bugger. I wanted that time to relax.'

'I'm sure you had your reasons.' She refused to believe Dad had anything to do with Mum taking off. And even if he had, no one left a child and a family over unrequited coursework.

So why *had* her mother left, then? Clare met her father's eyes, realising she'd never understood. In the days that followed Mum's departure, Clare had asked Dad over and over when she might return, and the answer was always the same: 'I don't know.' It hadn't been until a few years passed—and it was obvious 'when' was 'never'—that Clare realised she'd never asked why her mum had left. And by then, she'd told herself she didn't care. Dad had remarried, and the subject had been firmly closed. Clare had been only too happy to leave it that way.

'Anyway,' her dad continued, 'I'm not here to debate who did what—or not. But Clare, you can't run from memories, from the past. It's connected to the present, and that's something you can't change.' He ran his finger over the family tree. 'And that's why I think you'd benefit from seeing your mother. It might help you let go of the bad and remember the good again.'

Tam must have given him a tutorial before he'd come here, Clare thought. His words were almost the same as hers back at the house that day. Sadness flooded in as she remembered forcefully rejecting Tam's words, then shoving Edward and his email from her mind in a bid to prove her stepmum wrong—that the past should stay the past, and the key to moving forward was to keep things simple and uncomplicated. She'd tried that with Nicholas, and it certainly hadn't made her happy. In fact, it'd made her even lonelier.

A puff of air escaped Clare's lips. Were Tam and her father right, after all? She glanced down at the family tree again, tracing the line that lead to her unknown future spouse. And then—she squinted— what was that going vertically from both their names? Gradually unfurling the document, she followed a line that branched out to show . . . a son and daughter.

Her mouth fell open as she examined the boxes. She'd always thought she'd never wanted kids, yet here was evidence she had. Clare cast her mind back to Year Five—she'd only been nine, and Mum was still an integral part of the family. That was before she'd realised families didn't always live happily ever after. Okay, so she might have wanted children at some point. But what little girl didn't? It was how you were trained to think, before your own sense of self came into play.

Before Clare knew what she was doing, her hand slid down to her belly. An unexpected jolt of emotion hit as Dad's words ran though her head: the past was connected to the present, no matter how much you denied it. Was that why having children scared her? *Was* she letting her mother's actions affect her present—and her future?

Dad cleared his throat again, interrupting her thoughts. 'Have a think about what I've said, will you? Or at least tell Tam I convinced you. She keeps asking me if you've seen your mum yet.'

Clare forced a smile, picturing Tam's relentless prodding. When that woman wanted something, she went for it. Dad always joked that was how she'd got him to marry her.

'I will.' Gingerly, she touched her mum's name on the family tree. Try as she might, she couldn't blot out her mother. And maybe now, it was time to face Mum and all the emotions that went along with it—and to know why she really left.

If that didn't help Clare see things more clearly, God knows what would.

CHAPTER TWENTY-EIGHT

Poppy dragged herself through the front door of her flat Friday night, the pile of post greeting her like a reproach. Alistair was usually back before her, and he always sorted the mail when he returned. The flyers and leaflets clogging the entrance each day made her heart sink with the realisation that he still hadn't come home.

For the last two days—ever since she'd decided to pursue adoption—she'd tried frantically to reach Alistair. First, she'd left voicemail after voicemail, then sent text after pleading text. He'd finally responded saying he'd get in touch soon, but to please respect his need for space.

Poppy bit at her thumb as she considered for the hundredth time what to do. If she kept trying, it'd seem like she didn't respect his wishes. But she desperately needed to convince him she was ready to move on to other options! In fact, she'd stopped the injections and had starting reading online about the adoption process. Alistair was right: it was all straightforward, and if everything went well, it wouldn't take long to have a child in the house! Her heart flipped at the thought of a baby gurgling and cooing in the nursery. She would finally be a mum. The heartache at not getting pregnant would always be there, but she realised now that pregnancy was only the start of the journey.

The sound of the key scraping in the lock made her heart leap with hope. Alistair was home! Poppy turned towards the doorway, her pulse racing.

'Hey there,' she said tentatively, watching as he scooped up the post and sifted through it. She wanted to race over and throw her arms around him, but by the coldness of his face, it was clear he didn't feel the same.

'Hi.' His voice was almost robotic, and her heart dropped. 'I thought you'd still be at work. I've just come to get some things.'

'All right,' she croaked to his back as he walked up the stairs. *Shit.* He hadn't even looked at her! She swallowed hard against the rising fear. Okay, she'd messed up. Royally. But they could either recover and go on, or . . . Determination flooded into her. The longer this lapsed, the harder it would be to move ahead. It was time to put their marriage back together.

Poppy hurried up the stairs, her resolve growing with each step on the faded carpet. When she reached the bedroom, she was almost bursting. Inside, Alistair was neatly removing a bundle of socks from a drawer.

'Alistair,' she said, crossing the room and touching his shoulder. 'Please. I really have to talk to you.'

He swung around to face her, and her heart melted at the familiar floppy hair and stubble. 'Poppy, I'm sorry, but I told you: I need a break from all of this. Please let me have that.'

Poppy shook her head. 'No, Alistair. I won't. Because I don't think being apart is a good thing. We've—I've—let our marriage fade into the background to focus on getting pregnant, and more time away from it won't help.' She took a deep breath. 'I'm ready now to look at other options.'

'So you've said in your many messages.' Alistair raised an eyebrow. 'But do you mean it this time? Really and truly? Because I thought you were before, too. Are you only saying this now because you want me home again?'

Poppy dropped her head. She could see why he might think that. 'No,' she said, inching closer. 'I want you to come back for *you*. I miss you. I miss what we had together.'

Alistair ran a hand through his hair. 'Maybe you should have thought of that before deciding to go behind my back. Having a child is supposed to be about *us*, not you.'

'I know,' Poppy said softly. 'I realise that now.' She paused, daring to lay a hand on his arm, nearly melting with relief when he didn't shake it off. 'I'm sorry.'

The silence in the room was deafening as Alistair's grey eyes met hers; Poppy could barely breathe.

'I'm not doing the injections any longer,' she continued. 'I'm ready to move ahead.' She shook her head. 'Let me rephrase that. I'm ready to move ahead with you.'

A huge grin split Alistair's face and he held open his arms. Poppy scooted into them, leaning her forehead against his chest and breathing in his fresh clean scent. God, she'd missed him. He'd only been gone a few days, but it felt like ages.

'It's good to be home,' Alistair said as he stroked her hair.

'It's good to have you home.' Poppy swivelled out from under his arm. 'Nothing felt right without you in my life. No matter what happens, I need you here.'

Alistair drew in a breath. 'How would you feel about delaying things a bit on the adoption front?'

Poppy studied his face. 'What do you mean? I thought you wanted to get started straight away.'

'Well, I did. But I've been doing some thinking, too.'

'Okay,' Poppy said slowly, wondering where he was going with this.

'We both agree pregnancy overtook everything else in our lives. I think we should have a breather. Take a little time together, just the two of us, before we get ready to meet our child.'

Get ready to meet our child, Poppy thought, her heart filling up. What a wonderful way to put it. Although she wasn't keen on waiting, she knew in her heart Alistair was right. Parenthood was going to be a long road, and they needed to work as a team. Plus, now that he'd mentioned it, she *was* looking forward to living again—drinking wine and coffee, and maybe even going on holiday!

Poppy threw her arms around Alistair, burying her face in his neck. Then, she pulled back and grinned. 'That sounds brilliant.'

And as they fell onto the bed together, for once she wasn't thinking of anything to do with a baby.

CHAPTER TWENTY-NINE

Clare took a deep breath and pulled open the door of Carluccio's. After all these years, she could barely believe she was minutes from seeing her mother.

The second she'd returned home from meeting Dad at the café, she'd pawed through her handbag to find the contact information Tam had passed on weeks ago. With shaking fingers, she'd dialled the number, almost hoping her mother wouldn't answer and she could put it off for another few years.

But no, she told herself, listening to the tinny ring of the phone. She couldn't delay this any longer. Although her mother had been physically absent for ages, Clare could finally see the emotional connection had lingered. And now, she had to face it . . . if only to make her own future clearer.

'Hello?' Mum's voice had echoed down the line, and Clare sucked in her breath. With just one word, a powerful cocktail of emotions swept through Clare so strongly she had to sink onto the bed. That was the voice that had kissed Clare's hurts better—and the voice that had said she was leaving. Tears gathered in Clare's eyes at the memory of how she'd awoken early one morning and come downstairs to see her mother dressed and sitting at the kitchen table.

'Where are you going?' Clare had yawned, plopping onto a chair. 'And I can have some toast before you go?' Even now, she cringed at that memory.

Her mum had reached out for Clare's hand. Clare remembered how her mother's fingers had closed around her warm ones, squeezing them until they hurt.

'Mum!' Clare had tried to pull away, but then she'd noticed the liquid glistening in her mother's eyes . . . and the suitcases in the hallway. 'Mum?' she'd said, much softer and slower this time, confusion sweeping through her. 'What's going on?'

'Clare, honey.' Her mother paused, then breathed in deeply. 'I have to go.'

'Go?' Clare had rubbed her eyes. What on earth did she mean? 'Where?'

'Away. On my own for a bit.' She stood, then came around to where Clare was sitting and hugged her tightly.

'When will you be back?' Clare gazed into her mother's face, panic creeping in at the expression she saw there. 'Mum?' Clare had asked, clutching her mother's arm. 'When will you be back?'

Mum drew her in even closer, then pulled away from Clare's pincer grip and stood. 'I love you,' she said, looking down. 'Just remember, I love you.' Her lips had trembled as she gathered up her cases, and one tear had dropped from her chin. Then, she'd turned and was gone. Clare had raced barefoot out the door and onto the walkway to see her mother climbing into a taxi. She'd watched, frozen in place, as it drove down the quiet suburban street. Mum hadn't even looked back.

Now, Clare was finally going to hear why she'd left. Her mum had agreed to meet Monday night, and here they were. Or rather here *Clare* was, she thought as she scanned the restaurant. Still no sign of her mother. Was she even going to come? Maybe she'd bail on this, too.

Clare ordered an espresso, tapped her fingers on the metal table, then smoothed her hair and brushed a speck of lint from the sleeve of her jumper. She'd stood in front of the wardrobe for ages this morning, trying to decide what to put on. What did one wear for a meet and greet with the women who'd abandoned you thirty years ago?

'Clare?'

Clare glanced up from examining her sleeve, her mouth falling open as she took in the person before her. Far from the slim brunette with the chic swinging bob that had remained in Clare's mind, this woman sported a short grey crop and was pleasantly rounded, lines criss-crossing her face. In a million years, Clare never would have guessed this was her mother. The thought gave her a jolt.

'You still look like the little girl I knew,' the woman said in a familiar husky voice as she settled into the seat across from Clare. Her heart panged that after such a long time apart, her mum hadn't even tried to hug her. 'Although a much more grown-up version.' Her mother smiled, and Clare recognised the slate-blue eyes, though they were hooded now. 'It's wonderful to see you.'

Clare nodded, unsure what to say. With her mum in front of her, all the words that had bubbled up over the past few decades—everything she'd longed to express, but had never got the chance—stuck in her throat.

'I'm famished. What do you recommend?' Her mother picked up the menu, and Clare noticed it trembled in her hands. So Mum was nervous, too, she thought. Well, good. She should be! And despite all these years, the first thing she asked about was food? No surprise she'd put herself first, Clare told herself, trying to ignore the hurt circling inside.

'The carrot cake is nice,' Clare mumbled finally, sipping her espresso.

'Then that's what I'll have,' her mother declared, placing the menu on the table and meeting Clare's eyes. 'Tell me about you and your life.' The tone was casual, but she gripped the tabletop so hard her knuckles were turning white.

Clare shook her head incredulously. *Tell me about you and your life?* After three decades, where the hell should she start?

'Why don't you tell me first why you decided to leave,' Clare said in a strangled voice. The words sounded more bitter than intended.

Her mother swallowed, two small circles of red blossoming on her cheeks. 'Fair enough. I'll try my best.' She paused to nod at the waiter as he set a giant slice of cake before her. Cutting off a large slab, she placed it in her mouth and chewed.

Clare tapped her fingers impatiently on the table. She'd waited years for an answer, and now that her mum was here, she didn't want to wait a second more.

Finally, her mother wiped her mouth. 'I loved you, and I loved your dad. But . . . it's hard to explain. At the time, there were so many emotions inside me—I remember feeling so, so tired, and how your father would have to get me up every morning before he left for work. I used to lie in bed at night and cry for hours, thinking how I wanted a different life. I guess now, doctors probably would have diagnosed it as a sort of depression. But whatever it was, I just knew I had to get away.' She shook her head. 'Look, I don't know; maybe your dad and I should have waited to have children until I had a career. At least then, I'd have had a life outside of the house. But we both wanted to get started on a family quickly.' She made as if to take Clare's hand, then stopped herself.

Clare blinked, staring down at the space between their fingers. 'You could have had both, you know—a family and a career. I'm sure Dad would have agreed to help out rather than lose you.'

Her mother sighed, leaning back in the chair. 'It wasn't that easy. The thing is, I really didn't believe then I could have both.

Many women did, but they had to work for financial reasons or had husbands who supported them.' She set down her fork with a clang. 'I might have been able to convince your dad. But I wasn't sure I could face my own guilt at spending time away from family for my own career. I started to feel trapped, and that feeling grew and grew until the only thing that could fix it was leaving. I was convinced it was best for you, too . . . that you were better off having no mother than me.' Her eyes filled and she busied herself cutting off another slab of cake, then cleared her throat.

'And once I was gone, it didn't seem fair to keep inserting myself back into your life,' her mum continued, a few seconds later. 'I'd already left, and the last thing I wanted was to keep leaving. I missed you desperately, of course, and it was a high price to pay—a very high price, but I had to do it. Sometimes, when you're in a dark pit and you see a chance for happiness, you have to reach to it for all you're worth.'

'Do you regret leaving?' Clare held her mother's eyes as she awaited the answer.

A sad smile lifted her mother's lips. 'I regret the pain I caused, of course, and losing you in the process. But if I'd stayed, I think we'd all have been worse for it.' She took a bite of her cake, a faraway expression on her face as she chewed. 'You have a wonderful stepmum, from what I gather, and your father seems very happy. And I have a job I enjoy, as well as a terrific husband and a whole host of stepkids. I'd love for you to meet them one day.'

Clare drew in a sharp breath. Mum had another family?

'How could you have left me and Dad because you wanted space, and then dived back in again?' The question burst out before she could stop it.

'Oh, Clare.' This time, Mum did reach out and take her hand, squeezing her fingers the same way she had that morning so many years ago. 'None of this was about you, or Dad, or *family*. It was about me, and what I needed then.' Her eyes bore into Clare, as if willing her to understand. 'I love you. I never stopped, despite everything else.'

Clare stared down at her mother's hand, her mind spinning as she tried to absorb the words. Mum leaving had always felt like a rejection—any child would see it that way—and Clare had always thought it meant her mother rejected parenthood and family, too. But maybe, despite how she'd seen it for so long, Mum hadn't run from being a mother, exactly: she'd run towards happiness. It just happened that in her case, at that time, she couldn't see a way to do both. And while Clare couldn't understand how her mother could cut off all contact, she *could* understand wanting to find fulfilment.

'I'm glad we met up,' Clare said finally. She might never be able to fully forgive her mum for leaving, but uncovering the reason made her feel lighter, as if a brick had been lifted from her chest. She took a few deep breaths, relishing the air and feeling her whole psyche expand.

'Me, too.' The tightness of her mother's face relaxed, making her look years younger. 'Let's keep in touch, okay?'

Clare nodded. 'Okay.' Perhaps in time, they might even be able to have a relationship, like Tam had said. After chatting for a few more minutes about Clare's job and her mum's new London home, Clare looked at her watch.

'I'd better get going,' she said, shrugging on her coat. She didn't have anywhere else to be, but the long day and the accompanying emotion had completely wiped her out. She gathered up her things, then turned and smiled. 'Bye.'

Her mother smiled back. 'See you soon.'

Outside, pink tinged the evening sky as the sun set. The air was fresh but soft, and the smell of spring met Clare's nose. The perfect time for new beginnings . . . and new life, she thought, picking up the pace towards home.

She'd meant what she said earlier: she was happy to have finally met with Mum. Clare knew now that even though the past *was* connected to the future, it didn't mean the same events were destined to repeat themselves. Her mother's decision to leave the family was based on a situation miles from hers—they were in two totally different places. Clare had a career she loved, and she'd never rely on a family to fill her universe. There was no risk of that; she was already a complete person.

Clare froze as the realisation hit it wasn't *motherhood* that scared her. It was the emotional ties accompanying the relationship. Because of the past, she'd tried to shield herself from pain . . . and to stop others from being hurt by her. But the last few weeks—and her short-lived encounter with Nicholas—had shown she didn't want to wrap herself in protective layers. She wanted to feel, to have those bonds, despite the potential for pain.

Inside her right now was the opportunity for the ultimate bond. But was she ready to have a child? Clare started walking again, words echoing in her brain, from Mary's 'it's a gift' to Ellie saying that nobody ever feels prepared for kids. She pictured the lines on the family tree, connecting her to the past and the future; the people she loved then and now, and those she would.

Her hand moved down to her stomach. She didn't want to sever those lines. She wanted to make them even clearer, to fill in the blanks. There'd be complications and mess—and a hell of a lot of details to work out—but she was no longer confused about what the future held.

A smile spread on her face, growing larger and larger with each step. She was going to be a mother, and although the thought still made her quiver with apprehension, it was mixed with hope, excitement . . . and love.

CHAPTER THIRTY

Two days later, Clare tugged on a loose top and jeans, then glanced at the clock. Already six—she had less than thirty minutes before jumping on the Tube for another meeting of the No-Kids Club. If she timed it right, she could be there to sign in members, do a little schmoozing, then push off. Exhaustion dragged at her heels 24/7 these days, along with the ever-present queasiness.

Not to mention the thoughts of Edward keeping her awake at night, despite the fatigue. Ellie kept harassing her to get in touch, saying Clare should at least tell him she was pregnant. Clare had got as far as dialling his number, hanging up at the last second. Theoretically, her friend was right: now that Clare was pregnant, the issue that had driven them apart was resolved. But could she just call up and drop a bombshell like that? Raising a child together was a huge thing. And what if Edward didn't want to be with her anymore, baby aside? After all, she'd completely ignored his earlier email, and they *had* only been a couple for a few months.

Hopefully tonight would be a bit of a breather from all the voices in her head. It was funny; she'd thought the club would uncover a wealth of individuals similar to her: professionals with little time or desire for children. People like Anna, who'd chosen not to have kids despite a very traditional marriage, or Poppy, who simply couldn't, hadn't crossed Clare's mind. Just like life, the club was a cross-section of all sorts—even those who traded fertility tips and tricks. It certainly wasn't what she had envisioned, but people seemed to enjoy the group and that was the most important thing. Lord knows what she'd say when her belly started to blossom! Clare smiled incredulously at the thought of her child growing inside.

She was about to head out the door when her mobile rang.

'Hello?'

'Clare!'

Ellie's panicked voice came through the line, and Clare's grip on the phone tightened.

'You okay?' Ellie's due date was fast approaching. First babies were usually late, but babies weren't known for their predictability.

'No, I'm bloody well not!' Ellie huffed. 'My waters broke and bloody Graham's at his corporate away day in some Godforsaken place where they don't have reception!'

Oh, God. What the hell had Graham been thinking, taking off to the country right now? 'How long ago did they break? Are you having any contractions?'

Ellie broke off and released a groan in response. 'They broke this morning, and yes,' Ellie said, when she came on the line again. 'I was at work, of all places. You should have seen my boss's face when he spotted the puddle underneath my chair. He actually asked if I'd wet myself!'

Despite herself, Clare couldn't help giggling imagining the scene.

'Anyway, I rang up the hospital and they said if the waters were clear, I could stay at home until the contractions were about three minutes apart.'

'And how far are they now?'

'Damned if I know! Like I have the presence of mind to grab a watch and time them when it starts. These things are evil, Clare. Evil! And who the hell has a watch with a second hand, anyway?'

'When is Graham supposed to be home?' Clare asked.

'Just a sec . . . ' Ellie held the phone away from her and groaned again. Clare cringed at the awful sound emanating from the handset. 'They had some sort of teambuilding dinner,' she said breathlessly when she returned. 'And then it was about an hour back to London. He called from a landline to check in a couple of hours ago, but I didn't want to worry him and nothing much seemed to be happening. Apparently it can take ages from when your waters break.'

'Well, yes, it can, but it can also be quite quick. It really depends.'

'Anyway, I rang about thirty minutes ago, but they'd already left and I still can't get through to his mobile.' Ellie let out another yowl, and Clare held the phone away from her ear.

'Look, I'm coming over right now. We'll time the contractions, but by the sounds of things, we need to get you to the hospital.'

'Hospital? No! I don't have anything ready. I was supposed to have my bag packed, but work has been so busy, and nothing's done, and—'

'We'll get you sorted when I arrive,' Clare said firmly, cutting into Ellie's babble. 'If I catch a cab, I can be there in fifteen minutes or less. See you soon.'

'Okay.' Ellie let out a puff of air. 'Please hurry.'

Clare shoved the mobile in her pocket and rushed down to Fulham Road, hailing a taxi. One short ride—and a quick conversation with Poppy asking her to take over hosting duties at the club tonight—later, she was ringing the buzzer for Ellie's flat. The lights inside were blazing but there was no response. She rang again, heart in her throat. Was everything okay?

'One minute!' Clare heard Ellie's voice, followed by a low moan. Finally, Ellie swung open the door, brow covered in sweat and flushed face pinched with pain. 'Thank God you're here. Come in.'

Clare followed her friend into the lounge. The TV was blaring, the radio was blasting, and cup after cup of red liquid filled a variety of teacups dotted about the place. 'What the hell is happening here?'

Ellie lowered herself onto the sofa. 'My antenatal teacher said to try to distract yourself. You should see the kitchen—she recommended we bake cupcakes. Fucking *cupcakes*! As if that will distract me from the wrench squeezing my guts.'

Clare peeked into the kitchen—it looked like the Kitchen Goddess had an epileptic fit. Almost every bowl was removed from the cupboards, a gooey liquid oozed from a forest of utensils, and a fine layer of white powder covered the countertop.

'What's the red stuff?' she asked, pointing to a mug.

'Raspberry leaf tea,' Ellie answered. 'It's meant to soften the cervix and make delivery easier. The problem is I can't get through one cup without having a contraction, and then it gets cold.'

'Right, let me grab my phone and we can time your contractions. Tell me when you feel one coming.' Clare pushed aside a discarded tissue and sat down on the sofa. 'Still no word from Graham?'

Ellie clutched her stomach. 'It's coming!' She gave a growl, then leaned over. Her face closed off as if she'd gone to another place, and she sucked in air like she hadn't had oxygen for years. Clare bit her lip as she timed her friend, her hand sliding down to her own abdomen. *Yikes.* As a doctor, she'd seen many women in labour and even delivered several babies. But watching someone close to her was a completely different story—not to mention she'd be undergoing the same thing herself later this year.

'Okay,' Ellie said, straightening up. 'It's gone.'

'That looked like a strong one. We'll see how close the next one is, but I think we should make a move.'

'But I need to pack my hospital bag!' Ellie yelped, levering her bulk into a standing position. 'I know, I know, I should have done it already,' she grumbled as Clare helped her into the bedroom. 'Putting together the nursery and everything else is fun, but this . . . ' Ellie gestured at an empty bag in the corner. 'This is the real deal.' She turned a worried face towards Clare. 'What if I can't do it? What if—'

Clare put a hand on her friend's arm. 'You'll be fine, Els. You will.' It was nice to know doubt was normal, even if the baby had been planned.

'Okay, let's get this done quickly.' Clare started sifting through the pile of supplies beside the bag. 'Look, you've got most of the stuff already. Maternity towels, breast pads, nappies . . . ' She chucked it all in the bag. 'Just hand me a nightdress, maybe a T-shirt or two and socks, and I think we have all the essentials. I can pick up some things back here once we have you checked in at the hospital.'

'Just take it from the drawer.' Ellie was doubled over again, so Clare slid open the drawer and removed the items. She shoved them into the bag, grabbed a jacket for Ellie, and led her back into the lounge.

Clare threw on her coat and ran out to the street to flag down a taxi. Then, she helped Ellie put on her shoes, heaved the hospital bag over one shoulder, and took her friend's arm. The orange glow of the taxi only a few metres down the street seemed miles away, and Ellie leaned heavily on her arm. By the time they reached the cab, Clare's forehead was drenched with sweat despite the coldness of the night. She helped Ellie climb in and the driver started the short journey to Chelsea and Westminster Hospital, where Ellie had registered to give birth.

Ellie groaned as the cabbie went over a bump in the road.

'Sorry, love,' he grinned, meeting their eyes in the rear-view mirror. 'But that might help the baby along faster! Just as long as it's not in the car, mind. I had it cleaned last weekend.'

Clare didn't even bother responding. She couldn't—she was too busy trying to ignore the pain shooting through her fingers as Ellie clutched her hand.

'Should we try Graham again?' she asked, when Ellie's grip finally relaxed.

Her friend nodded. 'He should be on his way back, so hopefully his phone is in range now. It better be!'

'Don't worry,' Clare said, taking the mobile from Ellie's bag and scrolling through the contacts to find Graham's number before passing it to her friend. 'First babies do usually take ages to arrive. I'd say he'll be here with hours to spare.' Ellie's face contorted, and Clare crossed her fingers she was right.

'Here, you talk.' Ellie chucked the phone back to Clare before clutching at her stomach. 'Oh, God. Remind me why I wanted to do this?'

Clare couldn't help a smile as she hit "Call" on the phone. 'Just think of what you'll get at the end.' She patted her own belly, picturing her tiny baby nestled inside. Ever since realising it wasn't motherhood that scared her, she was becoming more and more excited to be a parent—even if she had to do it alone. The urge to call Edward flashed into her mind, and uncertainty flooded through her. Sighing, she pushed away the thought. She'd deal with it later.

'Hi, babes.' Graham came on the line and Clare nearly collapsed with relief.

'Graham, it's Clare.'

'Clare! Is everything okay? Where's Ellie?' Concern tinged his voice.

'She's right beside me.' Clare nodded to Ellie, who could only puff in return. 'Everything's fine,' she said quickly, not wanting to leave him hanging. 'But guess what—you're going to have a baby soon!' *Very* soon, if Ellie's contractions kept progressing so quickly.

'Tell him to get his arse here right now,' Ellie managed between pants.

'Oh my God.' Clare could hear the panic in his voice. 'Holy *fuck*. Please say you're joking.'

'Um, no. Why?' Clare kept smiling not to worry Ellie.

Graham let out a string of expletives. 'You'll never believe it, but I'm bloody stranded in the middle of nowhere waiting for my idiot workmate to come back with a can of petrol. He forgot to fill up his tank and we're stuck in the countryside outside London somewhere. God knows how long he'll be.'

Clare's eyes widened, and her mind spun to find a response that would transmit the urgency of the situation to Graham and not worry her friend at the same time.

'Well, the sooner you get here, the better,' she said finally, trying to keep her voice calm.

'Is Ellie all right? How far along is she? God, I can't believe I'm not there.'

'She's fine.' Clare gave Ellie's arm a squeeze. 'We're on our way to the hospital right now.' She glanced over at her friend, whose face had returned to normal. 'Do you want to talk to her? She's between contractions.' She handed over the mobile, then turned towards the window to watch the London night flash by.

'You get here as soon as you can,' she heard Ellie say as the cab pulled up to the hospital. 'And tell Pete I'm going to *kill* him when I see him next. What kind of moron runs out of petrol?'

Graham must have told her why he was stuck, Clare thought. Brave man.

'We're here, ladies,' the cabbie called back, just in case the glowing light of the hospital wasn't evident. Obviously he'd been serious about getting them out of the cab before they could think of sullying it.

221

Clare passed through a twenty-pound note, then scurried around the other side to open the door for Ellie. God, it was weird arriving here as a friend and not attending doctor. In her job, she was the one in control, the one with all the answers. Now, although she was trying hard to stay calm for Ellie's sake, adrenaline and fear raced through her.

'Let's get you up to the maternity ward and then you can relax,' she said, guiding Ellie over to the bank of lifts that led to the maternity ward. As they hobbled down the long corridor, Clare wondered what idiot architect had decided to put the ward so far away! It was like trying to get an elephant with PMS through a maze.

Finally, they reached the reception and checked in Ellie. A midwife guided them over to the triage unit, where they'd assess how far along she was.

'Just lie down on that bed and someone will be by shortly,' the woman said as Ellie gingerly lowered her bulk onto the bed, rocking forwards and backwards. Another contraction hit, and Ellie got to her feet, leaning against the wall and releasing a terrible cry. Clare cringed, watching her friend's face contort like something from *The Exorcist*.

'Don't worry,' Clare said, hoping Ellie could hear her through the pain. 'As soon as they see how dilated you are, I'm sure you can get an epidural. Or did you want to do it naturally?' she asked, realising how little she actually knew about Ellie's birth plan.

'Amanda gave birth to hers naturally,' Ellie huffed. 'She said it's the best way to do it and that anything else sullies the birthing process.'

Clare rolled her eyes. 'Sod Amanda. What do you want?'

Another contraction hit, and Ellie let out a low moan which was definitely 'epidural'. She repeated the word until the pain eased.

'Hello, there.' A smiling midwife pulled back the curtain. 'It says here your waters broke a few hours ago, is that right?'

Ellie nodded.

'All right. Just relax on the bed. I'll have a quick check to see how many centimetres dilated you are, and we'll go from there.'

Clare helped her friend clamber onto the bed, then swung Ellie's legs around and scooted back to hold her hand.

The midwife raised an eyebrow as she conducted her examination. 'My goodness, you're already seven centimetres. Let's get you assigned to a birthing room.'

Ellie turned a worried face to Clare before looking back to the midwife. 'What does that mean, seven centimetres?'

The midwife smiled. 'It means your baby should arrive fairly soon. You're well into established labour.'

'No!' Ellie howled. 'I have to wait until my husband arrives!'

The midwife shook her head. 'I'm afraid this baby isn't going to wait, dear. They come when they're ready, regardless if we are or not.'

Ellie's eyes filled with tears, and she swallowed hard. 'I want an epidural.'

The midwife squeezed Ellie's knee. 'We can give you one if you really can't cope, but you'll be able to start pushing soon. Why don't you see how far you can go under your own steam? In the meantime, I'll try to track down the anaesthesiologist and let him know you might want one—it's been a very busy night here so far.' She hurried off before Ellie could respond.

'This was not how it was supposed to be,' Ellie said, struggling to sit up. 'I'm so glad you're here, but Graham—' She caught her breath. 'Oh my God, here comes another one. I can't do this, Clare. I can't!'

Clare took her hand. 'You can, Els, and you will. You're doing great.'

The midwife was right, Clare thought as she watched Ellie's face close up with pain again. Ideal scenario or not, that baby was coming.

CHAPTER THIRTY-ONE

'Come on, Ellie. You can do it.' Clare crouched beside her friend as the midwife shouted encouragement. Ellie's face turned puce as she strained and strained. It was a wonder she could still muster any energy after the last couple of hours. As soon as they'd moved to the birthing suite—a room with dim lights and lots of contraptions designed to make labour easier (as if that were possible!)—the midwife had given Ellie the go-ahead to start pushing. And for the past hour, that's all she'd been doing.

Clare glanced at the clock on the wall. Just after midnight, and still no sign of Graham. He'd called almost every ten minutes or so, desperate for an update. The last they'd heard, he was coming down the M4 into the city and would be there in a matter of minutes. Clare bit her lip as her friend started to bear down again. He'd better get here soon if he wanted to see his child born, because—

'It's coming. I can see the head!' The midwife's excited voice broke into her thoughts. 'Okay, Ellie, I need you to give me one big push this time. Can you do that?'

Ellie nodded.

'On the count of three . . . ' The midwife counted and Ellie drew in a breath, then strained with all her might. The veins on her neck popped out, and Clare thought she might explode, too.

'Did I miss it?' The door burst open and in dashed Graham, his eyes wild and face panicked.

Ellie's eyes swung over towards him. Clare slid her fingers from Ellie's grip and gave her friend's hand to Graham. He clasped it like he'd never let go—not that he could, given the strength of her grasp—and brushed back a lock of sweaty hair from her face. The look of love that passed between them made Clare's breath catch.

'The shoulders are coming.' The midwife nodded, then glanced up at Ellie. 'Come on, now, one more big push.'

Ellie continued to strain, and then Clare heard a wail.

'You did it! Well done!' Grinning, the midwife gave the baby a quick wipe, then placed it on Ellie's chest. 'You have a beautiful boy.'

'A boy!' Graham looked so proud and excited that Clare's eyes welled up. 'Well done, Els. I'm so sorry I couldn't be here sooner.'

Ellie smiled over at Clare, her calm demeanour a sharp contrast to the past few hours. 'That's all right. Clare was amazing.'

Graham slung an arm around Clare's waist. 'I can't thank you enough for being here.'

'I can't think of anywhere I'd rather be.' Clare had seen many babies come into the world, but Ellie's baby was something she'd never forget.

Ellie gazed down at her son, her face filled with wonder. 'I can hardly believe it,' she said, running a finger across his cheek. 'I'm a mother.' She met Graham's eyes. 'We have a son!'

Graham leaned over to kiss her, then reached down and kissed the baby's cheek. 'I love you both so much.'

Clare backed away from the tableaux, closing the door behind her and leaning against the wall. Ellie had a family now; a tiny, tight unit. The love between them was so palpable she could almost see it hanging in the air. A feeling stirred inside, something so deep that at first, she couldn't identify it. The family tree flashed into her mind again, and Clare knew in a heartbeat what that feeling was: she wanted a family, too—to fill in all the blanks on that tree. The emotion grew so quickly it almost took away her breath with its intensity.

She closed her eyes and Edward's face swam into her head for the millionth time this week. She'd told herself over and over it was ridiculous to think they could overcome everything and be together—life didn't work like that. But now, with the euphoria of the past few hours, all the doubts and uncertainty faded. Edward might say she was crazy, but she had to try. This was her chance for happiness, and Clare wasn't going to let it slip away.

CHAPTER THIRTY-TWO

Clare's heart pounded as she dodged bleary-eyed commuters in Liverpool Street station the next evening. Despite the lack of sleep from last night's events and the long day shift, she'd never felt more clear-headed or alive. A huge smile lifted her lips, growing bigger until her cheeks hurt. She couldn't wait to see Edward and start sorting out their future together—if he wanted.

It would be a shock, she told herself, trying to keep her feet planted on the ground even as her mind filled with images of happy families. It was one thing to say you wanted a child, and another to be presented with one that was imminent! And after all this time apart, it wasn't a given he'd want to be with her, either, especially after she hadn't even responded to his email. Perhaps she should have called before coming? But no, this wasn't something that could be said on the phone. Fingers crossed he was in. Unless his schedule had changed, he usually returned from work by now.

She hurried past the restaurant where Edward had first taken her, unable to resist looking inside for old times' sake. God, that date seemed ages ago, and yet it was only a few months. So much had changed since then, including her own perspective on what she wanted from life. Clare watched the diners laughing and chatting, and her smile grew even wider. She couldn't wait to come here again with Edward.

A familiar face swam into focus, and she caught her breath. Well, that was a perfect timing—he was here now! Her heart beat faster as she took in Edward's short dark hair, olive skin, and the usual stubble she kept telling him to shave. A laugh escaped at the memory of how she'd once given him money for a haircut and professional shave, so she could have one razor-burn-free night. He'd taken her cash, got a haircut, and kept the stubble. Desire flooded in as she remembered the feeling of his face against hers, and how he always smelled just perfect: a mix of citrusy cologne and soap.

Trying to steady her nerves, she took a deep breath and quickly checked her reflection in the glass. She'd made sure to wear the turquoise coat he liked along with the earrings he'd given her for Christmas. Shame about the bags under her eyes, though. When the hell did that pregnant glow kick in? She looked more corpse than blooming with life.

Clare tugged open the door, adrenaline rushing through her body. With her eyes locked on Edward's solid back, she nodded to the maître d' before threading between the tables towards him. She couldn't wait to put her arms around those wide shoulders again . . . oh.

Clare stopped stock-still as she rounded a pillar that had partially blocked her view of his table. Edward wasn't dining alone, like she'd thought. Across from him sat a petite blonde woman, the very personification of cute. Were they together? Maybe she was just a friend and they were out for a drink. But in the next second, Edward teasingly offered the woman a morsel of food before reaching out to squeeze her hand, and Clare's heart dropped. There could be no doubt: he'd found someone else. In a second, her hopeful image of the future shattered.

Before the couple could spot her hovering mid-restaurant, Clare turned and forced herself to walk slowly towards the door so they wouldn't notice her. Tears blurred her vision, making everything soft and fuzzy. If only it could soften the ache inside, too.

Outside, Clare retraced her route back to Liverpool Street station, the sharp click of her heels echoing off the stone buildings lining the street. She walked faster and faster, as if the quicker she could get away from the restaurant, the quicker she'd escape the vision of Edward with another woman.

Breathless now, she entered the station and rushed onto the escalator, gripping the side as it transported her back down to the Underground. Despite the hurt piercing her heart, Clare didn't regret coming to find Edward. She'd have wondered forever if she didn't try to talk to him. They'd always be connected through the baby inside her, and Clare would get in touch eventually to let him know. She'd never deny her child access to a parent—she knew that feeling all too well. Edward would play a part in her life, although it wasn't the role she'd been hoping.

The carriage clattered into the platform, and Clare collapsed onto the seat, head throbbing and heart aching. She'd endured losing Edward once already, she reminded herself as the train left behind East London. She could endure this time as well.

Besides, she had more than herself to think about now. She had their baby, too.

CHAPTER THIRTY-THREE

'Here you go.' Ellie handed the baby to Clare, who held her breath as she awkwardly shifted the newborn in her arms. Jonas was so tiny she almost felt like one false move would break him. She stared down at the rosebud mouth and the squish of a nose, his soft eyelashes brushing chubby cheeks. 'He's perfect,' she said, smiling over at Ellie's expectant face.

'He is, isn't he?' Ellie grinned. 'I mean, I know I'm biased and everything, but he's bloody gorgeous.' Jonas let out a wail, and Clare turned a worried face towards Ellie.

'Don't look so terrified!' Ellie lifted the baby from her friend's arms. 'He's just hungry.' Clare tried not to stare as Ellie raised her top and expertly attached the baby to her breast. He slurped away with abandon. 'You'll have to get used to all this if you go through with the baby.' She stroked Jonas's downy head, then met Clare's eyes. 'Have you decided anything yet?'

Clare nodded slowly. Ellie was the first to learn she was pregnant, so it made sense that she'd be the first to know Clare was going to have the baby. 'Yes, I have.' She swallowed, the words forming in her head before releasing them into the world. Once they were out there, there'd be no turning back. Funnily enough, though, she didn't want to turn back. Fear wouldn't rule her actions any more.

'Well?' Ellie raised an eyebrow. 'Come on, then. Don't leave me hanging! My post-partum hormones are driving me crazy enough as it is.'

'Well . . . ' Clare smiled, enjoying the suspense. 'I'm going to have it.'

'Oh my God!' Ellie shrieked, cringing as baby Jonas came off her breast and started wailing again. 'Sorry, baby, sorry!' She hurriedly shushed him and latched him back on. 'Oh my God,' she repeated in a softer voice. 'Clare, that's amazing. I'm so glad. I mean, it's hard—it's *bloody* hard—but'—she stroked Jonas's head again, a tender look sliding over her face—'it's so worth it.' She grimaced. 'I know everyone says that, but it really is true.' She paused to lift up Jonas and switch him to the other side. 'What changed your mind?'

Clare toyed with the velvety ears of a soft toy rabbit. 'Well, I finally talked to my mother,' she said, watching Ellie's eyes widen at the news. 'Meeting her helped me see it wasn't being a mother that scared me. I just didn't want to cause the same hurt and pain, or feel that again myself. But we're two different people, with very different lives.'

Ellie nodded, then grinned. 'Wow! I'd never have imagined we'd be mothers together. It'll be great.' She reached out and gripped Clare's hand. 'I can't wait to share all this with you.'

Clare squeezed back. She was lucky to have a friend like Ellie.

'So . . . ' Ellie's voice trailed off and she tilted her head. 'You *are* going to tell Edward now, right? You have to. Straight away!' She gestured towards Clare's phone resting on the bed beside them.

Clare shook her head. 'I will once I have my first scan and make sure everything is fine. But, well . . . ' She pushed back the rising sadness. 'I did go to see him last week. I wanted to tell him about the baby, and to see if we could start over.'

'And?' Ellie was practically in her lap.

'And he was with someone else,' Clare said simply, trying not to show how much it had upset her. 'I saw them in the restaurant where he used to take me. He was feeding her a piece of food and then he took her hand.' Her throat closed off as she pictured the scene again.

'Oh, God.' Ellie's face dropped and she reached out to touch Clare's shoulder. 'I'm sorry. I can only imagine how that must have felt. But I'm so proud you went to him.' She paused to remove a sleeping Jonas from her breast. 'You don't know if they're together *together*, though. And even if they are, maybe it's not that serious. How did they look?' She plopped the baby on her shoulder and started patting his back.

An image of Edward's laughing face flashed through her mind. 'They were definitely together,' Clare responded firmly, not wanting to give Ellie any wiggle room to protest. 'Now listen, let me make up a plate of food for you. I've got bread, cheese, and some lovely prosciutto from Carluccio's.'

'Wait a sec, Clare.' Ellie put a hand on her arm. 'Listen, Graham and I have decided we'd like you to be Jonas's godmother.'

Clare's mouth fell open. 'Really?'

'You're always here for me when I need you,' Ellie continued, 'and that's the kind of person we want for our son.'

Clare's eyes filled with tears. 'I'd be honoured,' she said, voice husky with emotion. She reached down to kiss the new baby's cheek, her heart flipping over at the softness of his skin and the warmth of his breath. In half a year, that small seed in her belly would be exactly like this, cosy and safe in her care.

Clare put her arms around Ellie and Jonas. She might not have a partner, but she wasn't alone. Although she still ached at the thought of Edward, she had plenty of others who loved and supported her, from Dad and Tam to Ellie and maybe—in time—her mum.

This baby wouldn't be on its own, either. It would have her. The ferocity of determination mixed with overwhelming love was so strong it almost took her breath away.

'Welcome to my life, baby,' she whispered, unsure if she was talking to Ellie's newborn or her own little one. 'You're going to be very much loved.'

CHAPTER THIRTY-FOUR

Clare hurried up the stairs and into the already packed room of the pub. Laughter and chatter filled her ears and she stood still for a moment, letting the noise wash over her. Despite the slow start, the No-Kids Club was now a major success. More and more people turned up every week, and if things kept going like this, they'd have to find a bigger venue. Several members had approached her, asking if they could form chapters for their parts of London. Clare had been happy to say yes.

The club was taking on a life of its own, she thought proudly, watching members down drinks as they chatted and made introductions. That was a good thing, because tonight would be her last night. Her life was on another track to those around her now—not better, not worse, just *different*. Poppy had done a great job hosting the week before, and Clare planned to ask her to take over, at least until her circumstances changed.

Funnily enough, the club and its inaugural members had, in some small way, helped her see how much she wanted solid relationships and commitment. Clare shook her head at the irony of a group for the childless convincing her to have a baby. Never in a million years would she have predicted such a turnout.

'Hiya.' Poppy appeared at her elbow, clutching a glass of white wine. Clare's eyebrows rose at the sight of the woman drinking alcohol.

'Hello.' She tried to hide her surprise, but she was too late.

'I know, I know.' Poppy took a swig of her drink. 'Crikey, this is good.' She sipped again, then ran her tongue along her lips. 'I just wanted to say thanks for our chat a couple of weeks ago.'

Clare tried to remember what they'd talked about, but the recent past was a blur. 'Our chat?'

Poppy nodded. 'Yes. You told me how your stepmother was more like a mum than your real mother ever could be. Something twigged in mind, and I realised that I don't need to keep subjecting myself—and my husband—to failed IVF cycles. We can adopt and have a baby fairly quickly.' She grinned. 'I can't wait.'

Clare put a hand on Poppy's arm. 'I'm so pleased you're happy.'

'You know what? I really am—for the first time in ages.' She sipped her drink again. 'Until I finally decided to stop trying to conceive, I hadn't understood how much pressure I was putting myself and Alistair through. And for what? Like you said, being a mum is about mothering, not simply giving birth.'

Clare nodded, thinking how right Poppy was. She still felt sad her own mum hadn't been in the ideal time or place to continue the commitment to mothering, but she was finally able to accept it.

'Have you guys started the adoption process?' Clare asked.

Poppy shook her head. 'Not yet. We want to give ourselves time to recover from the past few years, to get back on an even keel. In a couple of months we'll start filling in all the paperwork. I'm excited, but you know what? I'm really enjoying just the two of us right now.' She paused, glancing at Clare's midsection. 'How about you, then?'

'Well . . . ' Clare smiled. 'I've decided to have the baby.'

Poppy's face almost split with the force of her grin, and she threw her arms around Clare. 'That's fantastic! I'm thrilled for you.' And despite her struggles to conceive, Clare thought she actually did look happy. 'So what are you going to do about the club?' Poppy asked, looking around the packed room. 'As founder and all, I'm sure people wouldn't mind you coming to the meetings, but they might find it a little odd with a baby bump.'

'I'm happy to take a step back,' Clare said, surveying the crowd. 'It's doing so well now, I don't think it'll make a difference if I'm here or not. Actually . . . how would you like to take over organising it for a bit?'

Poppy's eyes lit up. 'I'd love to! Alistair and I want to get out and meet people, have a regular social night, you know? And the members are all lovely, whether they want kids or not. We'll have a lot on our plate when we finally get our baby, so we'd best enjoy our freedom while we can.' She set her glass down on the bar. 'I'm off for another drink. What can I get you? Water? Juice?'

Clare shook her head. 'No, that's okay. Any liquid I have now will be through my bladder in about ten seconds.' She motioned towards the bar. 'You'd better get over there fast before the booze is all gone!'

Poppy smiled, then disappeared into the heaving room.

Clare leaned against the wall, glancing down at her stomach. A faint swell was beginning to show beneath her loose top, and she smoothed the fabric to eye its outline. Even now, it was hard to believe she was actually going to have a baby.

She was about to go mingle when a familiar face waved into focus. She blinked, thinking her mind was playing tricks, but the face remained the same. Edward was threading his way through the crowd towards her! Her heart started pumping as she watched him approach. What on earth was he doing here? Hastily, she let the material fall away from her belly and hunched her shoulders forward, trying to appear more concave.

'Clare!' His smile grew broader as he reached her side. She scanned the room for signs of the blonde woman he'd been with, but he seemed to have come alone. 'Hi, there. I was hoping you'd be here.' His face flushed and he glanced down before looking up again. 'I mean, of course you would be here, seeing as how you're the founder and all. I saw you on TV—you did a fantastic job.'

Edward's nerves made her relax slightly, and she returned his smile. God, it was good to see him. 'Did you come by yourself?' The words flew out and she wanted to kick herself. Why not just ask if he had a bloody girlfriend?

'Um, well, yes.' Edward's cheeks went even redder. He took her arm, propelling her over to a quiet corner of the room. 'Look, I'm sorry to ambush you, but I really have to talk to you. Clare, I spoke with Ellie last night.'

Clare sucked in her breath, her eyes locked on his as she tried to determine how much he knew. Bloody Ellie—she should have known her friend wouldn't be able to resist meddling!

'And?' she asked finally, not wanting to give away anything.

Edward's face softened. 'And she told me about the baby. About *our* baby.'

Shit. Clare's heart dropped. She was going to kill Ellie! 'Don't worry,' she said, glancing down to examine the threadbare carpet. 'I don't expect you to do anything. The last thing I want is for you to feel obligated, especially if you're with someone else.' Just the thought made her heart contract.

'There's no one else.' Edward took her hands, tipping her chin up to meet his gaze. 'Ever since we broke up, I couldn't help thinking we made a mistake. I'd always pictured myself with kids, but sharing my life with someone I love is enough to make me happy, too. I guess I should have said that in my email, but when you didn't reply . . . ' He shook his head. 'I went on a few dates, but I couldn't stop thinking of you. And then when Ellie got in touch, well, I couldn't believe my ears.'

Clare nodded. 'It was a bit of a shock for me, too.'

'I can imagine.' The corner of Edward's mouth nudged up in a smile before a serious expression reappeared. 'Why didn't *you* let me know, though? Why did I have to hear it from your friend?'

'I came to find you last week, to tell you about the baby and that I wanted to be with you, that I miss you.' Clare swallowed. 'But then I saw you at our restaurant with another woman.'

Edward's brow furrowed. 'Ah.' He waved a hand in the air. 'That was just a date.' He moved in even closer. 'I don't want anyone else, Clare. I want you.' He pulled her towards him and Clare relaxed into his arms, breathing in his scent. Something inside clicked into place, as if a crucial part of her had been missing.

'So tell me,' he said, pulling back slightly. 'How many months are you? Have you seen a doctor yet? Have you had any ultrasounds? Do you know if it's a boy or a girl?'

Clare laughed at the stream of questions and his palpable excitement. Which one to tackle first? But before she could say anything, Edward clasped her hands again, his face shining. 'I'm so glad I came tonight, Clare. I couldn't have asked for more. I have a baby, and I have you.' He gave her a hesitant look. 'Right?'

She nodded, joy gushing through her. This was it: her chance to have the future she wanted—the family she wanted—without fear or hesitation. 'Right.'

'You two okay over here?' Poppy appeared at her side, holding a huge glass of wine.

'Perfect,' Edward said, still gazing into Clare's eyes. 'Just perfect.'

Clare drew in a breath as all the confusion and hurt of the past few weeks—and years—fell away. Leaning into Edward's warm body, she shook her head, smiling at how things had turned out. Life now was the polar opposite of what she'd thought she wanted, but she couldn't have asked for more.

CHAPTER THIRTY-FIVE

Five Months Later

Clare leaned back on the banquette at Carluccio's, trying to get comfortable. Her belly swelled before her, a vast mountain pressing on her ribs and lungs. She ran a hand over it, marvelling at the tautness of her skin. Even after eight months, she found it hard to believe she was pregnant, doing a double-take each time she caught sight of her profile. Edward said he thought pregnancy suited her and that she'd never looked more beautiful, but the whole thing was downright bizarre.

Still, even the strangeness of it all couldn't diminish the excitement and anticipation of meeting her daughter. With a month to go, Edward had already starting decorating the nursery—Clare's only stipulation had been no pink. She smiled, thinking how well things were going between them. She'd never realised a relationship could feel so natural—that when you were with the right person, they weren't a weight that could potentially drag you under if you weren't vigilant. They'd agreed that keeping their own places was the best bet at the moment, and that Edward would spend as much time as he could with her and baby until they found somewhere that worked for both of them. They were moving at a pace that suited them, despite Ellie's constant eye-rolling that they should just marry, move in, and get on with it.

Clare took a bite of her carrot cake, reflecting on how wonderful Ellie had been through all of this. Smiling, Clare remembered her friend's shriek when Clare discovered the baby was a girl, rhapsodising how fantastic it would be when their two kids married. From helping amass supplies to lending Clare maternity clothes, she couldn't imagine this pregnancy without Ellie.

Despite all her medical knowledge of the human anatomy, there was still so much about babies she had to learn. But with Edward and Ellie—not to mention Tam, who was bursting with excitement at becoming a grandparent—she could just about do it. Having this baby was the definite antidote to wriggling out of attachments, she thought wryly. She'd even had lunch with Mum a few times, although she'd yet to meet the extended family.

'Hey, there!' Clare waved as Anna and Poppy came through the glass doors and settled into chairs across the table. She hadn't seen them for ages, and Poppy had wanted to catch-up on each other's news. Although they'd never be more than acquaintances, in a strange way, Clare felt like they'd been on a journey together.

'Wow, look at you!' Anna raised her eyebrows at Clare—or rather, Clare's belly. 'You look fantastic.'

What was it about pregnancy that compelled every woman to extol the virtues of the mother's beauty, Clare wondered? Especially when that mother looked like the Michelin Man on steroids. 'Thank you,' she said, hoping she sounded sincere. 'But you look great, too.' She meant it—Anna's skin was lightly tanned and her whole face glowed. Italy had obviously done her good.

'Thanks. I've been travelling back and forth between Venice for the past few months and I'm really enjoying it. Michael's been out several times and he loves the city . . . and listening to me speak in Italian.' She waggled her eyebrows and the women laughed. 'And of course the club is expanding insanely fast. I never thought Michael would enjoy being the leader of something like that, but I was wrong. He loves it.'

Clare nodded, remembering how surprised she'd been when Michael had offered to take over from Poppy and Alistair, who'd only wanted to run it on a temporary basis. He'd been doing fantastically well, and the organisation now had over two hundred London members and was spreading to other parts of the country. He and Anna were even working to organise a summer festival.

'And . . . ' Anna grinned as she removed a brightly wrapped box from her handbag. 'We had a whip-round at the last meeting, and the club got you a gift.'

'Really?' Clare raised an eyebrow. 'Wow.'

'They may not follow your lead on pregnancy, but you did bring us all together. They'd love for you to swing by sometime, if you can.'

'I'll try to drop in soon,' Clare said, tearing off the wrapping and lifting the box's lid. A smile grew on her face as she drew out a miniature sleepsuit sporting the slogan "Sh*t Happens", and a laugh bubbled out. Shit *did* happen, but with people she loved around her, she could deal with it.

'Okay, okay, sorry but I can't wait any longer,' Poppy broke in, her cheeks flushed and eyes sparkling. 'I've got news!'

'Well don't leave us hanging,' Anna said, turning towards her. 'What is it?'

'We've been approved for adoption!' She pumped the air in excitement. 'Isn't that just the best news ever?' Her grin nearly split her face in two, and Clare smiled in response. She was so pleased for Poppy. If anyone deserved to be a mother, it was her.

'That's fantastic, Poppy.' Anna gave her a quick congratulatory hug. 'So what's the next step?'

'The social worker will match us with a child. I can't wait!'

Clare leaned across the table as much as her belly would allow and patted Poppy's hand. 'Congratulations. You'll make great parents.'

'I hope so,' Poppy said solemnly. 'I can't believe I waited this long to get started.' She shrugged. 'I guess some things are hard to let go.'

Clare nodded, noticing Anna nodding across the table, too. It was funny: the three of them had come to the No-Kids Club hoping for a quick fix. Instead, they'd uncovered something else, something they'd never have anticipated . . . in her case, something she'd *definitely* never have expected. But as she glanced from Anna's glowing face to Poppy's sparkling eyes—then gazed down at her belly—Clare knew beyond a doubt that although they may not have found what they were looking for, they'd discovered something even better.

THE END

ACKNOWLEDGEMENTS

So many people helped this book come alive. First and foremost, a huge thank you to India Drummond, Mel Sherratt, and Glynis Smy. Your wonderful feedback and friendship have meant the world to me. Thanks to Emilie Marneur and the Amazon team for their support and encouragement—it's been fantastic working with such dedicated professionals. Thank you, too, to my agent, Madeleine Milburn, and to all my readers who buy my books, send emails, and offer such kind words.

Above all, thank you to my husband and son. I can imagine many things, but I can't imagine my world without you.

ABOUT THE AUTHOR

 Talli Roland was born in Halifax, Nova Scotia, Canada. By age 13, she'd finished her first novel and received very encouraging rejections from publishers. Talli put writing on hold to focus on athletics, achieving provincial records and becoming a Canadian university champion in the 4 × 400 meter relay. After getting her BA, she turned to writing again, earning a Masters in Journalism. A few years later, she left Canada behind and settled in London, where she now lives with her husband and their young son.

Talli writes fun and witty romantic fiction. Her debut novel, *The Hating Game,* was short-listed for Best Romantic Read at the UK's Festival of Romance, and her second, *Watching Willow Watts*, was selected as an Amazon Customer Favourite.

Talli's website is www.talliroland.com, and she blogs regularly at http://talliroland.blogspot.com.